DISCOVERY

I was certain we'd crash. Spray showered us like a waterfall. The shock of it made me shiver and gasp for breath. Squinting through straggles of hair glued to my face, I saw we'd avoided the foaming cavern and were rounding the rock wall on an aisle of racing water. I had no idea how Afton had prevented certain calamity, but it wasn't without effort. His shirt had pulled free of his belt and flapped in the wind generated by the surge. His hair stood out in all directions like a wild man's.

He turned slightly, his face gaunt, and said something I couldn't hear above the blare of the river. In that moment his daring fell aside, and I saw the vulnerability he tried to keep hidden. Empathy swept my feelings, as well as a startling awareness that Afton McCabe, whether he wanted it or not, owned a piece of my heart.

RIVER
of Our
RETURN

Gladys Smith

HarperPaperbacks
A Division of HarperCollins*Publishers*

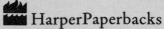 **HarperPaperbacks**
A Division of HarperCollins*Publishers*
10 East 53rd Street, New York, N.Y. 10022-5299

This is a work of fiction. The characters, incidents, and
dialogues are products of the author's imagination and are not to
be construed as real. Any resemblance to actual events or
persons, living or dead, is entirely coincidental.

ISBN 0-06-101144-4

HarperCollins®, 📖 ®, and HarperPaperbacks™
are trademarks of HarperCollins*Publishers,* Inc.

Cover illustration © 1998 by Peter Fiore

First printing: April 1998

Printed in the United States of America

Visit HarperPaperbacks on the World Wide Web at
http://www.harpercollins.com

❖ 10 9 8 7 6 5 4 3 2 1

To my husband and children
for believing in me.

To the early settlers who dared to live in the
Salmon River wilderness. The fact they
survived, even prospered, was proof
of their tenacity and grit.

To Tina Blaine

Best Wishes

& Happy Reading!

Gladys Smith

2003

Merry Christmas, Debbie!
Bought at Brenda, Az.
Love You, Dad & Mom

2003

1

Salmon River Canyon, Idaho, 1901

Two months had passed since Chester drowned beneath the river ice, and I still expected him to walk up the trail to the house, calling, "Hello, Hattie, I'm back." At times his voice drifted in on a breeze or rang echoing from the canyon walls. His face smiled at me from the spring's dark waters.

Wrapped in memories, I sat on a boulder near his grave, around me a grove of Ponderosa pine strong with the smell of rising sap. Sunshine from the cloudless May afternoon filtered through the trees and dappled the mound of earth beside me. One bright ray lit the cross. I needed to carve a fancy grave marker, but I hadn't the heart for it yet. I hadn't touched my carver's tools for weeks. Today, for the first time, I'd put a fresh jar of tulips and lupines on the grave without crying. My desolation had progressed beyond tears. I felt like a lump of flesh and bones, a clod of earth, a grain of sand. Indeed, the soil that cradled Chester's remains invited me to crawl in beside him and share his rest.

The grave lay at the top of a knoll that overlooked the Salmon River, its canyon so narrow and winding, I could see upriver only three hundred yards, downriver four hundred yards, and straight up pine and rock-studded slopes two thousand feet into the blue. An eagle soaring at the rim would view me as a tiny scrap of red gingham.

A short distance upriver, Weasel Creek tumbled down from the crags on the canyon's north rim and spilled into the Salmon, forming the bar on which Chester and I had built our homestead. The upriver half of the flat held the orchard, house and garden, barn and animal pens, the hay meadow, a pasture of nut grass and timothy. The lower half held scattered pine that ended at a cliff. Chester and I had put more physical effort than we'd thought possible into taming the half-mile-long bar. The resulting farmstead had become an extension of ourselves, born of our backs, our sinew, our sweat, our tears. Before Chester died I'd come to value the beauty and solitude of our wilderness home. Now that he was gone, that solitude held me prisoner.

Pebbles clattered down the slope behind me and rolled to a stop in a fringe of brush. High on the hillside, clouds of dust rose from a trail that snaked precariously down from the rim to the river's edge. The clouds screened the movement of animals on one of the switchbacks, but from the size of the dust-veiled figures and from the grate of metal on rock, I judged it to be a string of horses or mules. Lately, prospectors had been passing through on their way to the Thunder Mountain gold discoveries in the ranges to the south. Because of Chester's ferry crossing, this was the shortest route into the gold country. The nearest wagon road dropped into the canyon sixty miles to the east, another road fifty miles to the west. Trails were almost as scarce.

"Looks like we have customers for the ferry," I said to my collie and hound. They'd been lying at my feet, sad-eyed, heads resting on their paws, as if aware of my mood and of the reason for the mound of earth. "Better go see who it is." Alert to the activity on the trail, the dogs shot from their beds and sped across the sidehill of bunchgrass and pines to intercept the packstring.

Unlike the dogs, I was reluctant to leave, irritated to have my melancholy disturbed. I had no desire to tend the ferry, but I was responsible for it until John and Oakie, the young men who'd bought the ferry crossing, arrived in the canyon. I'd asked Len Johnson, a hermit who lived upriver, if he'd take charge until John and Oakie arrived, but he'd declined. He seldom ventured from his shack, though he'd come to dig Chester's grave, for which I was grateful. I took up my snake stick, made sure the fork at the tip hadn't split a tine, then poking at the grass, headed upriver along a deer path that followed the base of the hill. Young apple and pear trees growing between the path and the Salmon scented the air. The peach trees were yet to bloom. Downriver from the orchard, peas and lettuce splotched the earth green, and in the distance, timothy striped the hayfield. It seemed unjust the earth should continue to spin and nature to give green birth without Chester here to see, and smell, and appreciate it all.

Below the orchard, the Salmon rushed to meet the Snake without offering the slightest apology for taking Chester's life. As on most ice-free days from April to November, the river rumbled and spat defiance at the world. I viewed it with the same respect I'd give a precipitous cliff or one of the rattlesnakes that lurked in the shadows, a monster that exacted a toll from those brave enough, desperate enough, or foolish enough to call its banks home. At the moment, I considered myself one of the latter.

By the time I reached the ferry, a man leading a string of three pack mules had ridden down the last steep pitch of the trail. He seemed better prepared for months in the wilds than most prospectors. Some crossed the river with only a bedroll, shovel, and fry pan strapped to their backs. They'd leave homes, families, jobs behind, willing to risk life and limb to discover minerals gleaming on a hillside or the wink of gold in the shifting sands of a stream. Since the early 1860s they'd built gold camps all over central and northern Idaho, among them Elk City, the trailhead some twenty crow-flight miles north of the ranch. Now thousands of men crawled over the Thunder Mountain country, vying for a place to strike their picks.

I supposed the man about to ride onto the flat was no different than the rest, too seized by gold fever for conversation with a fifty-five-year-old widow. He sat a horse better than most, swiveling his hips with the loose-jointed motion of a practiced rider. A boy sitting behind the saddle slid around on the horse's rump like a saddlebag that had come unstrapped. On the trail above them, a rider on a buckskin bellowed at a string of mules to stop crowding his horse. The animals moved stiff-legged on the steep slope, skidding their hind feet and kicking up loose rocks and dirt.

The lead horse, a roan, grunted onto the flat, followed boulder-lined Weasel Creek across the head of the bar, past hills of gravel the previous owner had dumped from his placer operation, and slogged to a stop at a hitch rail near the ferry. Anxious to have a chance at water along with the rest, the second packstring hustled their wrangler down to the rail, where they heaved out their sweaty sides and blew great breaths. The dogs circled them, barking and wagging their tails. In the pasture west of the barn, my mare, Sadie, whinnied a welcome.

The men slid from their saddles, stretched their backs and flexed their knees to ease the stiffness brought on by the ride. I closed the distance between us and got a strong whiff of horse dander, sweat, and saddle leather.

"You look trail-weary," I said to the first rider. His appearance was that of a stringbean in clothes. A high-crowned felt hat matched the black of his walrus mustache. Lines radiating from the corners of his eyes and mouth creased into an easy smile.

"We're tired, all right. Left camp at dawn. And

that last bit of trail was a bone shaker." He lifted the boy down from the roan's towering rump. "This here's Toby. My name's Burdick." He jerked a thumb at the other rider, a burly redhead with a weedy beard and a hard, turned-down mouth. "That there's Jones."

"Where are you headed?" I asked.

"Thunder Mountain."

"There must be a city of prospectors up there, the way they've been coming through." I spoke to the men, but watched the boy as the dogs crowded him, licking his face. I missed having children around. In Lewiston, where Chester had a medical practice, neighborhood children had tramped through the house all day long, attracted by my cookies and the lemon drops Chester kept on hand in his office. Burdick tied his string of mules to the hitch rail and led the roan down by the ferry to drink. On the rise from melting snows, the frothy river slapped the ferry's hull and that of a rowboat used at times to retrieve the ferry from one side of the river to the other. Though John and Oakie had bought the ferry crossing, I hadn't yet changed the name on the sign tacked to the mooring post. It read, CLARK'S FERRY, 50¢ PER PERSON, STOCK $1.00 PER HEAD.

With Burdick down at the river and the dogs sniffing mules, the boy, Toby, looked abandoned. He stood with his back against the hitchrail, chin tucked into his chest, and peered at me from under the brim of a battered felt hat. His eyes were large and red-brown. From his size and the baby-softness that hadn't left his face completely, I judged the boy to be seven or eight, a slender but sturdy child. He was brown as a rain-spoiled cherry. Dirty, too. Bits of chestnut hair poked through holes in his hat. Something about the boy drew me, possibly the unruly hair and expression of innocence on the round face that reminded me of the child I'd lost to diphtheria.

"Aren't you a mite young to be out prospecting?" I asked.

Jones, the redhead, answered for the boy. He'd walked his buckskin down beside the roan, dipped a bandana handkerchief in the river, and was wiping the kerchief across his face and neck. "Toby ain't with us. We just give him a ride down from Elk City. Says he has an uncle placering here on the river."

"That must be Len Johnson," I said. "He has a shack about a mile upriver."

The boy shook his head.

"Then who? Johnson is the only one I know of." The boy mumbled something so softly I wondered if he was talking to himself. "Who did you say?"

A bit louder, "Afton McCabe."

"Good lord! How do you expect to find McCabe? He could be anywhere between Salmon City and Lewiston." I'd met McCabe when he stopped at the cabin once. I thought of him as old, but he was probably only ten years my senior. Each spring the Scotsman built a small wooden scow with sweeps at each end, loaded it with enough supplies to last the year, then worked his way downriver from Salmon City, placering for gold at sandbars and side streams. Sometimes he'd take the scow apart and use the lumber to build a shack for the winter. Other times he'd travel as far as Lewiston and spend the winter there. In the spring, he'd return by trail and wagon road to Salmon City, trade his gold for supplies, and begin another trip down the Salmon. I'd heard rumors a tragedy had brought him to the canyon in self-exile many years ago.

Burdick cut a quid from a plug of tobacco and let his cheek swell around the lump. "Haskel up at Elk City did some asking around when the boy showed up at his store," he said around the lump. "He found out McCabe put hisself up a shack last fall. Says it's about a mile downriver from here."

"And I didn't know! Guess the winter is to blame. We hardly budged from the house except to feed the stock. But you'd think McCabe would have told us he was settling nearby."

"Haskel claims the old guy's a loner. Probably doesn't want anybody bothering him."

If anyone knew about people in the backcountry, Haskel did. He thought Chester and I were crazy to settle in the canyon, thought we'd be completely out of place, but he didn't know about the fascination wilderness and rushing waters held for Chester. In Lewiston, Chester had spent evenings wandering the banks of the Snake, watching the currents interlace. He'd pore over maps of the backcountry and dream of making a home in the wilds. He'd retired from his practice to do that very thing. Perhaps the lure of the unknown and the solitude of wilderness waters had drawn Afton McCabe in a similar way.

"You must have wanted to see McCabe badly, to come into these wilds all by yourself," I said to the boy. "Where are you from?"

The boy continued to stand head-hung and shy, looking at me slantwise from under long, reddish lashes. He made no reply, just pulled his legs together as children do when their bladder is full, too timid to ask to be excused.

The redhead pointed to the outhouse Chester had built for those who used the ferry. "Toby, better get to the privy."

Burdick and Jones led their mounts back to the hitch rail and tied them with loose knots. "You ain't gonna get much out of the boy," Jones said. "He wouldn't tell Haskel a thing. All he knows is the stage driver about run over the kid somewheres between Grangeville and Elk City. I seen plenty of them like that—get shoved out of the house during hard times or get tired of the beatings. I know, I was one of them."

He loosened the buckles on his saddlebag and took out one of the leather pouches Haskel used for the mail, also a bundle of newspapers. He was handing me the pouch when the roan bit the buckskin's rump. The buckskin squealed, laid its ears back, and struck out with a rear hoof. Jones gestured impatiently toward the ferry. "Gotta get these yahoos to where they can feed. All right if we use the ferry?"

I explained that my husband was dead and that I'd never piloted the ferry. "You'll have to manage by yourselves. But I'll check the sweeps. The pivot holes have been getting a little ragged."

Chester had designed a ferry like those he'd seen on the lower Salmon and Snake, a flat-bottomed scow with side racks for restraining stock and sweeps at each end instead of oars. It drifted from bank to bank with the help of ropes and pulleys. Some of the prospectors who used the ferry weren't too careful with the sweeps, nor did they bother to clean out the manure. A pile of it filled one corner. I took a shovel and scooped it into the river.

Burdick and Jones had watered their mules and tied them to the hitch rail on the riverbank. They brought their horses on board the ferry and secured them to the side rack. Spooked by the bobbing of the scow on the water, the horses pulled on their ropes and thumped their hooves on the wooden deck.

"The pivots need new holes reamed," I said to the prospectors, "but they can make another trip without splitting the wood. It's a good thing you came early. Another month and the water will be too high to cross. Probably worse than usual, with all the snow in the high country."

I walked back on shore with the men. "Just take one string across at a time, otherwise the ferry will ride too low in the water. You can tie the first string to the hitch rails across the river."

Burdick led his mules on board and returned with a cigar box bound with several windings of string. "Almost forgot this. It belongs to the kid."

The boy had come from the outhouse, tightening his belt. When he saw Burdick hand me the box, he came on the run. "That's mine," he said, holding out his hand. The look in his eyes was one of urgency, yet he was polite. I'd known children who would have grabbed what was theirs.

"Of course it's yours, child. I was just holding it for you. Come along, I'll fix supper. Then we'll see if we can find your uncle."

I felt guilty leaving Burdick and Jones to unravel the mystery of cable and pulleys, but it couldn't be helped. The ferry crossing had been Chester's job. It seemed ages since he'd tacked the sign in place, ages since we'd left Lewiston. I remembered the day he'd told our grown daughters of his plans to sell his practice and move onto the Salmon. The younger one had exploded, "You're insane! The only people crazy enough to live on that stretch of river are mountain men or those running from the law."

The older girl had tried reasoning. "You won't like being so far from everyone. What will the grandbaby do without you?"

The placer miner who'd turned over his Weasel Creek claim to Chester in payment for services rendered had called the place a paradise.

Another miner, who'd come down the river in a small scow and wintered in Lewiston, had warned of the isolation. "Well, well, now. I don't know as you'll like it. You might get lonely. There's only an empty miner's soddy here and there, most of them from the stampedes of the sixties. But don't you worry, gold strikes are being made every day. There's bound to be more prospectors coming your way."

I hadn't taken much comfort in the forecast then. Nor did I now that it had proved true. If we'd listened to our daughters, I wouldn't be living alone, far from those I loved, vulnerable to the whims of strangers.

Five years of foot travel had worn the path to the house smooth and wide enough for the boy to walk at my side, but he lagged behind, the cigar box latched under his arm. He stopped now and then to pick up a pebble full of glittering mica or to watch a lizard scoot beneath a rock. As we skirted the orchard and garden I pointed out the different fruit trees, garden crops, and a few volunteer pear seedlings that stood lifeless outside the six-foot hogwire fence. Mountain sheep who wintered in the canyon's lower reaches had stripped the seedlings' bark.

The cabin stood halfway down the flat, with my garden of tulips, daffodils, and lilacs around the foundation. The logs had lost most of their bark and begun to gray, but the mix of mud and pine needles we'd stuffed between the logs still held firm. The cabin's lower level was an open sitting room and kitchen fitted with Chester's pine furniture, my patchwork pillows and curtains. The upper level was a sleeping loft. Today, the entire house smelled of the potato yeast bread I'd baked early that morning and left on the table to cool while I helped a doe deliver her baby goats. With Toby along, the cabin seemed more inviting than it had since Chester's death.

I hung my sunbonnet on a peg near the kitchen door, took a hurried look through the

pouch of mail, and at the headlines in the latest
newspaper: President McKinley to Launch Battle-
ship at San Francisco Harbor—Fifteen Thousand
Left Homeless After Fire (dateline Jacksonville,
Florida)—Andrew Carnegie to Give Away For-
tune. So much happening in the outside world, yet
here on the Salmon, such events seemed distant,
unreal.

My oldest daughter, Marybelle, wife of an
apothecary in Lewiston, sent us copies of the
Lewiston Morning Tribune. They piled up at Elk
City until a packer made a trip down onto the
river, or Chester made a trip out. The man who
delivered mail to the small mining camp of Dixie,
ten miles over the hump, didn't want his horse to
carry the extra volume and weight.

I set the newspaper on my rocker to read later
and fastened my braids back into a coil. They'd
slipped that morning when I'd acted as midwife to
the nanny goat and I hadn't bothered to reset the
pins. It seemed I'd always worn my hair in braids,
though now strands of silver threaded the black.
Chester had said if it weren't for my blue eyes and
light skin he'd think me a Nez Perce Indian. I did
have the prominent cheekbones and high, smooth
forehead of the Nez Perce, but stripped lean after
five years working the homestead, I lacked the
plumpness of some Indian women.

To make room at the kitchen table, I moved the
bread to the cupboard worktop, shoved aside books,
a box of watercolors and paper, wood-carving tools
that lay neglected. I'd tried to keep up with my art
since I'd attended the Academy in San Francisco,

but care of family had allowed only a few minutes now and then. My youngest daughter, Jennie, a teacher in Lewiston, had sent the paints and carving tools my first winter on the Salmon. "You'll have more time for it, now," she'd written. "You can paint a picture for my parlor."

I'd painted the picture to repay her kindness, as well as others during the winter evenings, though mending, darning, and sewing held first claim on the hours of darkness.

At the moment, sunlight streamed through the kitchen window, revealing dust I'd allowed to gather on the table since Chester's death. Somehow it hadn't mattered, but with the boy standing there, I felt shame.

"I'm sorry for the looks of the place. I—I've not felt like cleaning." I wiped the dust with the tail of my apron.

Toby took a wooden piglet from the table and ran his fingers over the snout.

"Do you like pigs?" I asked. He gave a vague nod. "I carved that one, but I need to do more work on it. The ears don't droop enough." I indicated a corner of the kitchen where I'd set a miniature barn carved from a slab of Ponderosa. There were several farm animals inside. "I made that barn to send to a grandchild, but you can have one of the animals, if you like."

While Toby fondled the animals, I stoked the coals in the range's fire box and added kindling from a stack beside the stove. I took goat cheese, pitcher of milk, and bean pot from the cooler at the back of the kitchen, put the beans into a pan to heat. By the time I'd cut several slices of bread, Toby had returned to the table and sat clutching a pony.

I set a plate of cheese and bread on the table. "Lordy, Toby! Your hands are so dirty you look like you're wearing gloves. I'll fill the basin so you can wash." I pulled a blue enamelware basin from under the wooden sink, poured it half-full with water from the pump, added hot water from the tea kettle. "Be sure you scrub with this." I set a bar of lye soap on the sideboard.

The boy didn't move.

"Come, child, a little water won't hurt you."

Slowly, he slid his rump from the chair and scuffed across the floor, his unreadable, red-brown stare fastened on mine.

"Don't be frightened. I haven't eaten a boy for ages."

I was certain he knew the words were said in jest, yet he thought awhile before he pushed his chest up to the sinkstand and dribbled his fingers in the water.

"Have you forgotten how to scrub?" Leaning over the boy, I rolled up his sleeves and plunged his hands into the water. He winced. I put in more cold water, working the handle on the pump attached to the sinkstand.

Toby watched with inquiring eyes. "Ma never had a pump in her kitchen. We had to carry water."

"Chester connected this to the spring out back."

"Who's Chester? Your man?" He glanced over his shoulder at the sitting room as if he might have missed someone. "Where is he?"

"He—he's dead, child." My voice thickened on the words.

"How'd he die?"

My thoughts flew to the day of the drowning. I saw Chester out on the frozen river, cutting ice. I heard the terrible cracking sound, like a rifle shot—heard Chester cry out as the slab of ice on which he stood broke free of the shore and bobbed up and down on waves caused by the break. I saw Chester teeter helplessly on the edge of the slab for an instant, then plunge into the black waters beneath. I saw myself sprawled on the shore ice while I ran my arm back and forth in the freezing waters, feeling for Chester's clothes, crying his name, crying again and again until my voice cracked from the strain, cracked from sobs that clawed their way up my throat. Now tears flashed in my eyes. "He drowned," I said simply.

Toby seemed to think about that. "My mom's dead, too."

I drew back so I could see his face. It remained inscrutable. "I'm sorry. You must miss her very much." Again that vague nod. I pulled a towel from a rack next to the sink and let him dry his hands.

"Are you an orphan, then?"

He shook his head tentatively, as if the mute answer needed further explanation. He gave none, just sat down at the table with the pony and precious cigar box close at hand. I put a glass of goat's milk and a bowl of beans in front of him, then sat across the table with coffee and my own plate of supper, observing him while he ate. He seemed to have gone a long while without care. His clothes belonged in a rag heap, and though we'd scrubbed his hands clean, dirt crusted his neck and ears. His hair was ragged, matted in places, his cheeks sunken in a round face.

"Do you want to tell me why you came looking for McCabe?"

He darted me a fearful look, said nothing.

"It must be mighty important."

Still no reply.

"Do you like goat's milk?"

"I like this. Mrs. Pardee's milk tasted like goats smell."

"She must have kept the buck with the does after the kids were born. They have to be separated, or the does pick up the smell of the buck."

"I didn't like her bread, either."

"Who is this Mrs. Pardee?"

He said nothing, merely scowled at his plate.

"I expect you won't have yeast bread down at your uncle's place. He probably makes all his bread from sourdough. Do you like sourdough?"

A nod as he wolfed down a spoonful of beans. "Ma kept a starter for hotcakes. Mrs. Pardee let hers turn too vinegary. I know 'cause I sneaked a taste of it once." The face he made revealed a mouthful of large, square teeth.

"You don't seem to like this Pardee person."

He wrinkled his nose. "Foster mother."

I felt surprise. Toby had implied he was no orphan. "Is Afton McCabe your only kin?"

The boy's gaze wandered, losing its focus. He swilled down a mouthful of bread.

"It's hard to be without kin," I said as I went to the stove to refill his bowl. The beans had stuck to the bottom of the pot. I gave them a stir. "I have family in Lewiston, and in San Francisco where I was raised. But they never come down here."

Toby raised his eyes, their expression part longing, part resentment sparked by some inner turmoil. "I got a pa. He's a sheep rancher."

I set the bowl of beans on the table. "Why aren't you with him?"

Anger flowed from the boy to spoon as he dug into the beans. "Pa don't want me no more. He farmed me out when Ma died."

I recognized the pattern. It happened when men found themselves alone with a brood to raise. I'd never approved of the practice, but times of loss in a place like Idaho made for tough decisions. "Maybe it was too hard for your father to keep you on."

"We woulda helped. He just didn't want us around. He was afraid we'd—" He snapped his mouth shut on the thought.

"You'd what?" Silence. "Who's 'we'?"

"My brothers and sister."

"Are they older or younger than you?"

"Younger. Some people took them to Oregon. I wanted to go too, but Pa made me stay at Lucile with Pardees." He jabbed the spoon into the beans in a sullen way.

I recalled the small settlement of Lucile, one in a string of tiny farm settlements between Riggins, where the Salmon turned north, leaving the

wilderness, and Lewiston, near the river's confluence with the Snake. "You came all that way by
yourself! How did you manage?"

"Walked . . . caught rides on wagons."

"I can't believe the Pardees let you do such a
thing!"

The spoon stilled. A mix of fear and guilt
showed behind the boy's eyes.

2

*I*t dawned on me that no responsible adult
would have allowed the boy to travel a hundred and forty backwoods miles on his
own.

"You didn't run away, did you?"

Toby squirmed, lowering his head, then
shoved his chair back from the table. He picked up
the pony and box. "Thank you for supper. I'll be
going."

"You did run away!"

"You gonna turn me in?"

"No." I put my hand on his sleeve. "I like children. I raised five of my own." He pulled his arm
away and headed for the sitting room. I followed,
saying, "Why don't you spend the night with me?
I can wash and mend your clothes so your uncle
won't think you're something the cat dragged in."

At the doorway, he stood, shifting his gaze
between my anxious face and the trail that wound
downriver.

I said, "You can put on some of Chester's

clothes. They'll bag on you, but we can roll up the sleeves and trouser legs. When I've washed your clothes and hung them on the line, I can bake a chocolate cake, and—" Realizing how desperate I sounded, I lowered my voice and calmed my frantic appeal. "What kind of icing do you like?"

Toby hung in the doorway awhile, seeming to consider more than the choice of icing. "Chocolate," he replied without turning to face me.

"Good. It's settled."

I put my arm around the boy's shoulders and drew him upstairs into the shadowy loft. To offset the lack of windows, I'd brightened the loft with splashy quilts of red and gold, braided rugs to match, and tacked my hand-loomed tapestries to the walls. Chester had built the loom our first winter on the Salmon and had found as much pleasure in it as I. He'd woven a rug to put at the foot of the Franklin stove in the sitting room, another to stand on after bathing in the metal tub in the kitchen, a third rug to front the chair he'd made by lacing deerhide to a frame of alder.

I lit the bedside lamp. From an oak cupboard I took one of Chester's shirts and a pair of dark gray trousers, the same pair he'd worn for a picture we had taken in Elk City four years before his death. The picture hung on the wall above the four-poster bed. I was dressed in my best green silk, several years younger than Chester and half a head taller, but feeling smaller than that splendid man. I looked a little heavier then, and very serious, though I recall wanting to break into a smile.

I would have selected a pair of Chester's work pants for Toby, but I'd worn them to spade the garden, and they were in need of a wash. I put the suit trousers and shirt on the bed and left the boy standing there, uncertain.

He looked like a circus clown when he clumped down the stairs and into the kitchen, carrying his dirty clothes. I'd put a tub of water on the stove to heat, and was shaving bits of soap into the water. I stifled a laugh. "You won't be able to do a thing with those sleeves flopping around. Here, let me roll them up." Folding the cuffs over and under, I rolled the sleeves until they were two-thirds their actual length. I did the same with the trouser legs. I was about to gather the shirttail into the pants when I glimpsed scars on the small of Toby's back. Raising the shirt, I saw row upon row of slender welts, some hard and scabbed over, others still raw, festering.

When Toby realized I'd seen his back, he whirled and stuffed the shirt into the trousers.

"Who did this to you?" I asked gently.

His eyes stretched wide. His voice turned breathy. "Nobody . . . just nobody!"

Next morning, Toby and I kneeled in the straw of the barn admiring the quartet of goats born the previous day. The smallest had tried to emerge from the birth canal with a leg turned wrong, and I'd had to help her out, so I felt a special fondness for her. She was Toby's favorite, too. He ran his fingers through her silky hair and smiled.

"She's cute. Has she got a name?"

"No. What would you suggest?"

"Umm . . . how about Nubbin? Ma always called little things Nubbin."

"All right, Nubbin it is."

As Toby giggled at the antics of the goats, he seemed unconcerned about what lay ahead. He'd refused to explain the scars on his back, though he'd let me treat them and cover them with gauze. All night I'd worried about the welts while I listened to the owls screech and the coyotes yodel on the canyon rim. I'd tossed and turned, turned and tossed, winding the bedclothes around my knees. I'd thought about the harsh life of most ranch children, no time for play or laughter, up before dawn, chores until bedtime, punished if they didn't perform, some boarded out and used as slaves.

Toby's momentary happiness made me wish I could give him one of the kids when they were weaned, but I'd promised them to the hermit Len Johnson.

Maisie, the doe, had been letting the kids suckle while she licked up the last of the grain in her pan. The stall smelled of her rich milk. Every morsel of oats gone, she stuck out her long tongue to lick the runt's ear.

"She's a good mama," Toby said.

"Yes, for it being her first litter. But animals usually are good parents."

"Not like people. 'Specially foster parents."

"I suppose foster parents can be mean sometimes, but you know, Toby, so can real parents . . . even the good ones. I always considered myself a good mother, but when my youngsters were small I'd get so tired I'd scold them more than I should."

"Pardees did more'n scold."

"You mean the scars?"

His eyes glazed over. "Don't tell nobody. Pardees might find out I snitched on them and come looking for me."

I put my hand on his shoulder and felt him flinch, a sign he'd been frightened often. "No one is going to come way out into the wilds looking for you, child. I wouldn't tell anyway. I can't imagine why anyone would want to whip you."

He hung his head and worked his mouth, taking a moment to respond. "They said I done my chores too slow. Said I was always dreaming 'stead of working." He took the cigar box he'd set in the straw and clutched it to his breast as if it gave him comfort.

The confession brought an ache to my heart. "You sound like my own little boy, Teddy. He was the greatest one to sit and while away the hours instead of doing his chores. I'd get exasperated and scold. Lord! How I wish I'd never raised my voice to the child. How was I to know he'd leave me, to do his dreaming in heaven?"

"He died?"

"He had diphth—" My throat clogged. I stared at the wall, suffering visions of the past, visions of a child like Toby with a love for animals, a shy child with soulful eyes and a smile that

warmed my heart. He was just eight when he died.
All of Chester's doctoring hadn't kept him alive.
The failure had crushed Chester for years after-
ward.

The runt nudged me for attention. I pulled
her squirming into my arms and absorbed solace
from her warmth, from the clean smell of her doe-
licked hair. Her pulse raced beneath my fingertips.

"You can dream all you want, Toby. I won't
scold."

With a sigh, I pulled myself back to the task at
hand. I released the wiggly kid and opened the
stall door, directing Toby to the opposite wall of
the barn where rows of spikes driven into the logs
held halters, bridles, and the like. Chester had
insisted that everything have its place and kept it
there when not in use. He'd arranged things on
pegs, in bins, in metal boxes, and had hung the sets
of harness from the roof to keep them from mice
and pack rats—the rats chewed the leather for the
salt absorbed from the mules' sweaty hides.

Toby closed the stall door and set his beloved
cigar box on a wooden oat bin near the row of
spikes. "You loved Teddy, didn't you," he said, as
I handed him braided halters for horse and mule.
"Ma loved me, too. She told me so. You wanna see
her picture?"

"Of course."

Toby strung the halters over a saddle that lay
astride a sawhorse, then loosened the many windings of string on the cigar box. The tintype he
handed me showed a thin-faced woman with sad
brown eyes and dark hair piled in coils at the

crown of her head. I was drawn into those eyes, wondering what hardships had caused their expression of hopelessness, their lack of sheen. I'd seen the same bleak countenance on farm wives riding rickety wagons into town, a mirror of the shadows in their minds, their feelings of dark misgiving and resentment.

One ranch wife had confessed to me of her loneliness and sadness. "I must bear all my troubles alone. Each day is the same old routine. Besides my house and farm chores, my husband expects me to run around after sheep all day long. It hardly seems like living." The eyes in the picture reflected a similar existence.

"Your mother was pretty," I said to Toby. "You have her features, except that your face is more round."

"That's what Pa always said. He didn't like me, 'cause he didn't like her."

The words startled me. I looked up from the picture and saw hate burning in the boy's eyes. "I'm sorry if your father gave you reason to think that. It's not good to harbor such feelings."

The boy shrugged his shoulders in a show of indifference.

His mother's face remained fixed in my mind as I watched him return the picture to the box and secure it with string. "What caused her death?"

Toby's eyes widened. He bit his lip as the fright of remembrance crept over his face. "H-her baby couldn't get born, and she—she got so tired she died. 'Least that what Pa said." Bitterness put a sharp edge on his voice. "But I know why . . ."

He closed his mouth on that thought and moved his lips silently on the next before he added, "Aunt Mary said Pa worked Ma into her grave."

The picture I had of Toby's father was of someone I could despise. I'd known others like him. The Idaho ranch and farm country had its share of men who'd settled the land, even made fortunes by breaking the backs and spirit of their women, men who took out their hatred for life on their wives and children, on the stock that toiled beneath their whip. To keep from saying something I'd regret, I raised the lid of the oat bin. Two mice scuttled from beneath the bin, where stray oats had collected. I ladled some oats into a bucket. The sweet, grainy scent filled my nostrils.

"We have what we need from here, Toby. Let's call in Sadie and Highpockets."

Toby seemed glad the conversation had changed direction. He skipped ahead of me into the barnyard, swinging the halters with a vitality he hadn't shown the previous day. The bawling of spring babies greeted us from the animal pens—piglets, calves, kids born earlier that year. Maisie had been late to drop hers. Napoleon, the buck, stood on the roof of his pen, bleating his authority. Toby wanted to spend time with the babes, but I hurried him along to keep warm. Several white leghorn chickens had left the henhouse and scuttled along the ground. They chased one another one minute, clucked and searched for seeds and insects the next.

The air had turned frigid during the night. Wind squealed up the canyon, pushing along woolly gray clouds that smelled of snow, one of those late storms that caught men basking in the promise of spring and touched their faces with frost. I feared for the orchard. Snow would turn the centers of the blossoms black and ruin the chance for fruit. Lettuce and radishes I could plant again, but the fruit blossoms had only one chance each year.

I made a yodeling sound when we arrived at the split-rail fence that separated the pasture from the corral and barn. Chester had always called the animals by tucking his lower lip under his teeth in a shrill whistle, but yodeling was easier for me. At the far end of the pasture, my horse and mule pricked up their ears and looked my way. I called again, and they came swishing through the grass, my sorrel mare handsome with her mane and tail fanned out in the wind. Highpockets, a grizzled old bay mule with white muzzle, followed a couple of lengths behind Sadie. He sped up as they skirted a low, tannish-gray mound of hay surrounded by a slat fence, the remains of last year's crop.

"They sure come to you good," Toby said.

"Chester and I turned them into pets. When I call, they know I have a treat . . . oats . . . pancakes . . . raisins. Chester made pets of all the animals, tame and wild. He kept a crow that liked to steal bright things. One time it hopped to where I was mending on the porch and flew away with the extra thimble from my sewing kit."

Toby laughed.

"Sometimes Chester would take a plate of left-overs from supper, set it outside on the ground and whistle. In no time, rock chucks, chipmunks, and camp robbers would come to eat from the plate, some from his hand."

"They knew he liked them."

A sigh tugged at my breast. "Yes . . . yes, they did." The horse and mule pulled up to the fence, their sides heaving from the run, and started snuffling the oats I'd dumped into their pans. They loved oats. In '97 a wagon road had been punched through to the mining camp of Dixie, ten miles northwest over the hump, and freight was delivered there in an open lumber wagon pulled by four horses—wheels in summer, sled runners in winter. After that, Chester was able to pack oats down from Dixie, rather than make the forty-mile round trip to Elk City, though we still went there for most supplies.

I crawled through the fence to stroke Sadie's neck and pull out patches of winter hair she was shedding. She and Highpockets had rubbed their hides on the slivery fence rails, and strands of hair clung to the wood.

"Is this mule a good packer?" Toby asked.

"He's packed just about everything you can think of, from rocking chairs to plowshares. He helped move us into the canyon."

"Bet that was a hard trip."

"I'll never forget it! The teamsters we hired at Lewiston drove their wagons only as far as Elk City. We had to buy stock there and pack our belongings down to the river. What an ordeal!" While I spoke, I slipped a halter over Highpockets' head and fastened the buckle. "Our two sons helped wrangle the mules. None of us had any experience."

Toby looked up at the canyon rim. "Bet you didn't like that zig-zaggy trail coming off the ridge."

"No! I still don't. I'm always afraid Sadie will step too close to the edge and we'll fall hundreds of feet into the river."

"I know what you mean. The horse I was on tripped a couple of times." Toby looked out over the pasture. "Where's the rest of your horses?"

"I sold them to prospectors . . . too many hooves for me to trim. The farrier comes twice a year—in spring to set the shoes, in fall to pull them. I never learned to shoe the animals. It takes a lot of strength."

"Do you ride Highpockets?"

"Sometimes. He's good under the saddle. I'll let you ride him down to your uncle's place." I'd put a halter on Sadie, and was opening the pasture's pole gate to lead the animals through. "I've only seen McCabe once, but as I recall he's pretty old to be your uncle."

"He's not a first uncle. He's my grandma's brother."

"How did you know where to find him?"

"I heard him talking to Pa last time he was at the ranch. He said he'd found this really good pay streak and was going to spend a couple of years working it."

I gave Toby the mule's rope, pulled the gate shut, and headed for the barn to saddle the horse. The animals felt the cold and clopped their hooves in double time on the barnyard's hard-packed earth. Sam and Bones, my collie and hound, had come in from their morning rounds and ran alongside, their tongues lolling out. In the past, Bones had lost half his tail fighting a coon, Sam the tip of an ear.

"I wonder what your uncle will say when he sees you so far from home?"

"I dunno. He doesn't know Ma died . . . or that Pa don't want me."

"Did you ever stop to think your father might regret letting you go." I didn't really believe that.

"Not Pa! He'd send me back to Pardees or do something—something really bad to me."

Looking across Sadie's nose at the boy, I saw that mention of his father had brought more fear to his face than talk of Pardees.

"What are you afraid of, Toby?"

He turned his eyes toward the ground. "Nothing—just never mind."

Saying little more, we saddled horse and mule, headed out past the house and flower garden and turned west on the river trail. Toby looked like a miniature drover astride the big mule. He handled the reins well and rode straight as a rod. Of course, the fleece-lined jacket I'd loaned him wouldn't allow a slack seat. The stiff jacket was Chester's, and with the collar turned up, only Toby's eyes showed. They peered out like brown coals from the woolly cavern.

To protect myself from the cold, I'd pulled a stocking cap down over my ears and braids, layered sweaters under my coat, and pulled on a pair of Chester's woolen trousers under my skirts.

The trail paralleled the Salmon about twenty yards above the water's edge. The river reflected the leaden sky, appearing more sullen than ever. Fed by snowmelt, a backbone of current piled up huge waves in midstream. The riverbank narrowed beyond the flat, and a trail of sorts followed slender strands of sand and gravel through beds of rock. Tracks in the sand marked the passage of deer and mountain sheep. Where the trail met the south-sloping hill, thickets of hawthorn and wild rose rustled with the movement of small animals and birds. Sam and Bones followed the line of brush, their noses an inch above the ground, testing for scent, swerving to avoid barrel cactus that brightened the gloomy day with fuchsia blooms. Now and then the dogs swung around abruptly to sniff a tangle of branches or a log where rabbit and grouse had left sign.

At one point on the trail, a granite wall sheered upward from the river for three hundred feet. The trail at the base of the cliff was barely passable through dumps of boulders that lined the stream bed. Rocks and sand, dampened before the cold night lowered the river, showed that snowmelt was causing the river to creep up the bank toward a high water mark eight feet above the trail. The source of the melt was the wilderness of knife-like ridges and jumbled canyons, tumbling creeks and wild, frothing rivers that stretched for scores of miles in all directions.

The main fork of the Salmon began as a trickle in the Sawtooth Range, a jagged upthrust of rocks located far to the south. From its source, the river flowed more than four hundred crooked miles before it emptied into the Snake on the line between Idaho and Oregon. Lewiston, the town where Chester and I had spent most of our married life, was situated near that confluence.

Sadie picked her way carefully through the rocks until we came to a creek that poured down a side canyon into the river. I knew the alder-lined creek and the bar that lay beyond. Each summer I picked orange currants at the back of the bar, also holly berries and purple serviceberries that grew on the hillsides. Now that McCabe had claimed the small flat, I wondered if I'd have the privilege.

As I'd expected, Sadie backed away from the churning creek and fought the reins. Every time I asked her to get her feet wet, it ended in a battle of wills. I let her backtrack a few steps, spun her around, and was about to charge the creek, when a huge Newfoundland tore through the willows and alders on the opposite bank and barked a warning.

3

The Newfoundland's black coat had a soft sheen, the hair neither long nor short. Sam and Bones weren't taken with the dog's good looks. They plunged through the icy water to the far side of the creek and circled him in a noisy dance of daring.

From up the creek, a gruff voice called, "Reb! Get back here!"

I said, "Sam, Bones, stay!" They did so with reluctance, yipping, hackles raised. They glanced alternately at the Newfoundland and at me for permission to start the chase.

The black dog ran several yards toward the voice, paused to look our way, then tunneled through the undergrowth toward a man barely perceptible through the branches.

I stung the mare's flanks with the reins. "Geeap, Sadie! We might as well get this over with."

Ears laid back in resentment, Sadie plowed through the water, Highpockets at her tail. On the far bank, she shouldered her way through a cross-weave of branches onto a flat about fifty yards deep and three times as long.

Startled by our sudden appearance, two Bighorn ewes and three lambs trotted down the flat a ways, then stopped, bulge-eyed, to look us over. Now and then they glanced up the creek where the Newfoundland's master had felled a huge, thick-barked pine across the creek, apparently for a bridge. The smell of resin was strong, the ground strewn with green needles, shattered bark, and limbs.

As we approached the man, the Newfoundland ran up to meet us, waltzed around Sam and Bones stiff-legged a minute or two, then coming to terms with the dogs, tore in and out the severed limbs in a game of chase.

Afton McCabe had straightened from limbing the tree and leaned on his ax handle to watch us ride up. The tall Scotsman was leaner and more stooped in the shoulders than I remembered. Years hunched over a goldpan and rocker could do that to a man. I thought he must be at least sixty-five, perhaps older. His clothes did nothing to make him look younger—a dirty stocking cap with a frayed edge, a sweater with holes in the elbows, denims with longjohns peeking through tears in the knees. The black-checkered mackinaw he'd thrown over a boulder seemed in better condition. Snow had begun to spit from the sky, scattering white pellets on the coat.

McCabe didn't know Toby in the nest of fleece until we slid from our saddles and faced him.

He lowered the wrinkled crepe of his eyelids in a long, narrow look. "What in the name of heaven brings you into the wilds, lad?" The Scottish burr was thick, rough, made more severe by a toothpick clenched between the teeth.

Toby eyed the ground and dug the toe of his boot into the dirt. He seemed about to turn tail and run. To provide reasonable escape, I gave him the mare's lead rope and told him to tie the horse and mule to trees with suitable girth.

While the boy did my bidding, McCabe and I locked stares, taking the measure of each other, my eyes almost on a level with his. I saw a determined survivor, impatient with human contact. I hadn't forgotten the face—long and harsh looking, a closed expression. The cheekbones were high, their thin covering of skin and flesh drawn tight as a mummy's. Above them, eyebrows jutted from the forehead like the wings of a bird. Snow pellets caught on the brows and on bristly whiskers that made a mustache and spade beard difficult to distinguish from the rest of the gray.

Judging from his scowl, McCabe saw me as a harbinger of trouble, a woman brazen enough to intrude on his privacy and meddle in his affairs. My eyes, I knew, held the glint of a woman who considered herself an equal, not the look of humility most men thought becoming to a woman. I steeled myself for his displeasure.

"Perhaps you remember me . . . Harriet Clark? I live a mile upriver."

"I remember." There was no tone of welcome in his voice.

"Could we talk alone?" I motioned toward a cluster of pines a short distance from where we stood.

McCabe's gray-green eyes filled with distrust. "I suppose, if we must." He shoved the ax aside.

"I didn't want to talk in front of Toby," I said when we were out of the boy's hearing. "It embarrasses him to speak of his problems. He told me his mother died and his father sent him to live with people who treated him badly." I went on to relate the little I knew of the boy's flight into the wilderness.

"He can't stay with me. I like the lad, but he must do as his father says."

"The foster parents whipped him. I saw the scars. And I gather his father is none too kind."

McCabe drew his eyebrows tight. "I can't help that. I had my share of whippings before I left home. 'Tis part of growing up. The boy must do his duty."

"He's only eight! What does he know of duty?"

"He must learn!"

I stared at McCabe in disbelief. "Then, you'll not take him in?"

"I'll be sending him back with the first packstring headed for Elk City."

"He'll run away before he ever gets there. How can you care so little about the boy?"

"His father is my nephew. I care that the boy does his father's bidding."

"His father's bidding is not right for the boy. And your reasoning is just as bad." I blew a gust of air, started to turn aside, turned back. "There's no chance you'll change your mind?"

"None at all."

"Then, if you won't take him in, I will!" I spun on my heel, intent on reaching Toby before McCabe could come between us.

He caught up to me in two long strides and turned me around by the elbow. "'Tis none of your business, Missus Clark. The boy is *my* kin, to tend to as I see fit. Now, leave us be!"

For a long, thorny moment our stares grappled in an anger neither of us cared to express in words, an anger I wasn't proud of but couldn't restrain. When finally I relinquished my stare, I went to where Toby waited long-faced and shy.

"Don't lose heart," I said, bending close to the boy. "You're always welcome at my place."

I kept a close watch on the river trail in the warm days that followed the snowstorm, but saw no sign of Toby or his uncle. After my outburst, I imagined McCabe would do his best to avoid me, but that wouldn't be easy. The rugged canyon allowed no trail downriver past his placer claim, nor up over the mountain back of the claim. He'd need to pass my house to intercept packtrains for Elk City. I thought he might have decided to keep the boy. Still, I couldn't help worrying. Whatever my task, Toby's face hung in my mind, soft, wistful, frightened. Some boys' eyes took on a callous look with adversity. Not Toby's.

After two weeks I could no longer stand the waiting. I put several dozen chocolate cookies in coffee cans, put the cans in a saddlebag along with a wedge of goat cheese and two loaves of bread, and headed downriver on Sadie. Sam and Bones streaked ahead. I knew McCabe wouldn't be happy to see us, but Toby and the Newfoundland might.

Swollen with melt from the winter snows, the river raged, carrying tree limbs and other debris it had snatched along the way. Water covered stunted willows that poked from between the rocks at shoreline. A foot and a half of roily water washed over the trail where it skirted the cliff. Sadie put up the usual battle before she waded the flood at the cliff.

McCabe's Creek presented an even greater challenge. Rocks, which during normal flow provided stepping stones, hid beneath a torrent of greenish-blue snowmelt. The raging creek reached the bottom of the log McCabe had felled for a bridge. Surges sprayed over the top. The log, hacked flat on top for ease in walking, was the only safe route to the other side.

Crouching, every muscle tense, the dogs crept across the log, then sniffed the air and ran toward the mouth of the creek. My only choice was to dismount and lead Sadie across. I expected to be shoved into four feet of rampaging ice water, but illogical creature that she was, Sadie balked less crossing the slick log than she had wading the high water at the cliff, though she quivered and rolled the whites of her eyes.

Following the dogs' lead, I found McCabe working his placer claim at the mouth of the creek. Rather than disturb him, I tied Sadie to a tree and settled on a driftwood log that overlooked the creek, a can of cookies beside me. Evidently something had distracted Sam and Bones. They were nowhere in sight. They must not have made contact with the Newfoundland. He sat at McCabe's feet. Whenever McCabe moved a short distance with his shovel, the dog followed, man and dog moving as one.

Over the years, the creek had deposited a wide band of sand and gravel at its mouth. McCabe had removed a section of the gravel down to bedrock, and he was busy with a shovel and trowel, scooping material from depressions and seams in the rock. Toby stood nearby, beside him a long wooden box patterned after a child's cradle. Every now and then he glanced up at me in his bashful way.

McCabe gave no sign he'd noted my presence. He'd dug his teeth into a toothpick, forming his mouth into a snarl. I wondered if the toothpick was the same hand-shaved splinter he'd had tucked in his mouth when I was there last. He seemed to use a toothpick like some men used chewing tobacco, as a salve for bile. At one time, he'd been a nice-looking man. He still could be if he'd shave, dress in something besides rags, and smile rather than glower.

Not until he'd filled the buckets to the brim and set them beside the cradle did he bother to look my way. He straightened, wiping his forehead with his shirtsleeve. "'Twas foolish to lead your horse o'er the log, with the water slicking it," he yelled above the rumble of creek and river. "Should of tied her on the other side."

McCabe was right about the log, but I didn't believe in tying Sadie where I couldn't keep an eye on her. I started to say as much, but shut my mouth on it. I knew McCabe wasn't the sort to accept excuses, nor was I disposed to offer them.

"I got to worrying about Toby," I said loud enough to be heard below. "How is he getting along?"

McCabe jerked his head toward the boy. "You can see for yourself."

Having deigned to utter those few words, he stooped back to his work, dumping a small amount of gravel from one of the buckets into a perforated hopper at the upper end of the cradle. With a coffee can attached to a long pole, he scooped water from the creek and poured it over the gravel in the hopper while Toby rocked the cradle. Slowly, the mound of material disappeared through the holes in the hopper like flour through a sifter, except that large gravel stayed in the hopper.

I'd watched placer miners enough to know the smaller pebbles and mineral-bearing sands washed through the holes in the hopper onto a piece of canvas stretched across a frame on the inside of the cradle. The canvas caught some of the heavy, gold-bearing sands, while the rest of the material escaped into a three-foot-long flume at the bottom of the cradle. Strips of fir nailed across the flume every few inches caught gold sediment that slipped past the canvas. To prevent loss of fine gold, McCabe had set a tub at the foot of the flume to catch the discharge. Later, he'd drain the water from the tub and pan out the sediment. In a year, he'd likely find enough of the light flakes of Salmon River gold to keep him in supplies, with a little left over for the bank.

Many prospectors had the mistaken notion they could get rich on Salmon River gold. Before his death they'd ask Chester, "Do you know where there's good color?"

He'd say, "Sorry, I'm no prospector. I hear lots of tales, but that's all they are, tales. I'd hate to send you on a wild goose chase."

Gold hunters were always suspicious when Chester showed ignorance. They sometimes questioned me in the same way, but not as often. They seemed to consider a woman's knowledge of such things limited. They were right.

For McCabe, placer mining was a way to earn a living, not a get-rich scheme. I watched him as he focused on his work, his expression one of intense concentration, yet something in his face hinted at a pervading loneliness. I'd heard rumors of a tragedy in his life, something about a sweetheart's untimely death. Evidently the accident had left deep scars on the man.

Toby bore scars of his own. He fixed his somber gaze on me as he worked.

"Do you like it here, Toby?" I asked. He nodded vaguely, shrugged. "I brought you some goat cheese and bread. That ought to fill the hollows in your cheeks."

The remark caused McCabe to look up slowly, deliberately. His eyes sparked from the tower that was his head. "Missus Clark, I don't mind you sitting there and watching if you have no better thing to do. But 'tis none of your business how the boy eats. Nor do we want your charity."

"I consider it an act of friendship! Children need proper food." The heat of anger rose into my neck and cheeks. I slapped my hand down on the coffee can. "I hope you won't think these cookies charity. I doubted you were set up to do much baking." I looked down the flat toward a shack set at the edge of a grove of pines. It appeared to have been built from the boards of a river scow. A stovepipe elbowed from the rear wall, held in place by wires attached to the roof. In addition to the stove that must be inside, a sheepherder's stove squatted in front of the shack—probably to cook on in hot weather. A food cache the shape of a large box hung from the branch of a pine.

McCabe noted my skeptical look. "'Tis no castle, but it keeps out the weather," he said with ill-disguised spleen.

"Yes, I'm sure," I said under my breath. I held up the can of cookies in another attempt at friendship. "Would you like to have some, now? They're really quite good."

McCabe turned to Toby, grimacing. "I can see this woman won't leave us be 'til we play tea party. Fetch a jug of water from the spring, and we'll have us a cookie."

While Toby went for water, McCabe climbed the pebbly creekbank and seated himself on a boulder near my log. He'd spit the toothpick from his mouth, softening his look somewhat, but his eyes remained slits of displeasure. His dislike charged the air and made my skin prickle. I squirmed, wishing there was more space between us.

"What's your interest in the lad, Missus Clark?"

I shrugged. "I like Toby. I'm concerned about his welfare."

"As I said before, the boy's welfare is none of your business."

I wanted to say something spiteful in return. Instead, I took the lid from the can of cookies, releasing the dark smell of baking chocolate. I held out the can. McCabe wiped his hands on his pantleg, leaving black sand embedded beneath his fingernails. He hesitated, then dipped his hand into the can as if it held worms. When he chomped down on a cookie, it was obvious he was struggling to keep from showing gastronomic pleasure.

I'd intended to wait until the cookies sweetened his disposition before I asked about his plans for Toby. Sensing there was little chance for a change of mood, I blurted, "Did you decide to let Toby stay?"

His steely eyes said he wondered what right I had to ask. It took a while for him to answer, then it was like pulling a stubborn weed from the ground. "I'll keep him at least through the summer. The lad can help me with the cradle. I'll send him back to his pa before winter sets in."

My spirits soared at the thought the boy would be near all summer. For an instant I saw McCabe as a human being, not the misanthropic canker he seemed. His motive might have been selfish, but at least he'd given Toby a short reprieve.

"I'll be happy to do the boy's mending," I said. "I can sew him a shirt and trousers from some of Chester's clothes. Chester would be glad to know some good came from what he'd left behind."

A peculiar look crossed McCabe's face, not so much an expression as a reflection of an inner thought. "Is your man dead?"

"Yes."

"You'll be having your hands full, then, without doing for us. I been managing all these years with no female help."

"But you haven't had a child to care for."

McCabe's glare scalded. "Are you saying I'm not able?"

"No—of course not—it's just that—I thought I could h—"

"We can do for ourselves! The boy's learned to do without. No sense coddling him now."

"At least I can make him a suit of clothes!"

I'd wanted to visit with Toby, but couldn't trust myself to stay longer without saying something I'd regret, something that might close my access to the boy completely. Determined to leave before I wore out McCabe's grudging hospitality, I took cheese and bread from the saddlebag and set them on the log with a second can of cookies.

"I must get back to my garden," I said as I untied Sadie. "Tell Toby to come see the goats when the river goes down."

"Are you going to stay on the river without your man?" McCabe's tone was razor-edged, critical.

I considered saying it was none of his business, but that would put me on his level. "I haven't decided. I might go back to Lewiston. My youngest daughter wrote, inviting me to stay with her, but I'm not sure living with family is what I want." I put my foot in the stirrup and heaved a leg over the saddle.

"Best go home to your girl, Missus Clark. That's the place for a woman. With her kin."

I held Sadie in check long enough to shoot a resentful glance over my shoulder. *You'd like that, wouldn't you, Mister McCabe! Well, I'll not give you the satisfaction. You can depend on it.*

4

The river reached high stage after my trip to McCabe's Bar. It covered the trail at the cliff with nine feet of water and turned the canyon into a riot of bilious green. It brought the Thunder Mountain traffic to a standstill, causing me to feel more caged than ever. The ranch might as well have been an eight-by-eight cell with iron bars. The only difference was, I had no keeper to speak a word of greeting. I longed to see Toby, even looked forward to arguing with McCabe. I wondered, though, if I'd ever see them again. With a snoopy widow nearby, McCabe might decide to rebuild his scow and move downstream.

John and Oakie, the new owners of the ferry, had arrived in mid-June and put up a cabin on the east bank of Weasel Creek, but had returned topside to ease their boredom with gambling and women. I wondered about the two men. They claimed to be loggers from Oregon—the muscles that bulged their sleeves appeared to prove that— but the men seemed to lack stability, as if they were ready to take off at a moment's notice. Once when I went to their cabin with a gift of eggs, I saw two frontier six-shooters on the table and all manner of guns hanging from the wall. I thought they might have fled debts, imprisonment, disgrace, or family, like others who sought escape in the backcountry. They might be remittance men, paid to lose themselves by someone who wanted them out of the way. Propriety prevented my asking. Chester and I had found that, in Idaho, one accepted a man at face value, especially in the gold camps and in the canyon. Still, my doubts about the men added to my feeling of isolation. I began to think it unwise to stay in the canyon alone, began to dwell on all sorts of imaginary dangers. On the other hand, I wasn't ready to leave the homestead for good. It was our home. Chester's and mine. His presence still pervaded every nook and cranny.

If it hadn't been for the garden, I might have run off to the settlements for a while. As it was, I had Johnson tend the animals and made a four-day trip to Elk City for supplies. I stayed at the hotel, a surprisingly large building for a gold camp—three-story frame with a long veranda, cafe, and bar. I enjoyed eating food I didn't have to prepare myself, but I was accustomed to wilderness silence and the racket from the bar kept me awake at night.

Back in the canyon, the dread of being alone expressed itself as fatigue and a lack of will to attack the scores of projects that cried for attention. I fed most of the goats' milk to the cats and dogs rather than make it into cheese. My paints and carver's tools sat idle. I did complete a suit of clothes for Toby, but left the treadle heaped with curtains to be mended and flour sacks to be hemmed for dish towels. A sweater I'd been knitting for a grandchild waited for sleeves.

I'd cut my plantings by half, but the need for a winter larder wouldn't let me ignore the garden entirely. While my fingers worked the soil, I wondered where the years had gone. They seemed to have passed me by as swiftly as the river sped past my garden. There were things I'd wanted to do, places I'd wanted to visit. It seemed fate never intended I visit the Louvre or the ancient pillars of Rome and Greece, but surely a visit to my childhood home in San Francisco wasn't beyond reason.

I'd wanted to return to San Francisco ever since Chester and I moved to Lewiston, but family and duty had always interfered. The tri-story house of my childhood, overlooking the Golden Gate, held such pleasant memories—laughter, scholarly conversation, the sound of piano and strings, the aroma of French cuisine wafting from the kitchen, the reek of paint and canvas from my mother's studio. As a patron of the arts, my mother had opened our home to all manner of musicians, actors, artists, many of them with an intriguing, often bizarre outlook on life. As a newspaper publisher, my father hosted dinners for important personages of the day. At one of those dinners, Chester met the naturalist John Muir, a meeting that fueled his interest in the wilds. After that, he spent as many hours as his studies would allow at the seashore, and succumbed to the call of the Sierra Nevadas, making several camping trips there.

Son of a carpenter, Chester struggled to pay for every bit of education and culture he absorbed, but he loved the arts as much as I. He knew how to stretch his mind and mine, too. We went to Elizabethan plays and the ballet, browsed through bookstores, attended the opera. In fact, we'd met at the opera. In my mind's eye, I could see us high in the balcony of the San Francisco Opera House, listening to the tomb-like voice of *Aida*'s Ramfis rumble out from the Temple of Vulcan. I saw us wandering the halls of the Academy, viewing the works of artists-to-be. I imagined my own paintings hanging there, as they once had. In another vision, we walked the trails of Golden Gate Park amid the floral tapestries, the fragrance of lush green lawns. Chester was delightful company. He had a deep curiosity about everything, a joy of living. His face was full of crinkling good humor even when he talked of serious matters.

Those years before our marriage had a fairy-tale quality when compared to the reality of life in Idaho. They seemed a dream, episodes I recalled from some book or the telling of a stranger's experience. They seemed so distant. If I returned for a visit, would San Francisco be all I remembered? Would it have changed? I had. Thirty-five years of marriage, most of them in a country town, the last five in the wilds, had formed habits and provided a rut for my thoughts. The noise of the city, the anxious bustle of humankind, the contrived architecture with its turrets and widows' walks, fancy shingles, and stained glass windows, might jolt my senses and jar my wilderness mind.

I'd need to decide what I wished to do while I had time and energy. When young, life seemed forever. At fifty-five, it seemed the blink of an eye. I thought of the brief moment my garden would feel sun and rain, and as I tucked each seed into the warm earth I wished it well. I saw the past in the soft, brown earth, the future in the seeds I held in my hand. I knew that later, when a seed burst through its protective womb and thrust a spike of green into the sunlight, I'd marvel anew.

Several weeks passed before I saw Toby again. He returned on a sun-drenched day in mid-July as I knelt among the rows of corn, tearing pigweed from the soil. The tinkle of harness bells came from the hayfield where Johnson, the hermit, was mowing the crop of three-foot-high timothy for shares. A small stir of breeze brought me the sound of his "whoas" and "gees" along with the scent of fresh-mown hay. I could hear Sam and Bones as they followed the mower, pouncing on mice that escaped their nests, the dogs' yips faint murmurs above the growl of the river. Though not as thunderous as during June, the river kept me from hearing footsteps until they were upon me. I looked up with a jolt.

"Well, glory be! It's you, Toby." I got to my

feet and hugged the boy. "I've been dying to see you! Is your uncle with you?"

"No ma'am. He's busy placering."

That surprised me. I'd thought McCabe too set against me to allow Toby to visit on his own. I held the boy at arms' length and looked him up and down. The bottoms of his trousers were wet, his bare feet plastered with mud. "Does the river still cover the trail?"

"A little at the cliff."

"I'm sorry you had to wade, but I'm glad you're here." I threw my gloves on the ground beside the trowel. "I'm about to fry. Come into the house, and I'll fix us some lemonade. I want you to see the suit of clothes I made."

"I don't mean to bother."

"Bother?" I gave a little laugh. "I don't know when I've been so glad to see anyone." I nudged him toward the house and closed the gate to the hogwire fence that kept four-legged thieves from the garden. "I'm happy for the change. I'm beginning to pick weeds in my sleep."

"Could I see Nubbin while I'm here?"

I smiled. "Oh, that's why you've come. Do you want to see her before or after we have our lemonade?"

"Before, if I could."

I'd left the chicken pen open, and a half-dozen Plymouth Rocks I'd bought in Elk City roamed the barnyard, scratching the ground for seeds, terrorizing one another. As we neared the goat pens, the chickens circled my feet and squawked for grain. The goats also saw me as a source of feed and came to their fences, expecting an armload of weeds. On warm days, when I had time to watch, I'd let them out of the pens to forage for themselves. Not Napoleon, the buck, though. On more than one occasion he'd eaten clothes from the line and chased me into the house. Chester had been able to make him mind, but all my threats had no more effect on the buck than on a fickle wind.

Toby and I slipped into Maisie's pen and closed the gate against the kids' nudging bodies. Nubbin had shot up like a dandelion on Maisie's milk, but so had the others. The difference in size remained. Maisie stood close, glancing protectively from one babe to the next.

Toby put his arms around the runt's neck and received a wet kiss.

"She's glad for your company," I said. "She doesn't get much play out of me. And the other kids bully her. I'm going to ask Len Johnson if you can have her for the summer. I'm sure he won't mind. Of course, you must ask your uncle if it's all right."

A smile traveled from Toby's mouth to his wide brown eyes. "Oh, he'll let me! He likes animals."

But McCabe was slow to decide about the kid. Toby visited the ranch every other day to play with her, taking her out of the pen on a halter until she learned to stay close. After that, they'd frolic about the ranch like wild things, one a true goat, the other a good imitation, skipping, leaping, bleating with utter joy and abandon. While they romped, I busied myself in the vegetable garden and supervised the play while hoeing or pulling weeds.

Several yards away, the river had settled into its summer bed, clear and rippling, its former growls turned to a loud muttering. On quiet days, clouds of newly hatched insects danced on the shiny surface and fish rose to them lazily. Tree swallows glided like shadows above the water, snapping up flies, then darted in and out of Chester's birdhouses to feed their last brood for the summer. The only time they touched the ground was to select wisps of grass or chicken feathers to soften their nests. Their legs were weak and tiny, but their fluid wings strong for the dart and glide.

One morning in early August, nearly three months after he'd come to the canyon, Toby ran to where I worked with shovel and homemade wheelbarrow, cleaning out the goat pens. He was hardly able to stand still long enough to tell me he could keep Nubbin at the diggings until fall and his return home. I suspected McCabe had begun to miss the boy's help with the placering and begrudged the days he spent with the goats at Weasel Creek. Nevertheless, I was pleased.

I wanted to make certain Nubbin arrived safely and McCabe understood her needs, so while Toby led Nubbin, I rode Sadie, behind the saddle a sack of grain for the kid and greens for McCabe's table. I wondered if McCabe would share the boy's enthusiasm for the goat. Her antics might demand too much patience.

I needn't have worried. The minute McCabe caught sight of Nubbin, his face wreathed into a smile. He put his hand on the kid's bony head and stroked her ears.

"Och, what a wee lass you be. But full of starch, from what Toby tells me."

I couldn't believe the change I saw in McCabe. The harsh expression had softened, a spark of kindness lit his eyes. An elusive quality had come to his manner, as though he no longer shut himself off from the possibilities of life. My heart opened a crack. If he could change, if he so loved animals, he couldn't be as mean-spirited as I'd thought.

I laughed from relief. "I'm glad to see you like goats."

"Aye. So much like wild lambs, they be. I've tamed the wild ones so they'll eat from my hands. Toby will vouch for that. Nubbin can keep us company while the sheep are gone to the high country."

Toby visited the ranch only twice in the next few weeks. He'd come skipping along the riverbank, leaping over rocks, while Nubbin dashed ahead. He'd chat awhile, munch the cookies I kept on hand, and hurry home with a gunnysack full of raspberries and squash. I had no idea when he'd visit again, so when the stringbeans burst in legions, I saddled the mare, stuffed beans in the saddlebag, and headed for McCabe's Bar. Hot enough for heatstroke, the late August sun blistered down from the ribbon of sky and radiated in furnace-like waves from the canyon walls. Sweat riffled beneath my bodice.

I could rouse no one at the placer diggings and shack, but Sam and Bones sniffed the premises and flushed Reb from the grove of pines at the rear of the flat. As I neared the grove, I saw McCabe through a tracery of branches. He appeared to toss shovelsful of earth from a shallow pit. Toby sat like a knob on a log nearby.

The minute I entered the grove, the reason for the pit became clear. Toby's shirtless back was toward me, but I could see Nubbin lying across his lap. Her bloodied head and neck hung limp from his knee.

I wanted to cry out. Trembling, I slipped from the saddle and tied Sadie to a tree.

5

Whatever the cause of the goat's death, Toby was hurting. Tears streaked his dusty face. I eased myself onto the log beside him and put my arm around his quaking shoulders. I felt the heat of his flesh, the heat of his sorrow. The runt's knobby knees rested on my lap, foretelling a growth that would not be.

I swallowed back my grief. "What happened, child?"

Toby said something unintelligible through his tears.

McCabe stopped digging and looked up at me for the first time, his face drawn, his cheeks gray-looking, a haunted look in his eyes. Sympathy for the man flooded through me.

"A cougar done it," he said. The words were thick, forced.

I gave a little gasp. "A cougar? So close?"

"Aye. He's been lying up on the outcrop for a bit each day, watching us. A young thing. Not much weight to him. Just seemed curious."

Anger stabbed through sympathy and grief. "You should have kept Nubbin nearby!"

McCabe slumped visibly beneath the straps of his coveralls. Without shirt, his mottled skin glistened with sweat. "Aye, we should. We'd been keeping good watch on her, we had. But this morning we cut a wide streak of color in the sands and forgot her for a bit . . . long enough she wandered off . . . and the cougar . . ." McCabe seemed to have forgotten I was there. Several seconds passed before a shudder took hold of his lean frame and he awakened to my distraught eyes. He went on as though he'd never paused. "I ran to the shack for me rifle, but the cat already had the kid by the neck and was dragging her up the mountainside."

"Did you kill it?"

"No. Just wanted to scare it off. It was doing what comes natural. It dropped the kid. But the poor wee thing was dead." He took a bandana handkerchief from his back pocket and wiped sweat from his forehead, tears from his eyes. "'Tis my fault. I should of taken time to build a pen."

Grief squeezed my throat. I felt as much to blame as McCabe for Nubbin's death. I'd let Toby bring the kid to a place of questionable safety. I should have foreseen the danger. Now the child must suffer the loss.

My arm sagged around him. "I'm so sorry, Toby. I'd give anything if this hadn't happened. It's hard to lose an animal you love." His chest swelled with a deep sob. "If it's any consolation, you can play with the other kids as often as you like." The offer had a hollow sound.

Reacting to the poverty of my words, Toby gulped out something I couldn't understand and burst into a flood of tears. I drew him close, letting him bury his face in my shirt.

When Nubbin lay in her grave, I held Toby's hand, and we viewed the mound we'd strewn with wild asters. Along the length and breadth, we'd laid out a cross of pebbles. I usually liked the smell of newly turned earth, but now it saddened. Not just because of the goat. It reminded me of the grave near my cabin. Behind me, the dogs whimpered, curled in beds they'd scratched in the earth. A hot breeze stirred the air. The trees soughed.

McCabe stood beside Toby, head bowed, cap dangling from his hand. He looked shaken. "Dear Lord," he said in lament, "we're sending you a little goat child this day . . . a sweet, cunning little th—" His voice cracked. He cleared his throat, went on with difficulty. "The wee thing didn't have long on this earth, so will you please see she has a green everlasting meadow to kick up her heels in . . . and . . . and see she has friends to keep the loneliness away."

The last phrase said worlds about McCabe. It told of his own loneliness and heartache, his yearnings, of needs pushed from mind, unsatisfied. In that moment I felt our spirits touch.

I sat on a slab of Ponderosa pine in front of McCabe's shack, he on another. He'd said he wanted to speak to me in private, so we'd left

Toby sitting by the grave, all three dogs curled at his side, Sam with his head resting on the boy's lap.

The door to the shack stood ajar, revealing the dusky room's austerity. A table and chair of rough-sawed pine stood in the middle of the earthen floor, on each wall a bunk barely wide enough to hold a man. I'd seen the box stove beneath the awning of McCabe's scow the time he'd stopped at the ranch. Now it took up much of the rear wall. On each side of the stove, shelves held personal belongings and an assortment of cooking utensils. A stack of *National Geographic*s and a dozen or so thick, leather-bound books leaned against the foot of one bunk.

Now that McCabe had shown his vulnerability, his heart, I felt his presence as acutely as I would had he reached out to touch me. He seemed just as aware of me. He fidgeted, pulled on his short beard, and darted a glance my way now and then. I couldn't imagine what he had in mind.

"I've brought you here to talk about Toby," he said after a silence that was far too awkward, far too long. "But first I want to thank you for your favors. I—I know I haven't treated you too kindly. But don't think me ungrateful. Understand?"

I nodded, unsure of what to say.

He ran a hand over his face and raised his bony shoulders in a sigh. "I been thinking, 'twould be no harm in letting the boy stay for the winter. He's told me a few things that make me think a year away from home would do him good."

My heart raced at the prospect of having Toby

near all winter. "Y-you're so right. It would do him a world of good."

"Trouble is, he'd miss school. He tells me they have three or four months of it at Slate Creek now. That's near the Pardees." He cleared his throat, once, twice. "I . . . I was wondering if you'd . . . so the boy wouldn't get behind in his schooling . . . that is . . ."

I wondered why men hated to ask favors, but I'd gotten the drift. "I can help Toby read and cipher, if you like. He can come to the ranch when the weather is good." I doubted my ability to teach, but I'd do anything to keep the boy from the Pardees.

A look of relief spread over McCabe's face. "That's what I was hoping you'd say. I can read and use figures myself, mind you. But a woman has more patience than a man."

"I'd enjoy it. It will give me something to look forward to. You could help . . . with the *Geographics*, I mean. I notice you have a stack of them. You could teach Toby about foreign lands."

"Umm . . . I suppose the boy and I could read them together of an evening. Aye, I think I'd like that."

In early November, I took time from Toby's lessons to make my last mail trip for the season. Dick Strong, an Atlas of a man we'd met in Elk City one winter, a man true to his name, had contracted to deliver mail and supplies from Elk

City to the mining camp of Dixie. I couldn't imagine anyone undertaking such a task in winter, but he'd done it successfully when there was no other way to get the mail from Grangeville to Elk City. If the temperature dropped to sixty degrees below zero there was danger of the horse's lungs freezing. When drifts of snow on the pass were too deep for the horse to pull a sled, Dick would wrap the cargo in rawhide and skid it over the snow. If the snow was too deep for the horse, Dick skidded the mail himself. One winter he froze the toes on both feet.

Unlike Dick Strong, I wasn't brash enough to make the trip to Dixie alone in midwinter. I might freeze to death or become buried beneath an avalanche without anyone knowing—though Chester and I had snowshoed the ten miles over the top and through the dense forests several times to escape cabin fever. Our arrival at Dixie had been met with playing cards, fiddles and mouth-organs, dancing partners, and jugs.

As it was, on this trip I had to travel the upper half of the trail on snowshoe, leading Sadie—the high country always received snowfall before the bottom of the canyon.

One reward of the trip to Dixie was back issues of the newspapers the boarding house kept on hand. This time, one of them told of President McKinley's assassination.

President McKinley was shot on September 6, while holding a reception in the Temple of Music at the Pan-American Exposition in

Buffalo. The assassin, Leon Czolgosz, a 28-year-old anarchist, was promptly arrested. McKinley was the third president to have been assassinated in the nation's history. The others were Abraham Lincoln in 1865 and James A. Garfield in 1881. Vice-President Theodore Roosevelt, a 42-year-old former governor of New York, and Harvard graduate, has been sworn in as the 26th President of the United States. He took the oath of office in the home of a close friend, after hurrying back by horse-back and rail from a mountain-climbing trip in the Adirondacks.

I recalled that during our first November in the canyon, Chester and I had snowshoed over the hump and cast our vote in the presidential election between McKinley and Bryan, the first election that allowed Idaho women the vote. I'd raised my voice for suffrage while in Lewiston, had spoken to the legislature in Boise, and I was anxious and proud to cast my ballot. In the Dixie gold camp, we didn't dare mention we voted for William Jennings Bryan, "the man of the people," who wanted to adopt silver as the monetary standard. As it turned out, McKinley was elected president, and gold became the standard. Now he was dead.

The news had two faces. It saddened because of the treacherous nature of the act, it also gave me one more reason to wish Chester were alive. He'd always admired Teddy Roosevelt, especially Teddy's affinity for the wilderness. He would have looked forward to seeing what Teddy could accomplish as President.

Short-lived animals and birds must have thought the winter an eternity. With the first snowstorms, deer and mountain sheep drifted down to the lower reaches of the south-facing slopes, their coats plastered with a layer of white. Squirrels and jays gave voice to their discontent, as if spring was too distant for hope.

Following its path in the southern horizon, the sun touched the south bank of the Salmon only where side canyons cut the steep walls, allowing the thin rays access. The sun shone on the north bank, where the homestead lay, for only three hours in midday, casting slender willow shadows against the pure white of the snow. From time to time storms rolled in from the west and northwest and dumped their load of snow, several feet on the rim, less on the canyon floor. In between storms the sun shone, sometimes in utter quiet, often through bitter, squealing winds that sent whirlwinds of snow dancing across the flat and swept streamers of snow from the mountaintops. The stock grew heavy coats of hair and huddled together against the cold, standing broadside to the sun.

The chickens didn't lay during the winter, but I fed them well and kept warm water on hand. I expected the no-egg-laying months, but when spring approached I'd tack a calendar on the wall of the henhouse and mark the last day I'd allow them to go without laying. "Girls," I'd say, "you start laying by that day or else you become fricassee." They always seemed to make the deadline, because I set it far enough ahead there was no danger they wouldn't lay. I'd always hated killing chickens, but I knew if I spent the money on feed, they'd have to produce.

This year, winter arrived in the canyon in late November, when an arctic storm spilled a foot and a half of snow and turned river, creek, and spring into sculptures of ice. Snow coated the canyon walls with a thick meringue. Icicles formed on the eaves, and frost painted florettes on the windows. When the thermometer reached thirty below zero, each breath pricked my nostrils and burned my lungs. I went about my ranch chores swathed in longjohns and layers of sweaters. A muffler that covered nose and mouth froze with my breath. Only Toby's visits kept me from wanting to go into hibernation.

Every other day the boy snowshoed the mile to the ranch for his lessons. He proved such an apt pupil in reading and ciphering, we took time to compose songs and illustrate stories with the paper and paints my daughter had sent from Lewiston. When our muscles cramped from sitting too long, we'd bundle ourselves for the cold, chop lengths of pine into stove size, and stock the kitchen woodbox.

Some days we'd drop a line through a hole we'd cut in the river ice to catch fish for supper and the icehouse—always alert to thin-crusted bubbles of air in the ice that could spell disaster. Other times we'd make a snowman or carry sleds to the hill back of the house and streak down the slope through pines standing black in their basins of snow. Ravenous and chilled to the bone, we'd return to the house for a dinner of steaming soup, stew, or beans.

McCabe came once a week to discuss Toby's progress and to share a midday meal. I fancied that an awakened need for adult company prompted his visits as much as anything. Talk still made him uncomfortable, but he relaxed when he sat in my rocker smoking the pipe that was his winter companion, listening to Toby sing out the words in his reader.

Sometimes I'd read aloud from books Jennie had sent. McCabe's favorites were Dickens' *A Tale of Two Cities* and James Fenimore Cooper's *The Last of the Mohicans*. The latter story appealed to McCabe's wilderness soul. In the first, Sidney Carton's hopeless love seemed to strike a responsive chord. I tried to bring the same drama to the reading as my mother had when I was young. I could still hear the parlor walls in my childhood home resound with the roar of the vulgar crowd as it ushered Sidney Carton to his death. Mother's reading of that scene would echo in my mind forever.

McCabe seemed never in a hurry to leave. The visits brought serenity to his face, a spark of good will to his eyes. I warmed to the man and allowed myself to think it was because of me as much as Toby he walked the snowy mile. When he stayed

home because of some ailment, I was terribly disappointed.

One day, we'd finished our meal and sat at the
table sipping coffee while Toby ate his third wedge
of cornbread. In the light of the sputtering lamp, I
observed the twisted hand holding the cup's handle, its dark-blotched skin stretched tight over
swollen knuckles. I noted, as I had many times, the
stooped shoulders, the look of endurance begun
so long ago. I wondered about men like McCabe,
schooled by the wilderness, toughened by adversity and hard work, with no one to care whether
they lived or died—that is, until now. My heart
swelled with a strange mix of admiration and
pity.

"How long have you been prospecting on the
river, Mister McCabe?"

"Umm . . . about twenty years."

"And before that?"

He took a sip of coffee, his eyes reflecting
inwardly on the past. "The first time I tried pan-
ning was in '65. I'd been working for a packer
headquartered in Salmon City . . . had a pal named
Archie who worked for the same man. We got the
gold fever and followed the stampede to Virginia
City—the one in Montana. We were sure we'd
strike it rich."

"Did you?" Toby said through a mouthful of
cornbread. His eyes had widened at the mention
of riches.

McCabe gave a snort. "Hardly! At first, at
every place we panned 'twas the same story. The
good stuff had already been filed on. There were

lots of crooks ready to steal any new claim that proved out." He scooted his chair to the side slightly and crossed his legs in an agitated way.

"Did they steal yours?" I asked.

McCabe dropped his gaze to the table, his eyes dark shadows. "The Plummer Gang did. Killed Archie, too."

"Oh, dear! I've read about the terrible things they did."

"Sired by the devil, they were. Worst thieving, butchering, desecrating scum I ever come across. They had the town fooled for a while . . . pretended to be saints while they stole everybody blind. They held most of the important offices. Everybody licked their boots." McCabe's eyes sparked with an outrage that had smoldered through the decades. He rubbed the knuckles on one hand as if he'd wear away the skin.

"Archie and me finally hit a rich pocket. While I watched over the claim, he took off for the bank in Bannock to convert our dust. The Plummers ambushed him. Put six bullets in his back!" He ran his hand across his forehead as if the image had weakened him, yet the horrid rush of memory had loosened his tongue. "I followed the buzzards to the coulee where the Plummers stashed Archie's body . . . had to kick the ugly black things off his back. Archie was the best friend I ever—"

He shut his eyes for a moment, coughed, cleared his throat. "'Twasn't bad enough the crooks stole our gold and our mule, they come back to town with a paper that turned our claims over to them—said Archie had signed it. 'Twas a lie. I tried to tell the miners' court what they'd done, but the court either didn't believe me, or was afraid to. The Plummers got off scot-free."

I caught myself reaching out to touch him, pulled my hand away. I hoped he hadn't noticed. "I—I'm sorry I brought up the subject. I didn't mean to stir up bad memories."

"Don't take much to stir them up. I never got over hating those Plummers. 'Twas one of the things that soured me on my fellow man."

"You can't blame all men for the foul deeds of a few."

"More than a few. It seemed every man that put a hand to a pan or rocker was out to cheat another or do him in. Gold does strange things to men. It can change honest ones into cold-blooded crooks that'd just as soon slice your throat for a bag of gold." He said no more, just sat hunched over his thighs, pursing his lips in and out in thought.

During the silence I went to the stove for the coffee pot. "I'm surprised you're still prospecting," I said as I filled his cup.

"What?" I seemed to have torn him from another time, another place. I repeated the remark.

"Ohh . . . I stopped for a while after Archie was killed. Kinda went it alone. I didn't want to be responsible for another death." He reached across to the kindling box, took a splinter, started to whittle a toothpick. "There were scoundrels wherever there was gold, especially in camps that sprouted up around strikes like the one in Leesburg, in the hills west of Salmon City. I followed the stampede there in '67."

"Was it a rich strike?" Toby said, the corners of his mouth yellow with crumbs.

"A wheelbarrowful of bedrock gravel brought a thousand dollars. I panned nuggets worth fifty dollars apiece."

Toby whistled. "You must of made lots of money."

"For a while, 'til the placer played out. From there I worked the Yellow Jacket country, then up to Hughes Creek. I worked there awhile crushing ore at the stamp mill. It was then I . . ." He let the rest trail off. Head bowed, he chewed on the toothpick, obviously reflecting on the past. As he stared at the blue-checkered oilcloth, an expression of deep melancholy crossed his face. I thought he might tell of the sweetheart. He didn't. "After that, I started floating the river. In '80 'twas. After one season, I couldn't stay away. It got into my blood."

"I've come to love it, too," I said. "Though I can't help feeling isolated, especially with Chester gone."

McCabe leveled his eyes at me in a steady, penetrating way. "You shouldn't stay on, not alone. There's bloody thieves in the backcountry, running from the law. They'd as soon murder you for whatever you've got. You need to be thinking about moving back to Lewiston."

"I know . . . but . . ." I looked at Toby wistfully. "I can't. Not just yet."

❧

After McCabe's talk of murderers, I kept a revolver on my nightstand. Whenever I returned from hunting rabbits or grouse to add variety to my meals, I made certain I oiled the Winchester pump shotgun in the way Chester had showed me, and loaded it before I returned it to the rack on the wall. As little confidence as I had in John and Oakie, I wished they were still in the canyon instead of holed up in Elk City for the winter. I could hardly wait for their return.

I was out feeding Sadie and Highpockets one day toward sundown—at least, I thought it must be close to sundown, the sun so low in the horizon it was visible above the rim only at midday. Sadie jerked her head from the pan of oats to look high on the snowbound ridge to the south, then whinnied. Her eyesight was much better than mine, but I made out several dark blotches working their way down the slope. It was impossible to see the Thunder Mountain trail for the snow, but I knew its course, and the blotches appeared to be following it.

Sadie wouldn't have whinnied at deer or sheep, and they didn't venture onto the north-facing slope in winter, the snow too deep, and little feed. They kept to the lower, south-facing slopes back of the homestead where wind blew parts of the hillside free of snow, and to the hay meadows, where they could stomp through the snow to stubble.

I brought Chester's spy glass from the house and focused on the moving figures. They took on the shape of five men and two mules, part of the time obscured by a forest of spruce and fir that found the north-facing slope to their liking. I saw the men wore snowshoes, their long coats easily visible above the snow. The poor mules, overladen with packs, floundered through the rotten snow of late March, sinking into it halfway up their flanks.

Only prospectors would be crazy enough to travel from the Thunder Mountain country this time of year, when snow avalanches were a danger. I supposed their provisions had become scarce and they were on their way to the settlements. It was the rare prospector who took enough food for the winter. These men would need to travel to Grangeville before they'd find much in the way of supplies. Elk City sometimes had to wait as late as June for the first freighters to arrive.

Dusk had fallen before the men reached the bottom of the canyon. I halfway expected them to ask to sleep in the barn—many prospectors did—but no one came. Normally, I would have walked up the flat to greet anyone coming down the trail in winter, Chester and I always had, but McCabe's words of caution put me on guard.

Curious about the travelers, yet fearful, the next morning I took the shotgun from the wall and headed up the flat toward the trail crossing. The sky had closed in during the night, and snow spit from the enveloping grayness. Sam and Bones bounded ahead, rolling each other in snow that had drifted along the orchard fence. A thaw had melted much of the snow that had covered the north bank.

When I reached Weasel Creek, I saw a pig's tail of smoke climbing from the chimney of John and Oakie's cabin, which stood among open pines east of the creek, the smoke strong with the scent of pitch. I couldn't believe the men had returned, not with snow still deep on the trail from Elk City. It could be the prospectors I'd seen on the trail. I'd need to check. John and Oakie had put a heavy padlock on their cabin door and asked me to watch for prowlers.

I crossed Chester's foot bridge, the creek ice swollen to the level of the bridge, and marched up the path to the cabin. Two ribby mules tied to trees near the door were stripping needles from the limbs. They must have been starving. I'd seen elk and moose eat pine needles when the brush was overbrowsed and the snow too deep to forage for grass.

Sam and Bones sniffed the mules, then, hackles raised, went around the side of the house, growling at strange scents.

I patted the chest of the nearest mule, murmured a few words of sympathy, then pretending courage, banged on the door to the cabin. I heard grumblings, a curse or two. A man's face appeared at the cabin's single window, then nodded someone to the door.

The door opened a few inches. A draft of hot air hit me in the face along with the smell of whiskey, the cheap, medicinal odor of John and Oakie's homemade liquor. They'd never mentioned the fact they had a still, but once I'd caught the smell of whiskey seeping from a shack at the back of the cabin.

A head moved into the space between door and frame. It was beardless, bristly with whiskers, smudged with dirt and soot. Bloodshot eyes stared out at me, suspicious, threatening.

"What do you want, lady?" The words dripped whiskey.

6

The expression in the man's eyes made me wonder why I stayed on that doorstep. Steeling myself, I said, "I saw the smoke. I thought John and Oakie had returned."

The man grunted, leaned a wobbly head against the door jamb, gave me an unfocused stare.

Someone inside asked in a guttural voice, "Who is it, Cole?"

"Uhh—some old gal looking for—who'd you say?"

"John and Oakie. They own this cabin."

"'Tain't here."

"Tell her to get the hell out o' here and leave us be," said the voice inside.

Liquored mutters of agreement rose from others in the room.

"I'll not budge until you tell me what you're doing here. John and Oakie locked the—"

"Shut the door, Cole, it's freezing in here!"

I shoved the barrel of the shotgun through the

crack to prevent Cole from shutting the door. "When are you going to leave?"

Cole's dark brows drew into wavering check marks. "When we're damned good and ready," he said in a slurred voice. "Now get out of here, before I get mad." He shoved the barrel of the shotgun up through the crack and slammed the door. I heard him push the bar-latch through the hasp.

"You'd better not do any damage," I yelled through the door. "John and Oakie will be back soon, they'll have your hide." I expected to gain little by the lie, but thought it worth a try.

I remained there a minute or two, uncertain what I should do next. I wanted to give the men further warning, but I was afraid they'd open the door and drag me inside. On the other hand, I couldn't let them trespass. In their drunken state, no telling what they'd do to John and Oakie's belongings. Perhaps McCabe could help.

I called the dogs and headed for home through the fresh snow. The storm had turned into a blizzard, the flakes so thick I could hardly see where to put my feet. That didn't bode well. If the snow piled up, the men in the cabin would have an excuse to stay until a thaw. I wouldn't be able to make it downriver to McCabe's. He and Toby wouldn't make it upriver. I'd be stranded with five toughs as neighbors—hungry men, no doubt, who'd deplete John and Oakie's stores and come after mine.

The storm dragged on for two—three—five days before the skies cleared, leaving snow piled three feet deep on the flat, the temperature near zero. I could imagine the size of the drifts on the trail to Elk City. The men in John and Oakie's cabin would stay on the creek for a while.

The falling snow had muffled the sound of their activities. Now I heard several rifle shots upriver. A herd of deer crossed in front of the house, wild-eyed, taking huge upward leaps through the deep snow. They had little chance of escape for long. Chester never shot a deer unless it had a sporting chance, and then he shot only out of necessity, if we were running low on food.

The next three mornings, shots split the air, sometimes far upstream, sometimes nearer my house. I was afraid the bullets might stray into the animal pens.

After lunch on the third day, I pulled on my wraps, took the shotgun from the wall, my snow-shoes from their nails on the porch, and worked my way along the orchard fence to Weasel Creek. Only the gray tips of the fence posts showed above the bright snow. In the slanted rays of the late winter sun, they cast a row of slender shadows, like soldiers on the march.

I found the men back of John and Oakie's cabin in a space they'd cleared of snow. They'd dragged a stack of dead pine boughs into the clearing—John and Oakie's store of wood on the cabin porch was nearly gone. The handle of an ax leaned against the stack of wood. Chips surrounded a chopping block. A snowshoe rabbit and the hides of two deer lay on the stack of boughs. At the back of the clearing, the bluish-pink hindquarters of one deer and the full carcass of another hung, frozen, from a pine, out of reach of coyotes and wolves.

Two of the men kneeled in the packed snow, skinning snowshoe rabbits. I could almost taste the smell of blood in the air. The rip of the men's hunting knives between flesh and hide sounded as if they were cutting parchment.

Three other men sat hunched on a log, looking like three grizzly bears bundled against the cold. They were talking, turning the snow brown with tobacco juice. It was hard to see features through their whiskers, but one, a blond, appeared much younger than the rest. I recognized another as Cole, the man who'd come to the door of the cabin several mornings ago. All wore holstered revolvers slung over their heavy coats, as if the guns were an accustomed part of their dress.

The quiet of the snow underfoot had made it possible for me to creep up on the men, unnoticed. Several seconds passed before Cole saw me standing on the edge of the clearing. Swathed in sweater and coats, the shotgun poised across my waist, I must have looked like a mountain man myself. Cole's hand went to his holster. Then relaxed at his side.

"Oh, it's you," he said. "What you got in your craw this time, Miz Snoopy?"

I tensed beneath my wraps. "I came to ask you men not to shoot so close to the animal pens. You might hit one of the goats."

Cole guffawed, jabbed the rough-looking fellow beside him in the ribs. "Hear that? Miz Snoopy's afraid we'll hit her goats. Must think our aim's not very good."

The other man laughed. "Too bad they ain't good to eat, or we'd make sure we hit 'em."

If they'd wanted to make me angry, they'd succeeded. "You needn't be so rude! I'm asking politely."

One of the men at the back of the clearing looked up from skinning his rabbit. He pointed the knife in my direction. "Well, now," he said with mock courtesy. "We're telling you politely to mind your own damned business. If we want to shoot near your place, we will."

The heat of anger surged from my neck to the roots of my hair. "If you take one step past Weasel Creek, you'll end up with buckshot in your leg."

"My! Ain't we brave," the man said with a sarcastic smile. By the time he'd risen to his feet, his expression had turned savage. He came toward me, knife extended. The sun glinted off the bloody steel. From the periphery of my vision, I saw the other men grin through their woolly beards.

I aimed the shotgun at the ground near the man's feet and willed my finger to close on the trigger. It refused.

My hesitation wasn't lost on the man. He wrenched the gun from my hands, then wagged the needle-sharp tip of the knife in front of my nose. "You come bothering us once more and you'll end up with this knife in a lot worse place than your leg." He jerked his arm toward the homestead. "Now git!"

That night, I brought Sam inside to guard the house and bolted the doors with fastenings I'd installed when Cole and his gang arrived in the canyon. Chester had never bothered to put locks on the doors. I was enraged at myself for not showing more courage that afternoon. I could still hear the men deriding me as I retreated down the path toward Weasel Creek, their words mocking, obscene. I couldn't bear the thought they remained on the creek, not three hundred yards away. They'd kept my shotgun, but I still had a revolver and Chester's Winchester rifle for protection. I hadn't shot either gun more than half a dozen times. For some reason, I preferred the thunder of the shotgun over the explosion of rifle and handgun on my ears.

A jittery mess, I didn't fall asleep until midnight. Shortly after, I awoke at a barking near the animal pens, the cackling of hens in the coop. I felt as if I'd been dragged from a deep well and squeezed through an opening too small for my body. Through my stupor, it occurred to me a starving coyote might be raiding the coop, perhaps an ermine or wolverine.

I pulled a woolen wrapper across my shoulders and headed down the stairs with a candle for light. Sam was already at the door, barking to be let out. I took my scarf and Chester's fleece-lined coat from a peg beside the door and pulled on my snow packs, slipped the Winchester from its scabbard on the wall, worked the lever to load the chamber, and stuffed extra shells in my pocket.

On opening the door, I decided not to bother with a lantern. A platinum wash of moonlight on the snow gave ample light.

"Come on, Sam, let's see what's out—" I saved my breath. The dog had already bolted ahead to discover what was causing Bones' upset.

I expected to find a wild animal digging under the henhouse door where I'd shoveled away the snow. Instead, I found Bones scratching at the door, barking and growling. Sam had joined the fuss. Inside, the hens cackled in a terrified way.

Lantern light shone through the space beneath the door and dirt floor, casting a narrow rectangle of light on the snow. The rag I'd stuffed in the space to prevent drafts lay at the edge of the path. Those horrid men must be inside! I didn't know which was greater—my fright or my outrage.

I yanked open the door, pointed the rifle inside. In the light of a lantern that hung from a hook in the low ceiling, I saw the young blond from John and Oakie's cabin. He was bent over one of the nests along the wall, putting eggs into his hat, some of the first layings of the year.

The dogs leaped across the threshold to snap at his ankles.

He flailed an arm and a leg, and swore.

Plymouth Rocks and leghorns fluttered from roost to roost, scattering straw. The coop smelled of their fright. I slammed the door shut before they could escape.

"Call off your mutts!" the blond yelled.

"Sam! Bones! That's enough." Sam backed off a step, but continued growling. Bones made another lunge at the young man's leg.

"Call him off!"

"Bones, heel!" Bones came to my side and stood with lips curled, snarling. I felt like snarling, myself. "What are you doing here?"

"What does it look like?"

"I mean, what right do you think you have to help yourself to eggs. Why didn't you ask? I'd be happy to give you a few. You don't need to sneak around and upset the hens."

"I'm used to taking what I want." His voice was sullen, and so was his face. His rough-spun clothes smelled of wood smoke, fried grease, an unwashed body.

"Stealing will get you in trouble."

"Already has."

I searched his round, baby-like face, saw a bit of character behind the eyes. His expression, though sullen, was more open, less menacing than the other men's. "Why did a boy like you take up with such a gang?"

He laughed as if I'd made a joke. "They're my brothers, except Cole. He's a cousin."

"You'd think they'd have more regard for your welfare." I considered giving a sermon on the consequences of thievery, decided it would fall on deaf ears.

I scanned the nesting boxes and roosting

ledges that lined the walls. The hens still flapped
nervously from roost to roost. "Take what eggs
you want. Then let's get out of here so the hens
can calm down."

The tiniest hint of gratitude slid over the
young man's face. "Uhh . . . thank you. I'll—" He
broke off as the door burst open behind me.

I spun into the black-eyed stare of Cole, his
heavy, fleece-lined coat buttoned to his bristly
jaws. He had my canister of coffee beans tucked
under one arm. The other hand carried a gunnysack bulging with heaven only knew what—probably things he'd taken from the house. He must
have broken the hasp on the back door and been
hiding in the kitchen when I came down from
upstairs, Sam too focused on Bones' barking to
smell a stranger.

The dogs charged Cole as soon as he opened
the door to the henhouse.

"Goddamned curs!" He lashed out with his
rugged boots.

Sam received a hard whack in the ribs, gave a
yip, and went ki-yi-ing into the night.

Bones set his jaws on Cole's foot, held fast
when Cole tried to kick him free. Cole dropped
the gunnysack and canister and pulled out his
revolver.

Before he could shoot I sent a bullet into the
floor at his feet. The explosion deafened. Hens
shrieked. The room smelled of spent gunpowder.
"You hurt that dog, and the next shot will be in
your leg," I said through the roar in my ears. I
jerked the barrel of the Winchester toward the

doorway. "Now, get out of here before I really lose my temper."

Cole's eyes became venomous slits. "Whyn't we take her to the cabin," he said to the blond, "show her what we do to women that make trouble. Get her gun, Jim."

"Aww, take it easy on her."

"I said, get her gun!"

I aimed the rifle at Jim, then at Cole. At the same time, I backed toward the nearest wall until my waist hit the edge of a laying box. My heart thudded in my chest. Perspiration dampened my armpits. I was certain I was about to be ravaged. I'd have to kill one of the men to keep that from happening. The thought paralyzed.

"Jesus Christ! Get her gun!" Cole yelled.

Jim set the hatful of eggs in one of the nests of straw, took a step toward me, hesitated. "She won't do us no harm."

"Shit on you, then!" Cole made a move to grab my rifle.

"Leave her be!" In a flash Jim pulled a pistol from his holster and aimed it at his cousin.

For a long, excruciating second, Cole stood his ground. Then slowly he backed away. An expression of loathing narrowed his eyes. "What's with you, Jim? First you try to save the skin of that old hag down in Nevada, now this one. You gone chicken on us?"

"Don't see no sense in shooting women. 'Specially old ones, like that gal in Elko."

Cole snorted. "I suppose you would of let her turn us in." He glared at Jim for a second or two, then picked up the sack and canister. "We'll settle this at the cabin," he shot a glance my way, "unless you want to hide behind this bitch's skirts like you did your ma's." He turned to leave.

Jim lunged, spun Cole around by the shoulder. "I never hid behind no skirts, you bastard!" His mouth twitched. His gun hand shook. I could smell the sweat of his anger. For a moment I thought he was going to shoot Cole.

Suddenly his arm went limp, dropping the pistol at his side.

Cole gave a snort. "Knew you were chicken." Turning his back on us, he went through the door and into the night. The squeal of his boots on the frozen snow drifted back to my ears.

Jim stood at the open doorway for a long while, looking after his cousin. He seemed to sort through his feelings, to gather courage. Then, lantern in hand, he picked up the hatful of eggs. "Thanks," he said with a grim nod and walked through the door.

"Thank *you*," I murmured under my breath.

Left in darkness, I stepped outside and shut the door on the hens. The outrage that had made me bold drained away, leaving me limp, too weak to move. I slumped against the rough planks of the door, breath steaming in the cold air, and watched Jim melt into the pines.

7

When I went into the house, I found cupboard drawers open in the kitchen, canned goods scattered on the floor, cornmeal and flour strewn about. The leather pouch that held money I kept on hand for supplies—money from the rental of my house in Lewiston and from the sale of the ferry—was where I'd hidden it, wedged under the base plate of my treadle sewing machine. I checked the sleeping loft and found nothing disturbed. Evidently Cole was more interested in food than money.

I was too weak in the knees, too distraught, to clean up the mess. I simply lay on the settee reviewing the night's events, hoping I'd seen the last of those awful men. I was afraid if they stayed, I'd end up a skeleton in baggy rags. Like so many who lived in the backcountry, tragedy had begun to stalk me like a predatory animal, waiting for me to weaken in mind and body.

In the Lewiston newspaper, I'd read of murders committed during acts of robbery or because of the insane hatred that can fester in the mind of those who live in isolation. I'd read of trappers and prospectors found lying in the wilds or in some remote cabin after suffering the agonies of disease, injury, frostbite, no one to offer solace. I knew of babies and mothers who died during childbirth, knew of one brave mother who put on snowshoes and fought her way through miles of blizzard to reach town before she delivered her child. There were those who lost everything to fire, nothing left of their stock but blackened corpses. It amazed me they had the courage and endurance to rebuild.

Possessed by such thoughts, I didn't stir to the task of cleaning until the soft light of morning lay beyond the windows. I washed the wearinesss from my face, brushed and braided my hair, and was busy sweeping up cornmeal when McCabe rapped at the door.

"I thought we'd better check to see how you'd survived the storm," he said as he removed his jacket and hung it on a peg beside the door.

Toby went into the kitchen area beyond the sitting room to look for sweets. He stopped and pointed at the floor. "What happened?"

"I was robbed. Some roughnecks broke into John and Oakie's shack and have been staying there. They've caused me no end of trouble."

"I thought they looked like outlaws." McCabe walked to the kitchen to see what had alarmed Toby and stopped near the table to keep from tracking meal.

"What do you mean they looked like outlaws? When did you see them?"

"They went past the shack shortly after dawn—were headed downriver on snowshoes." He turned to face me after surveying the mess on the floor. "I'd gotten up early and was on the river-bank, checking the morn. Those rubes had some fool notion it'd be easier to snowshoe downstream than up over the hump."

"They didn't take the mules, did they?" I worried about the rough ice lying beneath the snow. The river had thawed slightly during a warm spell in February and frozen again. The freezing surface of the river had jammed slabs of broken ice into piles that angled in all directions.

"No mules, just packs on their backs. Looked like they were carrying enough to last a year."

"Did you tell them how far they'd have to go to find another trail out?"

"Yes, but they didn't want to hold still long enough to listen. Seemed agitated."

I sighed onto one of the kitchen chairs. "Guess I was lucky they didn't stop at the house to do me in. I've never seen five such hateful men. The youngest wasn't so bad. He saved me from harm."

Perplexity dawned on McCabe's face. "I saw only four."

"Then where's the other?"

"He might have gone out over the top."

"Possible. Or . . ." A horrible thought came to mind. "If he's set up housekeeping at John and Oakie's, he'll be up to no good. Especially if it's Cole."

McCabe considered that a second, pulling on the folds of skin beneath his chin. "I'd better

go have a look. Toby, you stay here with Missus
Clark." He needn't have bothered with the last.
Toby had taken the cookie jar from the cupboard and was stuffing his mouth with a raisin
bar.

I put a restraining hand on McCabe's arm.
"Be careful. It could be dangerous."

He turned his eyes on mine, seeming to note
my concern, to examine other feelings my eyes
may have revealed. He twitched a smile. "Don't
you worry your head about me. I'm too stubborn
to die."

An hour later, McCabe walked into the kitchen,
his face haggard. I stood at the stove, turning
eggs for Toby's second breakfast, my first. For
the moment, the boy was outside with the goats.

I glanced at McCabe, then back at the eggs.
"What did you find out?"

"The bugger won't be causing trouble. He has
a bullet in his back."

I dropped the pancake turner, looked at
McCabe in shock. "Why would they shoot one of
their own?"

"Who knows? Probably had a falling-out."
McCabe took a cup from the shelf, poured coffee
from the pot on the stove, then sat at the table
waiting for it to cool. "The lad didn't have a
weapon on him—no money purse. The others
must of taken them. They'd jerked a watch from
his pocket—the keeper was torn."

"Horrid men!" I took the pancake turner from the floor and washed it at the sink. "What about John and Oakie's guns?"

"Took them all, except the old flintlock that used to belong to John's dad."

I groaned in anger at myself. "And I was supposed to watch out for the place! How was the cabin?"

"A mess. Whiskey spilled around, a couple of jugs broke, stinking plates."

I set a platter of eggs on the table with a loaf of bread on a cutting board. My knees felt like mush. My conscience hurt. "John and Oakie are going to be mad as hornets. They'll blame me."

"What could you do? One woman against the likes of them. I think I know who they were—a real bad bunch. The dead fella had a name engraved on his belt buckle—Jim Harper."

I looked up abruptly from slicing bread. "Oh, dear! Why couldn't it have been one of the others. I think Jim might have turned his life around if he'd had a chance."

"I doubt that. His gang is already in deep trouble with the law. Everybody was talking about them the last time I was in Salmon City—the Harper Gang. They left a string of robberies behind them in northern Nevada and southern Idaho, a murder or two. You're lucky it wasn't you with a bullet in your back."

I felt suddenly faint, giddy. I nicked my finger with the bread knife, sucked the cut. "We should bury him."

"I did—in the snow. We'll dig a grave when it

thaws." He tried the coffee, sipped gingerly at first, then took two or three large swallows, wiped his mustache with the back of his fingers. "By the way, I found a dead mule. Looks like it'd starved to death. The ravens were working on him, fast as they could. I scared off a couple of coyotes. I brought another mule back with me—all skin and bones. I put it in the barn with some hay and oats."

"I hope you didn't give it too much."

"I know better than that. Just gave it a little, 'til it gets used to eating. I don't know what you're going to do with it . . . just one more animal to sell when you move out."

"Move out?" I had the feeling McCabe had read my thoughts.

"You won't be wanting to stay after this, will you? Like I said before, you'd be better off with your kin."

Last year I'd resented the suggestion. I'd thought McCabe wanted to be rid of me. This time, I knew he had my interest at heart. I had to agree, the wilds were no place for a widow. I'd need to give serious thought to a move. The question was when? And where?

After the incident with the Harper Gang, McCabe and Toby came to the homestead each day, Toby for his lessons, McCabe to make certain I was safe. I was thankful for their company and felt lost when they returned to McCabe's

Bar. I asked them to stay at the house, but McCabe thought it improper.

Toby had thrived on the winter activities and grown an inch and a half. I let out the cuffs of his pants and the seams of his coat. McCabe ordered the boy a larger boot from the Sears Roebuck catalog. Because of the boy—and McCabe, I'm sure—April seemed to arrive more quickly than usual. The sunshine grew warmer and slowly melted the snow and river ice. The last thin sheets that fringed the shore broke free and joined the flow of dirty white flotsam. Even the icicles on the north side of the house melted down to thin spikes and lost their winter-long hold on the eaves.

Instead of the profound silence that rang in the ears on winter's windless days, rushing waters filled the air with sound. The breezes smelled of damp earth and the tangy sweetness that signaled spring. Buttercups poked their heads above the soggy ground, providing a yellow carpet for deer and mountain sheep that wandered the flat, nibbling bits of emerald green. Prospectors wandered into the canyon and crossed the river on their way to gold country. McCabe and Toby returned to their placering. I succumbed to the lure of the garden.

The arrival of spring, with its feeling of hope, pushed thoughts of the Harper Gang to the back of my mind and made me want to consider a long while before I left the canyon. Chester lay buried here . . . and there was Toby. I hated the thought of leaving him.

One night toward the end of May, I woke to a pounding on the door. I sat up, aware of my heartbeat, its pulsing so fast I dizzied. Who could it be? Not the Harpers! What would anyone want in the middle of the night? Prospectors wishing to sleep in the barn had sometimes come to the door of an evening, but never this late. The dogs were outside. If they'd barked, I hadn't heard them. Why weren't they sounding the alarm?

Another rap at the door. A voice called my name.

Stiff from fright, yet annoyed, I lit the candle I kept on the bedstand, drew on slippers and wrapper, and took the Colt .45 from the bedstand. With the revolver in one hand, candle in the other, I stole to the foot of the stairs.

I aimed the Colt at the door. "Who is it?" My voice shook.

"Afton McCabe."

At this hour? Something must have happened! My thoughts raced from one dire imagining to the next.

I pulled the heavy bolt free of the keeper and opened the door. McCabe stood at the threshold, a lean silhouette in the pale moonlight, his eyes owlish in the shadows cast by the candle.

8

hatever brings you here in the middle of the night?" I asked McCabe. "Where's Toby?"

"He's sick."

"Oh lord! What are his symptoms?" The question seemed to come from Chester's mouth, not mine.

"He's running a fever. Real weak and all that."

"When did it start?"

"'Twas midafternoon. We were cleaning the cradle, when all of a sudden he keels over."

"It could be the grippe, but where would he catch it?" Remembering my manners, I motioned McCabe inside. He followed me into the warm kitchen and watched while I lit a kerosene lamp that hung from the ceiling above the table. I thought I must look a fright in wrapper and cap, nightbraid hanging down my back like a Chinaman's queue. Sleep glued my eyes half-shut. I tried to smooth my hair. McCabe had removed his cap and was doing the same.

I pulled out chairs and sat across from him, my hands limp on the table. He watched my every movement, obviously seething in his worry.

"Any sign of Toby feeling ill before today?"

"He's been complaining of a headache and stiff neck. Been doing a bit of shoveling the past few days, and I thought the ache was from that."

"What have you done for him?"

"Give him a spot of quinine . . . put him to bed. I—" He bit off what he was going to say, shook his head. "No man on earth hates to ask a favor more than I do, but I'd appreciate it if you'd nurse Toby. I know nothing about treating youngsters. And I'm sure he isn't up to making the trip out to see the doctor."

My relationship with McCabe had come a long way since May of last year. Then, I think he would rather have died than ask a favor. I smiled reassuringly. "I'd be disappointed if you hadn't asked. I'll get dressed right away." I pushed back my chair to rise. "You can put a stick of wood in the stove to warm the coffee."

Before I left the kitchen, I took Chester's satchel of medicines and herbs from a cupboard, stuffed the satchel with laundered flour sacks, and set it by the front door. "You might call Sadie and Highpockets in from the pasture and tie them in the barn," I said as I started up the stairs. "Oats and halters are to the right of the door, also a lantern. The coffee should be hot by the time you get back."

A wild barking came from within the shack when we arrived. McCabe unwound the wire that fastened the door hasp, and Reb burst through the doorway, beating our legs with his tail in his happiness to see us.

Outside, the air held the sharp, herbal scent common to the small hours of morning, but the inside of the shack smelled of smoke from the woodstove. Wisps of it drifted through the circle of light a lantern cast over table and earthen floor. Toby lay on his bunk beyond the glare of the lantern. He moaned and turned his head from side to side, his face white as paste except for two spots burning on his cheeks. He reminded me of my own child lying on his deathbed, except the putrid smell of diphtheria was absent.

Toby opened his eyes, squinting with pain at the light. He mumbled something I couldn't understand.

I put my hand on his forehead. "I'm sorry you're ill, Toby. Tell me how you feel."

He licked parched lips, tried to clear his throat. "My head and neck hurt something awful, my back, too."

"Poor child. I brought some medicine that should help."

I rummaged around in Chester's satchel, best black calf with brass fittings. He hadn't removed anything since his days in Lewiston, and the bag still held a copy of *Gray's Anatomy*, a book on medicinal herbs, as well as stethoscope, bandage material, a set of surgical knives, quinine, laudanum, morphine, carbolic ointment and acid, hop bitters—good for many ailments—herbs of all kinds, and sulfate of zinc for use as a disinfectant.

I poured a spoonful of quinine and put in a drop of laudanum to help the headache. Toby swallowed it under protest and made a face.

"Now I need to cool the fever." I took three flour sacks from the satchel and turned to McCabe, who was stoking the fire under a tea kettle. "The boy's head is as hot as a flatiron. I'll need some tepid water." McCabe pointed to a bucket of water in a corner of the room. "If we were at my house, I'd wrap him in a damp sheet. These cloths will have to do." There was no such thing as a sheet at McCabe's.

As I lay a wet cloth on Toby's forehead, I noticed a scabbed-over swelling in the soft spot beneath his ear. "What caused this, Toby?"

"A tick," he mumbled.

"Swollen bigger'n a shoe button it was," McCabe added. "I had to put a match to its rear end to make it let go."

Toby put his fingers on the fiery lump. "It still itches."

"I have carbolic ointment in the satchel. I'll put some on the bite after I take your pulse."

At his wrist, I found a rapid beat, irregular in strength. Of greater concern were flat, reddish-black swellings beneath the skin. I ruled out pox, as pox usually started on the face. "Have you had the measles, Toby?"

"Yes'm."

Then what could the eruptions be? I drew back the blankets and saw that blotches had spread across the boy's waist above the band of his underwear. My chest tightened.

"Mister McCabe, bring the lantern," I said abruptly. "I need to look for something in Highpockets' saddlebag." I stepped outside onto grass slicked by a gathering frost.

McCabe stared out at me stupidly. "Highpockets doesn't have—"

"Mister McCabe, come! And close the door. I don't want to let in the cold air."

When McCabe stooped outside, his displeasure showed in the glow of the lantern. "For a woman, you sure know how to give orders. What do you mean about Highpockets'—"

"I had to get you out here some way. I didn't want to talk in front of Toby, and I knew he'd seen Sadie's saddlebag on the floor."

"What's the problem?" His voice was harsh, concerned.

"I'm afraid Toby has spotted fever."

"The devil he has!"

"The rash is just beginning, but it looks like spotted fever to me. I've helped Chester treat cases of it. I had a friend die from it. I'd swear it's the same rash."

McCabe's face turned savage. "No! I won't let it be!"

"Then you look at it. Do you know the rash?"

"Ought to. The fever nearly killed me! Took most of the summer and fall at the hot springs to get back on my feet. Good God, I hope you don't catch it."

"It's not contagious. They say it's caused by

drinking snowmelt. But Chester was never convinced of that."

"Aye. That's a bunch of hogwash. I got the fever in mid-July. Not much snowmelt then." He turned to re-enter the shack. "No sense staying out here in the cold."

I put my hand on his arm. "Be careful what you say. We don't want to frighten the boy."

McCabe bent over Toby a long while, speaking to him softly, checking the rash. When he'd finished, he came to the stove where I worked and gave a slow, grave nod. The dreaded confirmation brought a hard knot to my stomach. My mind wheeled, sifting through its files for all Chester had taught me about spotted fever. It would require all my skill to keep the boy alive.

A glum McCabe stared at the pot of water and herbs I stirred. "What's that you be making?"

"A decoction for Toby's fever. It's a Chinese potion . . . Jade Girl . . . sort of like a soupy tea." I continued to take pinches of ground herbs from vials and put them to steep in the boiling water. "I have to let it simmer awhile to thicken."

"What would you be knowing about Chinee medicines?"

"Chester learned about them from his Chinese friends in Lewiston. These herbs are called Sheng-di . . . Sheng-shi-gao . . . Zhi mu . . . and Gan cao." I held up each vial as I pronounced the names.

"Don't matter one bit what they be, just so they work."

I lowered my voice. "I don't want to mislead

you. The herbs won't cure the illness, just help the fever. We'll give Toby a spoonful whenever he wakes, another grain of laudanum with the first dose to ease the pain and help him sleep."

A cloud spread across McCabe's already stricken face. He leaned toward me. "What are the lad's chances?"

I shrugged, fighting my own anxiety. "He's young and has the strength to fight it. But there's always a chance he . . ." The rest of the words caught in my throat. I knew Toby's chances to survive were slight, but whatever the odds, he must, he *would* live.

I sponged him with tepid water and gave him a spoonful of the decoction when it had thickened and cooled. It didn't take long for him to doze off. I sat beside his bed in a half sleep. Reb sprawled on a matted quilt at my feet, his paws scratching the floor in some dreamed chase. The only other sounds in the room were the sputter of the lamp and the snap of coals in the box stove.

Sitting there, keeping watch, reminded me of the times my own children lay sick, of the hours I spent helping Chester tend the ailing, their feverish eyes filled with trust, admiration, gratitude. I'd lost track of the times we'd taken a buckboard into the country to care for the sick, struggling up rough, crooked roads, through mud and snow, fighting bitter winds that shook the wagon box, sometimes for miles, to ramshackle homes with pale wives and runny-nosed children, little food, no medicine. Chester knew he'd never be paid, but he didn't care.

I'd seen him mend a rancher gored by a bull, the man's stomach ripped open in a way that made me retch. Chester just shuddered, went about cauterizing the wound, and sewed it up. Another time he amputated the leg of a child caught in a mower, then fashioned an artificial leg from wood, ordered new ones made as the child grew. Last time I saw the boy, a young man now, he walked as if the leg were his own. On one occasion a neighbor beat his son, his face bruised and bleeding beyond recognition. Chester wrestled the man to the floor so the boy could escape, then brought the boy home to stay until the man was sentenced to jail. Keen of mind, courageous, tender of heart, Chester was always crushed when a patient slipped beyond help, and crucified himself for not knowing enough. How I wished he were here to help me now!

Outside, a robin trilled. A puff of breeze stirred the frigid pre-dawn. McCabe hunched on a stool near the stove and, at times, would catch his head bobbing with drowsiness. After one such jerk of the head, he shifted his position and put long, gnarled fingers over his mouth to stop a yawn.

"Mister McCabe, go lie on your bed. I'll sit with Toby."

"That wouldn't be fitting. You're the one doing the favor. You be the one to rest." He hauled himself to his feet. "I'll smooth out my bed so you can lie."

"I wish you wouldn't. I'm all right."

Ignoring my protest, he pulled rumpled blankets over a mattress of gunnysacking filled with moss and tree lichen. A piece of the chartreuse lichen poked through a hole in the sacking and gave off a yellowish dust when disturbed.

"Come Missus Clark, you'll be needing your strength to tend the lad. I'll watch him." As he lifted me by the elbow, his weariness passed through my cotton sleeve into my own tired flesh.

"Be sure to wake me if he needs care."

"Aye, I'll do that."

I must have been exhausted, for when I woke, the sun had already topped the ridges to the east, and a dazzle of rays streamed into the shack. The spitting sound of the river drifted through the open doorway. McCabe stood in the pool of sunlight, turning bacon in a cast-iron fry pan. At the back of the stove, a Dutch oven smelled of sourdough biscuits. A coffee pot steamed the aroma of dark coffee. The lid on a saucepan puffed up and down, suggesting oatmeal.

I slid my legs over the edge of the bunk and sat up, rubbing the sleep from my face. "I didn't mean to stay in bed all day."

McCabe gave a brief thaw of a smile and mumbled a good morning. Dark puffs sagged in wrinkles beneath his eyes. On the opposite wall, Toby lay in his ivory pallor and breathed pitiful sighs.

"Did he wake?"

"Twice. I give him some brew and cooled the head cloth."

"You should have wakened me."

"'Twas nothing I couldn't do."

"I know, but I feel responsible for the boy since you asked me to care for him."

McCabe forked the bacon into a tin plate, set the plate on the table, and turned toward me with a curious, slantwise expression. "Tell me about your own boys again. I can't remember what they do for a living?"

A sign of old age. I'd spoken about the boys many times. I could see them in my mind's eye. Alan, twenty-eight, had inherited my black hair and blue eyes, my high cheekbones, a serious, dreamy young man. Walter was thirty-three. He looked like his father, his straw-like hair parted in the middle and combed to each side, a generous nose, a spark of humor in his blue eyes. Despite their terrible misgivings, the boys had helped us pack our belongings onto the river. Before they returned to their homes, Alan had helped me break ground for a garden and had planted fruit stock. Walter had helped Chester fell trees for the cabin and skidded them to the building site. I sighed, wishing I could see them soon.

"Alan attends Stanford on a graduate fellowship and rooms with an aunt," I said to McCabe. "He's a twin of the daughter who teaches in Lewiston. Walter, the oldest boy, is trying his hand at farming in eastern Oregon. He has two little boys." While I spoke, I checked Toby's fever and found it still raging. I wanted to disturb him as little as possible, so I simply dipped the cloth in water and returned it to his forehead. I'd wait until he woke to give him the Jade Girl.

"And the oldest girl? I forget where she is."

"In Lewiston. She married a gentleman who owns an apothecary shop. She has two little girls."

McCabe spooned some oatmeal into his bowl and sat. "I never could figure why you settled so far from your girls . . . aren't you lonely?" I felt a strange shyness at the question, at the note of concern in McCabe's voice. Having lain in his bed, though alone, I was aware now of an intimacy between us, circumstantial, but . . . I averted my gaze.

"I didn't want to disappoint Chester. I think you knew Jake Burns—a prospector. He worked a placer on our flat."

"I don't recall he took out much gold."

"He's in Alaska now, but when he signed the land over to us, he raved about the upper Salmon, said it was a paradise." I'd moved to the doorway, and was washing my face and hands in the basin of hot water McCabe had set on the wooden slab outside the door. It seemed we'd had this conversation before, but it was a relief to talk. "The more Jake carried on, the more Chester wanted to live on that piece of ground. Chester called it heaven, but from what I'd heard about this section of river I thought it would be more like Hades . . . so far from everything . . . so hard to get in and out."

McCabe's gritty voice found its way through the folds of the towel I was using to dry my face.

"'Tisn't good to move someplace against your will."

"I wanted to try it for Chester's sake. It was difficult for me at first. But before Chester died, I'd come to love the place . . . except I missed seeing my children and friends." Breathing hard from washing, I hung the towel on the slab. My body hadn't yet taken a hold on the day.

McCabe had moved the clutter from the small table and set me a place. While he munched on a biscuit, he watched me with twitchy, sideways glances. "If you want gruel, there's bowls on the shelf. You can help yourself. It's best to leave it in the pot to stay warm."

I wouldn't be ready for breakfast until I freshened my braids and fastened them at the nape of my neck. I was putting the last pin in place when Toby awoke and asked for water in a weak, breathy voice. I gave him a drink with a spoonful of Jade Girl and quinine and asked about his symptoms in as quiet a manner as I could. After I'd tended his other physical needs and dropped a kiss on his cheek, I settled at the table opposite McCabe.

I wanted to whisper a comment about Toby's condition, but McCabe had already picked up the thread of our conversation. I couldn't account for this rare desire of his to talk and question. He seemed as ill at ease at having me in his shack as I was to be there. Perhaps conversation was a way to hide the fact.

"It must of been hard on you to find your man dead."

I reflected a moment, saddening. "The most difficult thing I've ever faced. I couldn't get word to my family about the burial. Chester's body was in such a state when I found him washed up on the shore, I asked Len Johnson to bury him right away." I fell silent, trying to push the memory aside, forcing myself to eat the thick oatmeal.

McCabe drew a deep breath, relaxing visibly.

His eyes steadied, became sympathetic, thoughtful. "The river is a hard place for a woman alone."

I nodded. "For men, too, I'm sure. Yet you chose to stay here, far from other humans. Why?"

An expression of melancholy darkened McCabe's face like a slowly drawn shade. "Sometimes a man has a need to be alone . . . to forget . . ." His gaze wandered, settling on the world beyond the open doorway.

"You mean the girl?"

He spun his head around and looked at me, squinty-eyed. "If you knew, why were you asking?"

"I—I'd heard there was a girl . . . some kind of an accident . . . nothing more."

He frowned, an expression of reflective thought rather than anger. "No matter. 'Twas a long time ago."

He rose, started to clear his plate and bowl from the table. I thought he'd say no more, but as he scraped biscuit crumbs into a pan for Reb, he went on as if there'd been no gap in his muttering. "A storekeeper's daughter in Salmon City, she was. One day, drovers was running a bunch of longhorns through town, and the lass didn't know it. She stepped out of the store just as a steer went wild busting things up . . . and the beast . . . I—I could do nothing to save her . . . she . . ." He clamped his mouth shut, breaking the low, rueful thread of his speech. He looked spent, as though that one incident had so crushed him he'd never been able to rise above it.

"I'm sorry. I shouldn't have asked."

He set the pan outside the door for Reb to

find and returned to the stove. "No harm, woman. I didn't have to tell you." Something approaching warmth flecked his eyes.

Remorse sat heavy on my breast. I shouldn't have questioned McCabe about his past. His approval had become important to me. I sat a long while sipping coffee, trying to think of a way to repair the damage I might have caused. "Do you suppose you could call me Harriet, instead of 'Missus Clark,' or 'woman'? After all, we've known each other awhile."

"Harriet doesn't fit you."

"What do you mean, fit me?"

"Harriet is too stuffy . . . like a woman who spends her time giving tea parties. With your height and pluck, I'd think something like Hilda or Gertrude would be more suiting."

"I hate those names!"

He laughed. "I could call you by your middle name. Do you have one?"

"It's Isobelle, and I hate it!"

"I could call you Belle."

"I'm not a Belle sort of person."

I couldn't have imagined a more foolish conversation, but McCabe seemed to derive some pleasure from it. "I suppose you could call me Hattie, like Toby and Chester."

"I like that better than Harriet. More friendly. And you can call me Afton, but it's kind of a sissy name." He broke into a grin that disarmed me so completely I had to smile.

❧

Our watch over Toby lasted one anxious day after the other, each night's vigil more tiring and worrisome than the last. Afton had draped a canvas sheet over a tree limb for a shelter, pegged the sheet to the ground, and laid a pallet of fir boughs inside for himself so I could use his bed in the shack. He took the late watch each night while I rested, though if I slept at all, dreams of Toby, Afton, and death troubled my rest. It was better to be up tending the boy.

Every day I rode Sadie to the ranch to gather eggs, feed and water the stock, milk the goats, weed the pea vines, and see that nothing had been disturbed. I insisted Sam and Bones stay to guard the place, but though they spoke volumes in their own way, they weren't able to report on trespassers.

John and Oakie had cleaned the wreckage in their cabin and lived there most of the time, but couldn't be counted on to keep watch or do the chores. With the river on the rise, they'd soon return to the outside to satisfy their cravings. If I continued to stay at McCabe's Bar I'd have to ask Len Johnson to tend the stock, as the trail from McCabe's would become impassable at the cliff.

In spite of our care, Toby seemed to slip away, his pulse the tiniest of flutters, his wrists little but bone beneath their loose skin. We continued to cool his fever with wet cloths and sponging, gave him a sip of the decoction every hour, even if we had to wake him, and small doses of quinine and laudanum. I disinfected his underwear and the sponge cloths in a solution of zinc sulfate and table salt. The horrid spots covered nearly every inch of his body, even the palms of his hands and the soles of his feet. In his delirium he cried out for his mother. At other times he screamed his father's name over and over in a frightful way. I wondered what his father had done to cause such terror.

The tenth night at McCabe's I dreamed a thief had me by the shoulders, threatening to harm me if I didn't reveal where I kept my savings. I woke to find Afton's hand on my shoulder.

"Sorry to wake you, Missus Cl—I mean, Hattie. I cannot get the boy to take his medicine. It just dribbles from his mouth."

I rose so quickly I lost my balance and fell back to the bed. With the next attempt I was able to take the spoon and cup of decoction from Afton and cross over to Toby's bunk. I spoke the boy's name. No response. When I shook him, his head wobbled on his neck like a broken doll's. I searched for a pulse, but could find none. With Chester's stethoscope I heard the same faint rasping I'd heard for days. Losing hope, I dipped my fingers in a cup of water and lay them on the boy's cracked lips, willing him to live.

9

*fton and I sat a long while, watching the almost imperceptible rise and fall of Toby's chest, his body so small and frail it scarcely swelled the covers. His breath seemed a mere wisp of life, a broken spider web stirring in the faintest breeze. The swollen river roared in front of the shack, but in my concentration I barely heard anything, save the boy's breathing and from time to time Reb's elbow bumping the floor in a scratch. I knew that in these wee hours of the night Toby would remain with us, strengthened by some unfathomable will, or he would leave us, alone in a wilderness of sorrow.

"It's inconceivable Toby might die, isn't it?" Grief hurt my throat, yet I must speak. "He's come to mean so much to me, I don't know what I'll do if he dies. Before he came to the river I'd nearly given up on life . . . he gave me reason to live . . ." I knew such morbid thoughts were wasteful, but I couldn't push them from mind. I raised my unseeing eyes and turned them on

Afton. "I expect it will be hard for you, too. You must love the boy as much as I." A look of compassion passed between us. The look grew in tenderness and complexity, until, embarrassed at our feelings, we looked away.

"Toby tells me you lost a laddie to diphtheria." Afton's voice was low, thick with feeling.

"Yes . . . and there was another . . . a baby at birth. I don't think I felt any worse about losing them than I'll feel if Toby dies. Have you lost anyone who meant as much to you as Toby?" Recalling Archie and the girl, I thought the question stupid after I'd asked, but my muddled brain could do no better. "In your family, that is."

"I had a baby sister born dead . . . I didn't grieve much . . . not like my mother. How could I mourn for something I never knew?" He thought awhile, staring at the floor as if it were the source of his past. "A brother got the chills and died. Real close, we were. After that I ran away from home . . . was just thirteen. By the time I was nineteen I'd come to America and got left out of the buryings back home."

"What about your sister and her husband, Toby's grandparents? Toby said his father and his Uncle Will took over the ranch when the grandparents died of the flu. That must have been one or two years before Toby was born."

"On the river I was at the time, and heard about the funeral too late. The same with Toby's ma. I never seemed to be around at burying time. Always here and there on the river." He turned his gaze on Toby, watching him with wide, sad eyes.

"Maybe this is Providence's way of making me pay for my neglect."

The heartache reflected in Afton's face wakened a frightening thought that slept in a corner of my distraught mind, one that surprised me with its import. If Toby died, not only would I lose that joy, but Afton, too, might fade from my life.

Despite our will to the contrary, Toby showed no improvement. For the next twenty-four hours, his pulse was barely discernible, his breathing a filament of foul air, the translucent hollows of his closed eyelids as blue as river ice. I'd almost given up hope.

On the morning of his twelfth day in bed, I sat beside his bunk in haunted silence, mentally listing what Afton and I must do to prepare for a burial. The weather was cold and overcast, and the shack smelled of the cotton and flannel burial wraps I'd washed and spread to dry by the stove. From behind the shack came the rip, rip, rip of Afton's saw, cutting slabs of pine for a coffin.

So deep were my musings, I hardly noticed a whisper that rose from the folds of bedding. "Hattie . . ."

I thought my troubled mind had played tricks. I bent over the bed, listening. "Toby?"

A faint quiver passed over the boy's face. He moaned.

I put my hand on his forehead. It had cooled. His pulse? Stronger than it had been for days.

A gurgle rose from his throat. "I'm thirsty."

With a gasp of relief, I turned my eyes to the ceiling, back to Toby. "Bless you, child! You can drink the spring dry, if you like."

I put my arm beneath his head and held a cup of water to his lips. He took a few sips and slumped back to the bed. A moment later his lids raised over dull, sunken eyes, and he drank again, draining the cup.

"I'm hungry," he murmured.

My heart swelled with relief. "That's the best news I've had in ages. We'll start with chicken broth. I've kept a jar of it cooling in the creek in case—that is, for when you improved."

"Did you think I was going to die?"

"No, dear boy," I lied. "I—I was just terribly worried because you weren't getting well as fast as I'd like." I squeezed his hand, letting gratitude flow from my flesh into his. Quiet tears slid down my cheeks. "I'm so glad you're feeling better. I can't remember when I've been so glad."

May had slipped into June. Snow in the high country was melting fast. The river had gradually covered the trail at the cliff, causing Sadie to balk more each time we went home to do chores. Her stubbornness, coupled with my need to get seeds and hotbed tomatoes into the ground, prompted me to suggest to Afton that I take Toby to the ranch during the month of high water.

He agreed, with sadness. "I'm willing to grant

he'd be better off with you. I'm not all that great
for bathing and fussing over the boy. And you
have a feel for caring for others. I'll miss him,
though . . . and you."

And me? The thought surprised, pleased.

So we moved Toby to Weasel Creek, and while
I planted seeds and pulled weeds, he watched from
his cot on the porch or sat in an old rocking chair
with Sam and Bones at his feet. I knew it was
impossible, but I couldn't help wishing I could
keep Toby with me the rest of my days. I was
beyond the point of childbearing, but the need to
nurture—touch—hold—lingered on.

Because of my encounter with the Harpers,
both of my daughters had written, begging me to
move in with them, but I delayed making a decision until after Toby had regained his health. As
much as I wanted to throw my arms around my
grandchildren and give them hugs and kisses, living at my older daughter's house with noisy toddlers romping about might fray my middle-aged
nerves. Living with my younger daughter, the
teacher, would be easier, but I'd rather live in my
own house, especially if Toby were with me.

If Toby were mine, I'd take him to places I
loved, places I'd never been, places unknown to
me as yet. We'd visit the cities, museums, concert
halls, art galleries, zoos. We'd walk seashores Toby
had seen only in his imaginings. We'd learn
together, wonder together, laugh and cry
together. We'd sit on the porch of a summer
evening and gaze at the stars strung across the
heavens, trying to see into the ages, his body

strong and tall beside me, his mind eager, discerning. I imagined his child's voice changing subtly to that of a young man. If only I could be with him when that happened.

Toby gained strength, and wandered the flat with the dogs, playing and teasing as boys are wont to do, imitating the Plymouth Rock rooster when it crowed a lusty challenge. He wanted to take the new kids out to play, but I hadn't tamed them, and they were too full of vinegar to let out of the pen, except for one brown runt who had Nubbin's white muzzle and stockings. I let the boy take her out on a halter rope, much to Napoleon's displeasure. I kept the large buck in a pen by himself this time of year, but he wanted his herd next door where he could keep track of things important to a buck. If ever I took a kid or doe from the neighboring pen, he'd rant and rave.

One morning I was in the garden, shovel in hand, channeling ditch water into furrows—Chester had built the diversion from Weasel Creek to the vegetable garden our first summer on the homestead. The day was pleasantly mild for July on the river, a few wispy clouds, a light breeze from the east carrying the scent of lush greenery that grew along the banks of Weasel Creek.

Toby had taken Daisy, the runt, for a walk around the outside of the garden fence. From time to time, I'd stop in the midst of my irrigating to toss her a juicy weed. The other goats bleated in their pens, irritated at having been left behind. Napoleon stood on the roof of his pen and blattered his outrage.

I'd bent over to scoop a mound of silt from a furrow when I heard hooves clatter on the hard-packed earth of the barnyard. I straightened in time to see Napoleon streak along the garden fence and corner Toby and Daisy in a thicket of wild roses. The goat had often jumped from his pen to wander the flat, returning when his craving for oats outweighed his desire for freedom. This time he had something in mind other than free-dom.

"Call him off!" Toby screamed.

"Hang on! I'm coming."

Clunking along as fast as I could in my muddy boots, I threw open the garden gate and ran to the tangle of briars. Napoleon was pawing the ground, giving Toby the evil eye.

"You damnable goat! Leave the boy alone." I swung the shovel. "Put Daisy in the pen," I told Toby. "Then go to the house."

While Toby backed out of the briar patch, I swung the shovel at the goat to keep his attention. I jabbed him, sidestepped when he charged, swung again, hit him once or twice. Sweat trickled from my scalp into my eyes. My heart pounded against my ribs.

When I heard the gate to the pen close, I looked over my shoulder to tell Toby, "Be sure the hook is all the way—" I broke off with a cry, think-ing someone had struck my hip with a two by four. I fell to the ground, my knee on a rock, my outstretched palms on the thorny runners from a rose. My pride was as bruised as my hip and knee, as badly torn as my hands.

"I hate you!" I shrieked at the goat.

Napoleon seemed to revel in my humiliation. He stood with his head lowered, a devilish glint in his eyes, pawed the ground and snorted, waiting for me to rise so he could ram me again.

I picked myself up and gave him back glare for glare. "You beast! You're not going to win this time." I referred to the day he'd chased me into the house and followed me all the way upstairs, forcing me to hide under the bed until Chester returned from a fishing trip.

From the corner of my eye, I glimpsed Toby on his way to the house. Curious about what was happening to me, he wasn't moving as fast as he should.

Napoleon must have thought him easy prey. Forgetting me, he tore after the boy and rammed his way through the yard gate before Toby could shut it.

"Crawl under the porch!" I cried. I didn't dare tell him to run into the house. Napoleon would have been right at his heels, giving him no chance to close the door.

By the time I entered the yard, the buck had pushed Toby to the ground. The boy crawled along like a crab, fending off the goat with one hand. When he reached the porch, he rolled into the space beneath the floor. Napoleon dropped to his knees and jabbed his horns at the boy.

I headed for the door. "Don't be afraid, Toby. I'll get my gun."

It took but a minute or two to grab the Winchester and load a shell in the chamber, yet when I came from the house, Napoleon had already discarded thoughts of Toby and had buried his muzzle in a bed of petunias at the edge of the porch. My favorite lavenders were disappearing down his gullet. Nothing could have enraged me more. I raised the rifle, pulled back on the hammer.

The buck seemed to recognize the click of the hammer as the signal for an explosion, such as those that had killed varmints invading his pen. Before I could draw a bead, he spun, tore through the gate and down the hayfield without stopping.

I tried a running shot, but missed. The thunderous clap of the rifle deafened me momentarily, made my ears ring, and swelled my anger.

"Go ahead, run off!" I screamed at the goat. "I hope a cougar finds you."

Toby scrambled out from under the porch and stood beside me, wiping cobwebs and dirt from his face. "I don't like that goat," he said with typical understatement.

"Are you hurt?"

"Don't think so."

I saw that his face was scratched from briars, nothing serious. "Come, let's sit down." I dropped to the porch step, leaned against the roof support, and closed my eyes. The adrenaline had drained, taking my strength with it, unstringing my nerves, leaving me ashamed I'd considered killing the goat. The anger I'd felt gave way to tears of frustration that welled over my eyelids and trickled a hot path down my cheeks.

Toby sat down beside me and took my hand. "Why are you crying?"

I sucked in a breath, wiped my eyes with the corner of my apron. "It's hard enough to keep this place going without having that ornery goat around. Chester could make him mind, but I can't. He bullies me every chance he gets. Sometimes I think I'll turn the entire herd loose, and good riddance. Then I'll leave here and never come back."

"You can come live with Uncle and me."

I smiled through bleary eyes, patted his hand. "I'm sure Afton wouldn't like that."

"Then I'll go with *you*."

"I'd love to have you, Toby. But Afton wouldn't approve of that either."

He tucked his lip beneath his teeth and sucked it in and out as a look of apprehension crept over his face. "I don't want you to leave."

The words struck me like a revelation. Toby blurred before my damp eyes. I threw my arms around him and squeezed. "Dear child, I wouldn't think of leaving you. I was just feeling sorry for myself. It was stupid. Forget what I said."

Our conversation on the porch made Toby's days at the homestead more precious. I tried to make time stand still, but it refused, and soon it was mid-June, the river at its highest stage, spilling its scourings down the canyon. Now and then a prospector would come from Dixie or Elk City to check on the water, then return to the mining camps to spread the word the river was too high to cross. Our only other contact was Len Johnson, the hermit. We took the trail upriver to check on his goats and ask if he wanted the Harpers' mule, now in good health. He said he did.

McCabe was still isolated west of the cliff.

Because we'd had so little company, I could understand the excitement in Toby's voice when he came running into the kitchen one hot afternoon. I'd cleaned a hen too old for laying, and stood at the stove adding onion and spice to a fricassee.

"Hattie, somebody's coming!" the boy cried.

"That's nice," I said offhandedly, too busy counting cloves into the pot to look up.

"One's a lady."

That news made me raise my head with a start. In my six years on the flat, I'd seen as many women in the canyon.

I put the lid on the Dutch oven, pulled off the apron I'd dirtied cleaning the hen, rinsed my hands at the sink, then turned to the little mirror that hung on the wall by the window. Through the windowpane, I saw a man in city clothes ride up to the gate on an underfed buckskin—the livery stables at Dixie and Elk City were always short of hay this time of the year, probably next to nothing in storage until the new crop was shipped in. Fifty yards behind the man, a woman sat astride a sorrel, her skirts up to her knees.

I smoothed straggles of black hair from my

face, fastened the braids more securely at the nape of my neck, and went out to the gate. Toby stood just inside the fence and was staring at the man in his shy way, answering questions in monosyllables.

"Good afternoon," I said.

The man tipped a gray derby. "Afternoon." He dismounted with the clumsiness of someone unaccustomed to riding, tied the horse to the fence. "This is a trip I don't intend to make twice," he said, clapping the dust from his vest and trousers. "There's as much dust on me as on the trail. I prefer to do my traveling from the seat of a buggy."

He seemed out of place—his shirt linen, the gray vest and trousers well tailored. The high polish of his boots shone in places where the dust hadn't gathered so readily. He removed the hat to wipe his damp forehead, revealing thick red hair pomaded and combed into a sleek center part. The mustache that ran the length of his massive jaw was waxed and curved upward into sharp points.

He helped the woman from her horse. She displayed the same stiff awkwardness as he. She was dressed in a green plaid skirt and white shirtwaist, high buttoned boots, green silk gloves. Again, not the garb of mountain people. The veil on a green alpine hat partially hid her features.

"Mother, has it been so long you don't know me?"

My heart skipped a beat. "Jennie? What on earth are you doing here?" I stood with mouth agape, looking the fool, I'm sure. I couldn't believe my youngest daughter had ridden into the wilderness. She disliked horses, had always been too cautious to attempt anything as dangerous as the slippery trail that dropped onto the river. But ride onto the Salmon, she had.

I hurried through the gate, my arms spread wide. "Come here, I want to squeeze you."

10

*J*ennie and I exchanged hugs and kisses.

"Didn't you get my letter?" she said. "I wrote the middle of May." Her voice had the same soft quality as Chester's, her eyes the same crinkle of humor.

"It's probably waiting at the Post Office. There's not much travel this way when the water's high. And I haven't been able to leave the ranch." I held her at arms' length, searching for the changes six years had wrought. "My lord, it's good to see you!" She was still the prim, immaculately dressed girl I remembered, though coated with dust at the moment, and clearly sweltering in the heat. I saw myself when I looked into her face— the same high cheekbones, fine-grained skin, ebony hair and blue eyes. Unlike me, she wore her hair in a pompadour that was the new fashion.

"Mother, you look wonderful," she said through my scrutiny.

I laughed, conscious of my faded gingham. "Not dressed for visitors, I'm afraid."

"But rosy-cheeked and healthy."

"Homesteading has its advantages. And you—you seem so—so grown up." Strange, I always remembered Jennie as a sixteen-year-old, all sweet smiles and thoughtful conversation, the scholar, the painter, the musician. She'd returned to Lewiston from the Normal School in Cheney, Washington the year Chester and I moved onto the river.

While Jennie and I talked, the man stood to one side, his face drawn into an expression of fatigue and impatience. He was much older than Jennie, perhaps forty-five, a tall plank of a man who seemed impressed with himself. I wondered what Jennie was doing this far from home in his company.

He cleared his throat for attention.

"Carl, forgive me." Jennie linked her arm in his and looked up at him with uneasy pride. "Mother, this is Carl Foreman, my fiancé."

The news jolted. Jennie hadn't mentioned a new beau in any of her letters.

She noted my expression of shock. "I didn't intend for it to come as a surprise. That's why I wrote."

"I'm sorry. It—it's just so unexpected." And to Carl, "I tend to think of my family as they were when I left Lewiston. I haven't been home in such a long time." I extended my hand. "I'm happy to meet you, Carl." The gesture of good will obviously caught the man off guard—most women thought it unseemly to shake hands.

Toby tugged at my skirts. He was standing at

my side with the expression of abandonment I'd seen on his face before. I slipped my arm around his shoulders. "This is Toby McCabe. His uncle lives down the river a ways."

Toby held out his hand toward Carl. Carl just nodded, but Jennie took Toby's hand and held it. "I'm glad to meet you, Toby. Mother's told me so much about you, though I must say, she hasn't written for a while."

"I plead guilty. I—I've simply had too much to do." Also, I'd put off making a decision about moving in with her. To avoid saying more, I motioned toward the house. "Come, I'll fix us something cool to drink. Or would you prefer coffee?"

"Coffee would suit me," Carl said. "Maybe first I should unsaddle the horses and give them some water."

"By all means. Use the corral next to the barn. Toby can show you where we keep the oats and hay. I'd let you turn the horses into the pasture, but Sadie is a domineering sort. She'd run them around in circles—not give them a minute's rest."

Carl took a large, heavily stuffed saddlebag from the rump of Jennie's horse, struggled to drape it across the fence, then did the same with his leaner bag. "I'll carry these into the house when I get back," he said as he gathered his horse's reins. "They're kind of heavy clothes enough for a week."

I turned to Jennie. "Just a week. Oh, I wish you could stay a month."

Carl had taken Jennie's summer-weight coat

from behind the saddle and tossed it across the fence. I took the coat, gave Jennie another hug, and directed her toward the privy out back. "I'll fill a basin in the kitchen so you can wash."

When she entered the cabin, I stood at the drainboard, grinding beans for a fresh pot of coffee. "What a cozy house," she said. "It's so—so rustic." I could tell by her tone she was disappointed, though I didn't know what she'd expected to find in the wilderness.

She took the pin from her hat, loosened the veil, and set the hat on the table. "I've never been so tired and dusty." She ran slender fingers over her hair, an artist's fingers. "I can't believe you ride that trail every time you go out for supplies."

"And I can't believe *you* traveled it. It scared me half to death the first time I rode down."

"I almost turned around at the top, but Carl wouldn't let me. It's just as well. I wanted you to meet him before we married." She dipped her hands in the basin of water I'd put on the table and worked up a lather from a bar of soap. "You must come to the wedding. It's in October. I wanted to hold it before school starts, but Carl is going east for a few months."

My baby daughter planned to marry. The thought tugged at my breast. I lost myself in nostalgic memories of Jennie, the quiet child, the girl blossoming into her teens, the confident young woman going off to college.

"Mother? Is something wrong? Surely, you're not upset with me for marrying."

"No . . . of course not. It's just hard to think of you as a matron."

"You haven't been around to watch me . . . shall we say, 'mature.'" She laughed. "I'm sure my first graders think of me as ancient."

I took the drawer from the coffee grinder and sniffed the grounds before I put them in the pot. The dark aroma helped to brace me for the reality of the wedding. "Will it be a large affair?"

"Oh, yes. Carl has become well known since he moved to town. For business reasons, he'll want to have everyone there."

"And what is his business?"

"He's a lawyer."

I thought about that while I filled the coffee pot with boiling water from the tea kettle. One of Chester's best friends was an honest, respected lawyer. There was another lawyer in town, who couldn't be trusted. I wondered into which category Carl fit. I hoped the former, but probably some gray area in between.

"And who will you invite?"

"Mainly close friends and family. Walter will give me away. Marybelle will be my matron of honor." A mix of excitement and uncertainty showed in her voice. I recognized the pre-wedding jitters from my own experience thirty-six years ago.

"It's too bad Marybelle didn't come with you. She'd have enjoyed the canyon." Unlike Jennie, my older daughter, Marybelle, had always loved things physical, things that pertained to the out-of-doors. Jennie would sit inside and read on a nice day, while Marybelle played cowboys and Indians with the neighborhood boys, or hunted toads.

"She wanted to come, but she had nowhere to leave the children. Do you have a towel?" I handed her a clean white one from the cupboard. "I'm glad she didn't take the chance. She's expecting again."

"So soon after losing the last one. That wasn't wise. Now she'll have three little ones under the age of eight."

"You know Marybelle. That's the way she likes it."

So had I at one time, I recalled, though I was more organized than Marybelle. The house could tumble down around her shoulders while she played with the babies, and she'd pay no heed. After living in the solitude of the canyon, the thought of moving into that confusion had little appeal, though I wanted to see the babies often and was willing to help around the house.

"And what have you ladies been talking about?" Carl had come into the house after stomping the dirt from his boots.

I didn't want to mention Marybelle's pregnancy, so I said, "I was telling Jennie she was brave to ride down that trail."

He brought up a scornful laugh from deep in his chest. "Brave! Hardly. She wanted to turn around at the top. I told her no woman was going to get me this far into the damned boondocks, then turn around before she'd done what she came for."

I could understand his feelings, but I didn't like the critical way he expressed them. Perhaps he was just tired. "I'm glad she had reason to make the trip. I doubt she would have otherwise. It was good of you to bring her." I motioned toward the saddlebag Carl held in his arms. "You can put Jennie's bag up in the sleeping loft. She can sleep in my bed. I'll sleep on Toby's cot. I'll lay pallets there, in the sitting room, for you and the boy." Propriety kept me from offering the cot upstairs where Jennie would sleep.

Carl looked down at the floor with a snort. "Guess it's better than sleeping in the barn with the mice." Grunting beneath the weight of the bag, he mounted the stairs to the loft.

Jennie seemed embarrassed at her fiancé's remark. She leaned toward me and whispered, "You'll have to forgive Carl. He's hot and tired. He didn't want to make the trip, but I told him I wouldn't marry until you'd met him."

"I hope it doesn't depend on my consent. I may think of you as my little girl, but you're old enough to make that decision without me."

"Mother, I'd never marry anyone if I thought you disapproved. I value your judgment."

"And I love you for that." I was so happy to have Jennie near I couldn't keep my hands from her. I gave her another hug. "But you must realize, a man Carl's age might resent a mother's interference."

"He's only forty-four."

"Old enough to want his way, without my butting in." The coffee had started to boil up through the spout, so I pushed the pot to the lip of the stove. "He's been a bachelor all this time?"

She seemed uncomfortable with the question. "He was married once . . . when he lived in Spokane Falls. But . . ." I expected her to say more. She didn't, just stood, biting her lip. She seemed relieved when Carl descended the stairs, and followed him outside solicitously as he went to retrieve the other saddlebag.

I went about setting coffee cups on the table, my thoughts on the impending marriage. I was pleased that Jennie valued my advice. But I didn't like the position of consent-giver. Something about Carl Foreman made me wonder if I could find much in him to like.

That evening, after supper and a visit to Chester's grave, we sat on the porch in his lodgepole furniture, sipping brandy I'd kept on hand for a special occasion—until then, I hadn't had an excuse to open the bottle. Toby was in the yard tussling with the dogs, giggling. A Lewis' woodpecker rapped at a pine near the gate. At river's edge, the flooded willows gave birth to a cloud of mosquitoes.

Carl slapped a mosquito that lit on his hand. "I hope these don't carry yellow fever," he said with a snort of humor.

"We'd be in a bad fix if they did. I feel sorry for those people who live in the tropics."

"Did you read the latest newspaper report on the fever?" Jennie asked.

"I did. Can you believe it's caused by an organism so small it can pass through a fine porcelain filter? It's frightening. Viruses, he calls them."

Jennie shooed away several mosquitoes with my favorite Japanese fan. "Dr. Reed showed courage to continue the study after his associate died from the fever. I don't think I would have stayed on."

"It was stupid, if you ask me," Carl said. "Why risk your life for a bunch of ignorant natives?"

The heat of resentment flared in my cheeks. "What if your life were at stake, wouldn't you want someone to make the effort? And what about the whites in the area. Don't they count? Little progress would be made in medicine if someone weren't willing to—" Fortunately, a squeal from Toby interrupted my tirade. Looking his way, I saw the dogs jump for a stick he was about to throw.

"He's a nice boy," Jennie said, smiling. "I brought him a copy of that new book I mentioned in my letter, *The Wizard of Oz*. The children at school love it."

"I'm glad America has a fairy tale of its own."

Carl gave another of his cynical snorts. "What the younger generation needs is cold, hard facts, not fairy tales. No good witch is going to put bread on their table."

"Good witch? You read the book?"

"Hardly! Jennie was telling me about it."

"I meant no offense," I said, flushing again. "I understand the book is popular with both young and old."

What was it about Carl Foreman that made anger rise so easily? I studied his face, the hard jaw, the piercing green eyes with their look of scorn. I watched while he bit the tip from a cheroot, struck a match on the sole of his boot, then sucked the cheroot to life.

"Tell me, is it easy for you to put bread on the table?" I made no attempt to hide the sarcasm.

His expression said I was prying where I shouldn't. He let smoke string from his lips, obviously deciding whether to answer. "The kind of cases I handle make me a good living," he said after a bit. "I work for the banks—mortgage foreclosures, bad loans. I represent mining interests in suits against the competition, in the takeover of claims. Not lofty pursuits, but they pay well." So far, I couldn't fault Carl for lack of candor. "Lately the owners of large cattle ranches have come to me to bring suit against the wool growers."

"I understand there's been a lot of trouble over range land since I left. That's too bad, the two factions ought to be able to get along. It seems to me the cattlemen are Janus-faced. They use barbed wire to protect *their* land. Cut it, if it's protecting a sheepman's land."

Foreman studied the fiery ring at the tip of the cheroot, sucked on a tooth. "I'd say they have a right. The sheep graze the grass down to the roots, then cut the roots with their sharp hooves. It makes the cattlemen breathe fire and fury."

"They tell me the sheep ooze a sticky fluid from a gland between their toes," Jennie put in.

"The cattle don't like the smell and won't eat where the sheep walked."

I laughed skeptically. "That's a fairy tale in itself. If it's true, why do sheep and cattle graze together on small farms?"

"It might be a fairy tale, but it brings me business," Carl said with greed in his voice. "Trouble is, some cattlemen don't bother to sue. They're too impatient to wait for court action. They take the law into their own hands."

I shook my head with disgust, recalling reports I'd seen in the newspaper. "Vigilantes! They murder sheepherders—club and dynamite sheep—even drive them over cliffs."

"It's called rimrocking," Carl said with a glint of approval in his eyes. "A means to an end."

I couldn't believe his callousness. That, along with his choice of clients and the implied lack of ethics, made me dislike the man intensely.

He tilted his head back and blew a ring of smoke. "Jennie tells me she asked you to come live with her," he said, changing the subject abruptly. "That was one of her reasons for coming, to ask your wishes in the matter."

I squirmed in my chair. I wanted to say it was none of his business until he was married, but settled on, "I haven't decided."

"I . . . uhh . . . suppose it's still possible," he said in a condescending manner. "Of course, you might be a little cramped at her place. I intend to close off part of the extra bedroom to make myself a study."

So! He intended to move in with Jennie,

rather than provide her a home. I didn't say I couldn't possibly live under the same roof with a man of such arrogance, of such questionable motives. Instead I said, "I wouldn't think of imposing. Especially on newlyweds. If I leave the river, I'll rent a flat. If my renters can find another place to live, I'll move into my own house."

Jennie reached across the space between our chairs and touched my arm. "Mother, be reasonable. You don't want to live alone."

"I've lived alone for the past year and I rather like it." My belligerent tone surprised me. Perhaps the statement held a truth I'd kept from myself.

Jennie looked hurt. "If you don't want to live with me, then think of Marybelle. She needs your help. They've bought a bigger house to have space for the baby. And there'll be a bedroom for you."

Knowing Marybelle, bless her heart, I'd become a nanny, a housekeeper, a cook. I was willing to help, but there were other things I wanted to do with my time.

"It's not a matter of not wanting to live with *you*. I've suddenly realized, it's a matter of not wanting to live with *anybody*." Except Toby, I thought to myself.

"Hattie, can I take Daisy out of the pen?" the boy asked from the yard.

"Yes, but be on the watch for Napoleon." I suspected he'd followed the receding snows into the higher elevations to dine on succulent herbs, but he might return any time.

Carl watched Toby head for the pens. "Why is the boy here?"

I explained Toby's illness. I'd told Jennie when Carl was upstairs resting and I was putting the finishing touches on supper.

He frowned. "You're too generous. If you like nursing children, you should be in Lewiston caring for Marybelle's, not some urchin who dropped into your life from nowhere."

Urchin! How could Carl possibly think Toby an urchin? And what right did he have telling me what to do? Resentment crawled up the back of my neck. "You do Toby an injustice. He's a fine boy—smarter than most—loving—willing to work. He's more respectful than many children I know. If I could, I'd adopt him as my own. You and Jennie will be fortunate to have a child as nice." I immediately regretted the spite that crept into the last few words. Jennie had come all this way so I could meet Carl. And I couldn't be civil to the man.

Carl replied in kind. "Thank God we don't have to worry about that!" he said with barbs in his voice. "I had an illness that prevents me from siring children."

Jennie darted me a look that showed her discomfort with the topic.

I tried to blunder a way out. "You—you can adopt. There are always children in need of a good home."

Carl glared. "That's the last thing I'd—"

"I have all the children I need at school," Jennie blurted—I supposed to bring the subject to a close. "I think of them as my own."

"I—I'm sure they love you for it, dear. I can

imagine how lovely your classroom must be, with all the artwork and the like. Tell me . . ." I went on to ask how she approached the teaching of drawing and painting, about other subjects on the first grade level, anything to center the conversation on her professional rather than her private life. I knew I'd have to watch myself during the week ahead to keep from treading on Carl's toes. Jennie had put out a great effort to come visit. I didn't want to spoil the occasion.

The weather cooled during Jennie's stay, became quite pleasant, with soft sunshine and gentle breezes, making it easier to keep her away from the house and her fiancé, making it easier for me to restrain my tongue. We talked while I tended the flowers and vegetable garden, the animals. We strolled up and down the flat and passed many hours reminiscing in the grove of Ponderosa near the cliff. Carl Foreman didn't seem to mind. He spent most of each day in the hammock at the side of the house, sleeping and reading dime novels he'd brought with him.

At mealtimes and after supper when we sat on the porch, I tried to avoid conversation that would cause argument or put Carl in a bad light, but it was difficult. There was little we could talk about that didn't reveal him as a mean-spirited, grasping individual. I wondered how Jennie, a girl with so much decency, so much respect for others, could marry such an ass in lion's skin. What manner of carrot had he dangled before her eyes. Perhaps at twenty-eight she was afraid of spinsterhood. Yet, as a girl, she'd rejected beaus I'd found charming. Perhaps she'd been looking for an older man like Carl, obviously secure in his profession.

He appeared to like Jennie—I doubted him capable of love. I gathered from things said outright, some hinted at, that he had political ambitions, and I suspected he considered Jennie—an educated, pretty woman, who knew all the social graces—a valuable asset in reaching his goals.

Despite an honest attempt to find some good in the man, I decided I wanted as little to do with him as possible. If necessary, I'd stay on the river to avoid letting my feelings interfere with the marriage, to avoid watching the unhappiness he was certain to bring into Jennie's life.

The moment I'd been dreading came the day before their departure for Lewiston. Jennie and I sat on a log beside Chester's grave, recalling patients he'd treated in the past, people who revered his memory and continued to speak of him to Jennie.

"I miss those years in Lewiston," I said with a sigh. "I miss Chester. I feel only half-alive."

Jennie put her hand on my arm and squeezed it gently. "That's why I'm marrying Carl. I don't want to spend the rest of my life rattling around the house, alone."

"I doubt there'd be much chance of that. You've always aroused men's interest."

"I know . . . but . . . I'm not sure what it is . . . I could never really care for any of them. In fact,

I'm . . . I'm not sure I care for Carl . . . you know . . . in a feminine way. Maybe I'm afraid of intimacy."

"I think most women are before they marry. I remember I was—as much as I loved Chester."

"I hope I get over it. I look at my girlfriends and their young families, and I feel it's time I married *someone*."

"And children?"

"I'm not the Marybelle type. I'm happy rearing children at school." She paused to look out over the river, its waters rumbling along in their rush to the sea. She pursed her lips, ruffled her brow. "Tell me, Mother, what do you think of Carl?"

Panic! What should I tell her? The truth? No, not entirely. The truth might hurt too much. I thought I'd prepared for that moment, but I had to fish for words.

"He . . . ahh . . . has some good qualities." I tried to think what they were. "He's obviously intelligent, educated, nice-looking. He can provide for you, if you should tire of teaching." I thought there was little chance of that happening. "But there is quite a difference in your ages. Men get set in their ways. For that matter, don't we all. The main point is, when he's sixty, running out of time on this earth, you'll be the age he is now, with many years ahead of you."

"I've thought about that. But lots of young women marry older men and it seems to work out."

"It depends on the circumstance." I thought of women in a farm community like Lewiston. Life was hard on them. They'd die, leaving a husband

and children. The men looked for younger women to take their places. Then the younger ones would die from overwork.

Jennie squirmed on the log. She obviously didn't want to discuss age difference. "What I really want to know, Mother, is, do you like Carl? Do you think I could be happy with him?"

"What I think of him doesn't really matter. You're the one who must decide. But I caution you to consider marriage to Carl with an open mind. Is he someone you want to live with for twenty years or more?" I forced a smile. "I know it's hard to be rational when you're emotionally involved with someone. I recall I wouldn't listen to criticisms my parents had of Chester—mainly that he came from a poor family."

I paused, saddening. Jennie had come to me for reinforcement and I couldn't give it in good conscience. I slipped my arm around her shoulder. "Jennie, dear, I don't want to influence your decision. As far as that goes, it seems you've already made it."

She turned miserable blue eyes on mine, gave me a wan smile. "You don't fool me. I know you don't like Carl. But, Mother," she raised her arms in a gesture of frustration, "sometimes I don't like him, either. He can be insufferable. Sometimes I think marrying him would be a mistake." We sat in silence for a long, aching moment before she went on. Her chin trembled. Tears welled over her eyelids. "One thing," she said, pressing my arm fervently, "if I go through with the marriage. Promise you'll be there."

I threw both arms around her and held her tight. "Of course I'll be there. I promise."

Suddenly, I felt a desperate yearning to be near my daughters, to be a mother again. I'd been away too long. By coming to the homestead, Jennie had shown a hunger for my support and advice. I vowed that whatever she decided, I'd be on hand when she needed me. If that meant moving to Lewiston, so be it. At the least, I'd spend some time there each year.

11

I spent the rest of June pondering the problem in endless circles. My girls needed me—I needed them—Toby needed me—I needed him. And Afton? Should I stay on the Salmon? Leave? What should I do? The decision would take time. And time was flying past with its usual lack of concern.

After several scorching days in early July, the river had dropped to its seasonal flow, and the gentle rains trailed off to the summer pattern of thunderstorms every fourth or fifth day, some storms a mere grumble and bluster with little rain, others fire-spitters and bursting clouds that set snags afire and drowned the canyon with runoff.

One morning, Len Johnson hitched Sadie and Highpockets to the buckrake, hoping to gather the windrows of mown hay into stacks before the next storm. Sam and Bones followed the rake and caught mice, while Toby and I bent our backs in the rows of pea vines to harvest the last of the pods. The rake's clatter had been drifting to my ears on the breeze, but it stopped abruptly. I caught the change along with Johnson's, "Whoa!"

Squinting in the direction of the hayfield, I saw Afton's lank figure standing beside Johnson's smaller one. My heart gave a leap. I'd been so busy with Toby and chores, I hadn't realized how much I'd missed the man.

"Look, Toby! It's your uncle."

Toby tossed a handful of peas into the bucket, streaked through the garden gate, down the flat, and into Afton's arms.

When I met the two at the cabin, I wondered at the change I saw in Afton. He'd dressed in clothes I'd never seen him wear—black cheviot pants and vest, a black bowler, shiny black boots, the suit coat thrown over his shoulder. He'd taken pains to shave cleanly around his mustache and narrow spade beard, and the sun had put a blush on his bare cheeks. At first glance he seemed hand-some and fit, but on closer scrutiny, I noticed a grayness around his eyes, the same grayness at the corners of his mouth.

The look of regard he gave me said I'd been missed. I felt strangely reassured and vowed to see the man often, now that the trail had opened. I wanted to tell him how glad I was to see him, but I had no chance. He'd brought Toby a baby rac-coon on a leash, and the animal sat on the boy's shoulders and squeaked at me.

"Where in the world did you get this little thing, Afton?" I reached out to pet the coon's rough coat. "I hope you didn't steal it from its mother."

"The mother's gone. High water took the tree she was using to nest her babes and floated it downstream. This little tyke might of been thrown from the tree when it fell." He picked the coon up by the scruff of the neck and curled his fingers around its rump. The coon's black eyes glittered.

"What do you call her?"

"Chitter, because of the sound she makes. I'd been giving the coons the cleanings from my fish, but they'd not let me touch them. I had to throw a net over this one and grab her with my heavy gloves to keep from getting scratched." He set the restless coon on the ground and scolded the curious dogs away.

Tired of standing still, Toby hurried the coon down to the river, the dogs barking after them. As I watched them play along the shore, my joy ebbed. I'd been content having Toby for company. He'd brought laughter into my life, had made the days pass more quickly. Now he'd return to McCabe's Bar. I'd be left with my loneliness and endless chores.

Pushing aside my regrets, I invited Afton into the house for coffee.

He removed his hat and fingered the brim nervously. "I need to ask you something first. Whether I have time for coffee will depend on your answer." His twitch of a smile wavered to a look of apology. "I—I was wondering if I might use Sadie and Highpockets to go to Elk City. I can't wait for Gulecke to deliver my supplies by river." As always, asking a favor seemed torture for the man. "I know how you feel about your stock. And I wouldn't blame you none if you was to say no."

I studied Afton quietly, wondering what unspoken need had prompted him to humble himself. He'd put me in a dilemma. He was kind to animals, and I knew he hadn't asked the favor lightly, but I hated to let anyone take my stock off the place.

"You can use them if you wish," I said with obvious reluctance, "but Len needs to finish gathering the hay. The animals will need to rest after that. They should be ready by noon. Can you wait that long?"

"If you don't mind having me about. I want to see John and Oakie anyway." His look turned more sheepish. "Would it be asking too much for me to leave Chitter and Reb with you whilst I take my trip?"

The question caught me off balance. I'd enjoy having Reb, but the only dealings I'd had with coons was when they'd raided the henhouse and melon patch, and then I'd felt considerable hostility. "Why—why, I suppose so, if you're sure the coon will stay around. You can pick me up some flour and sugar in exchange."

Reb caused no problem while Afton was gone, but Chitter turned the ranch into a circus, performing in all three rings. I had no empty animal pens with chicken-wire roofs, so the first night I kept her in the house. She pulled the lid off the flour barrel and slung flour across the kitchen floor. When I scolded her for that, she ran upstairs, tore tapestries from the upstairs railing and threw them down into the sitting room, then took the lid from a box of talcum powder and made a white trail over bed and floor. From that disastrous beginning she went on to commit general mayhem.

After two nights of coping with the coon's tricks, I shut her in the barn, hoping the little terror wouldn't find a crack large enough to escape. I should have put her in the barn to begin with. The next morning the only visible signs of mischief were a scattering of grain on the barn floor and spots of blood and fur where slain mice had spent their final minutes.

Afton was gone four days. It was late afternoon when he rode onto the flat and reined Sadie to a stop at the garden fence. Creamy white thunderheads had begun to pile up behind the ridges to the south, but the sun had broiled down all day. Afton looked parboiled, as did Sadie and Highpockets. I straightened from my carrot-thinning crouch and stood massaging the ache in my back.

"How was the trip?"

"Too long—too steep—too hot." Afton groaned from the saddle and stooped to rub his knees. "Remind me never to ride that trail again. I'd rather go without, or wait for Gulecke to deliver my needs."

He'd stuffed Sadie's saddlebags with supplies and packed the mule high. Two long saws were strapped to the outside of the canvas packs. I watched as he loosened a complicated four-way hitch on the packs and removed the saws.

"What are you going to do with those? Build a house?"

"There you go with your questions. Always questions. Didn't anyone ever tell you about the old woman who got her nose stuck in a knothole when she was snooping on her neighbor?"

There'd been a time in my short relationship with Afton McCabe when I would have taken affront, but I'd come to recognize the humor hidden behind his squinty eyes. "The day I stop being nosy will be the day I die."

"I believe that, Hattie. Aye, I do." He leaned the saws against a fence post and turned to gather ropes that dangled from the packs. "Get Toby to run up to John and Oakie's cabin. Tell them the saws are here. I'll unpack the flour and sugar at your house."

I walked over to the hogwire fence and threw a handful of carrot seedlings on the outside for the cottontails to find. "I suppose you'll not tell me what John and Oakie want with the saws."

McCabe coiled the ropes without replying. He often left my questions unanswered. For that matter, when he asked questions of his own, he acted as if he didn't expect an answer.

"All right for you," I said, "then I won't tell you what that coon of yours has been up to."

"Been a mischief, has she?" Afton tied the last coil to the packs and let his gaze wander the flat. "Where is the little demon? And the boy?"

"They're out roaming the hayfield with the dogs."

"Good. I need to talk to you alone."

"Might as well come into the house and rest awhile. I baked a dried apple pie this morning."

Inside, Afton sat hunched at the kitchen table, heavy-browed and somber. He'd eaten two wedges of pie, the edge of the crust shiny with apple juice that had seeped through the dough. Now he alternately drank coffee and ran calloused fingers around the rim of the cup. Once in a while, he responded to my nervous chatter in monosyllables. I feared Toby would return from his play before I learned what the man had on his mind, but I knew I couldn't rush him into conversation.

At last, he said without preamble, "I've decided to send Toby back to his pa."

I set my cup down with a clatter and fixed my eyes on Afton with such ferocious disbelief he should have looked up or stirred uneasily. He did neither. "How can you even consider sending Toby away after treating him as your own! After nearly losing him to the fever."

"The illness was what decided me." He looked up then. "'Tisn't fair to keep the boy where there's no doctor at hand."

"A doctor would have done nothing more than we did!"

"Och, Hattie! You're making excuses to salve your heart. And what about schooling? The boy is bright. He needs to learn more than we can teach him. He needs to be with youngsters his own age. He needs to get out into the world."

"You're a great one to talk about getting out into the world! How can you have one standard for yourself and another for Toby?"

Sparks flashed in Afton's pale eyes, then quickly lost their glow. His face saddened. "I've come to love the lad, and I want what's best for him. He needs to make peace with his pa. I don't want him to make the same mistakes I did. 'Tis wrong to leave hard feelings . . . I'll go to my grave regretting the things I said to my Mum and Dad."

For the first time, I got a full sense of Afton McCabe, of his feelings toward life, of the guilt he'd been living with for so many years. But his intentions for Toby had stunned me speechless. I had to admit his arguments had merit. I knew of rebellious youths who'd left parents behind, heartbroken. I knew of children who'd died from the ravages of illness because no doctor was near. I knew of children who were left to fend for themselves when a mother took ill and died far from medical help. I'd felt their heartache. On the other hand, I knew of fathers who'd disappeared without a trace, leaving families who needed them, other fathers who'd beaten their children until they'd run away. Children were always the first to suffer. Now it appeared Toby might be open to more pain.

The clock on the wall ticked loud seconds before I could loosen my tongue. "Toby's father would send him back to the Pardees. You've seen the scars. You know how they'd treat him. If his father kept him, the boy's lot would be the same. I wonder when people will begin to see children as humans, not work animals to use and abuse."

Afton's gaze remained fixed on his cup as he traced the rim. "I understand what you say. Living with Toby has let me know him as a child. . . . I've seen his needs. But his best chance to grow into a person of worth is to come to grips with life, to make amends."

"Will his father make amends?"

"I can't say. But we'll have to give him the chance."

I sat awhile, trying to control my inner tremblings, trying to think rationally. I found it difficult. "When will you send Toby out?"

"I'll not send him out. I plan to deliver him to his pa myself."

"I thought you hated the trail."

"I don't plan to go by trail. I'm going to build me a scow and take him down the river."

My lips parted with a gasp. "It's not safe! I won't let you go by boat!"

Afton's eyes narrowed. A relic of the old harshness came to his face, the old formality to his voice. "You have no say in it, Missus Clark. I've already made arrangements for John and Oakie to saw my lumber. They're readying the old pit behind their cabin."

"Without telling me! That saw pit is part of my homestead. Chester built it." Later, I realized how uncharitable my words sounded. At the moment I spoke without thinking. "And I suppose you'll build the boat here, where I'll have to watch it go up each day."

My anger brought a quirky smile to Afton's face. I knew I'd disappointed the man, but in my outrage, I didn't care. He regarded me in silence for a disturbingly long time. When he spoke next, his tone was overlain with regret. "I just might raft the lumber down to my diggings." He rose as if he carried a great burden on his shoulders. "Now that I've upset your day I'll be going. I'll pick up the lad when I return your animals."

12

My spirits plummeted at the thought of Toby and Afton floating down the Salmon River in a scow. I'd heard many a grisly tale about placer miners who'd caught the river at the wrong time, men who never made it to the last mooring, or who'd lost their lives trying to cross from one bank to the other. Cap Gulecke, a mountain of a man whose scows carried freight downriver from Salmon City to Lewiston, had lost oarsmen in the whitewater. Even when boatmen survived the trip without mishap, the deadly rapids kept them from returning upstream, so they tore their scows apart at the end of the run to make shacks for homesteaders or timbers for mines. For that reason they'd given the Salmon the name "River of No Return." The river had taken many lives, including Chester's. Toby and Afton might be next.

Despite those terrible thoughts, a morbid fascination drew me to John and Oakie's to watch the preparations. When my ears caught the rasp of crosscut and ripsaw, I'd slip from the garden, walk the pole bridge over Weasel Creek, and follow the path to the saw pit Chester had built at the base of the hill. I had to admire the skill with which the ferrymen had redesigned the pit. The loggers seemed to have waited for a project worthy of their training to move themselves from their hammocks.

The men had extended the saw frame to the side of the mountain and were able to roll green logs from the slope onto the frame. Since the downhill end of the frame was slightly taller than a man, Oakie, the shorter and brawnier of the two, stood beneath the frame and pulled the crosscut and ripsaw through the saw logs from below, while John, the lankier man, stood on the platform and pulled the saw on the up-stroke, a strain on back and shoulders for both. Now and then, one or the other failed to put the necessary bit of arc at the end of the stroke, and the blade stuck fast in the channel. Forgetting I watched, they'd let loose with a, "Goddamned, sonofabitch of a log." Or, "Christ! Watch what you're doing, you damned hillbilly!" Or "Yankee," whichever fit.

Despite my will against it, the men completed the sawing, ripping, and trimming, and were ready to float the lumber the mile down to McCabe's Bar. Having rafted logs down the Clearwater River, they knew how to build a sturdy raft. They tied the lumber into twelve-inch stacks, fastened the stacks side by side to make the floor, tied two cross-poles the breadth of the raft to hold it rigid, and attached sweeps at each end for steering.

Hoping secretly the lumber would be lost on the way downriver, I rode along the shore with Afton, following the progress of the raft. John and Oakie proved too skilled for accident. By the time the side-current had delivered the raft into the grip of the river, their legs had rediscovered the art of balancing on a bobbing craft with the river slapping at their feet. Hunched over the sweeps, they guided the raft around rocks and whirlpools as though they were part of the raft rather than land creatures who could easily slip and drown.

Afton and I had to prod our lazy mounts along the trail to keep ahead. Afton led the way, and from his vantage point on Highpockets' tall back, warned the rafters of rough water or of a drop in the river. Meanwhile John and Oakie kept a commentary running between them.

"Watch out for that rock to starboard, Oakie." "Keep her heeled around, John." "Christ-a-mighty! There's a cross-wave coming at us!" And after a particularly tight squeeze between rocks, "Nearly changed the measure of your lumber on that one, McCabe!"

It seemed they'd hardly started before they'd negotiated the mile to McCabe's Bar.

At first, I was glad Afton wasn't building the scow where I could see it from house and garden, but I soon began to wish he was. Though I fought against it, my anxiety led me from the demands of the garden down to McCabe's Bar and the wide stretch of shore where the men had beached the raft. A grassy bench above the building site offered a Ponderosa pine for shade and a large boulder in the shape of a seat with back. There, I could escape the fry of the sun and the smell of silt and waterlogged debris, could distance the ring of hammer on nail.

The dogs followed me each time I traveled to the bar, and when I settled on my rock they'd move off to sniff the fringe of brush at the foot of the hill. The coon lumbered behind, turning somersaults in the air to get their attention.

Afton had laid several sixteen-foot planks side by side, and nailed six-foot boards across them to make a double hull. I'd seen his last scow when he stopped at the ranch a few years back. The new one was to be the same, a sixteen-foot boat, six feet wide with three-foot gunwales, not one of the thirty-foot-long scows the daring Cap Gulecke used once or twice a year to deliver supplies to mines and sourdoughs between Salmon City and the Salmon River wagon road some one-hundred-fifty crow-flight miles to the west.

Only a person like Cap Gulecke would attempt to run freight down the Salmon through the string of deadly rapids. He was a man of great strength and agility, and there was little he feared. On his route he delivered tons of machinery to mines located along the way, carried coffee, dynamite, sugar, flour, tobacco, and bacon to miners and prospectors. He'd delivered my wood range, Franklin stove, harness, plow, and other farm implements.

Afton's scow would be somewhat easier to manage than Gulecke's; still, the trip to his nephew's ranch near Lucile would demand all the strength and skill he could muster.

Each day I watched Afton and Toby with hungry eyes, noting every gesture, each change of expression so I could bring the images to mind after they left for Lucile. Toby squatted on his heels and handed his uncle nails, his face as glum as when he'd first arrived on the river. Knowing how he dreaded the return, I watched the shaping of the hull with a heightened sadness.

Then a new worry rose to burden my mind. Afton would often slouch on a driftlog, head hung, chest heaving, until he had to give up on work. I suspected he had a problem with his heart.

One day he slumped onto the gunwale he was shaping, took off his cap to wipe his brow, then sat cradling his head. He'd removed his shirt, and beads of sweat trickled from his shoulders. "Be a good lad and bring a jug of water from the spring," he said to Toby. Shirtless, the boy looked his uncle's miniature in the coveralls I'd sewn from some of Chester's.

I saw the measured way in which Toby picked up the jug, the way he watched Afton, and sensed he, too, worried about the man. He shot me a troubled glance, then dragged himself off to the spring on the hillside, the hot wind ruffling his hair.

High above the canyon, the eastward wind drove clouds shaped like puffs of cannon smoke. On the river bottom, it rattled the brush, rippled the sleeves of my blouse, and thwarted a hummingbird that hovered over a clump of bobbing thistle.

When Toby was out of earshot, I climbed down the bank, set a board across a nail keg that stood by the nearly completed gunwale, and sat. Watching Afton for signs of illness, I saw the trembling hands, the downward curve of eyes and mouth. He still cradled his head. "I wish you'd forget this idea of yours. You're not well enough to make the trip."

"I'm in fine fettle. I can ride the river easy, I can."

"I doubt that. I've watched you grab your chest."

"Och, you're the limit. Always finding new worries to add to your pot of stew. I tell you, there's nothing wrong with me. 'Tis just the heat."

I pulled the keg nearer and leaned forward to make his gaze meet mine. "If you won't think of yourself, then think of Toby. It would be bad enough if he was fit, but he's still on the mend."

Afton looked up, a snap in his eyes. "You've seen how much taller he is than when he first come. And strong enough to lift a log. He'll be fit as a gamecock by the time the scow is ready. The trip will be the making of the boy."

"Or the breaking!"

"That's right! Make up fool excuses to keep me from giving the boy an adventure."

"Adventure! More like suicide, if you ask me. If you must take Toby back, why don't you go by packstring and stage instead of risking both your lives?"

Afton glared at me for a second, then hauled himself to his feet and gave vent to his irritation with hammer and nail. When he spoke, his voice was as grainy and grudging as when we first met. "Go back to your rock. And if you must watch the boat-building, just use your eyes and keep your mouth clo—" He stopped hammering and pulled at the air as anger mixed with problems of the heart to squeeze his lungs dry.

Despite our differences, my insides wrenched to see him suffer. I'd talked of my concern for Toby, but my fear for Afton was just as great. How could I convince this man he was gambling with his life?

When he'd caught his breath and resumed hammering, I continued my plea despite the warning to be still. "All right, suppose you *are* up to it. And suppose Toby *is* well enough to make the trip. You still might capsize. Wouldn't it be better to ride downriver in Cap Gulecke's big scow?"

Afton straightened from his work until his back was stiff as a rod. He turned slowly, deliberately to face me. "Are you doubting my skill, woman?"

"No, it's just that—"

"I'm too old? Dimwitted?" He shook a finger in front of my nose. "Let me remind you, I've come down the river fifteen times, and I'm here to tell of it. I'm among the few to make the trip at all. And unlike the rest, I've never lost a scow. On top of that, I don't have the money Gulecke asks for the trip." He turned back to his hammering. "I don't care what you say. I aim to deliver the boy myself."

The sense of impending loss kept me returning to the building site. I didn't question Afton again about the advisability of the trip, but there was a strained note in our conversations, because I worked to avoid the subject and he was wary lest I might not. Enough of our friendship and our need for each other remained that we wanted to keep the peace.

Every day I brought along my carver's tools and a high relief of Toby and Afton I'd started that spring. At the time I began the carving, I'd thought it fitting to carve their faces side by side on the slab of pine. Now that Afton was forcing Toby to return home, I wondered at my reasoning. I'd completed the outline of Afton's head, but I hadn't started the face. Some carvers drew in features with India ink, but I preferred to work without a pattern. Freehand, I put in the details of Toby's face. I'd set aside mallet and chisel and with penknife was treating the more intricate contours, such as the folds in the eyelids. I wanted the carving to show a happy child, but Toby gave me little model. Dread of the return home had soured his face.

A similar dread, one of the river, disrupted the boy's silence. He questioned Afton repeatedly about the safety of the boat and the dangers of the trip.

"Is the boat going to be good and strong?" he'd ask.

"Of course it will. I been making scows a long time. I know how to make them sturdy."

"You sure you can get through the rapids?"

"I'm half fish. I can always tell where the current's best."

"Will they be real scary—the rapids, I mean?"

"They might make you wet your pants. And I wouldn't blame you none. But there's lots of smooth water between rapids, and those smooth parts make it all worthwhile."

And so they'd talk, Toby dragging every ounce of scare he could from Afton while he learned about the river and about the building of a boat—the way to measure and saw the planks, how to angle the cut to make the outward slant of bow and stern. Afton's patience with the boy amazed me. Certainly his tolerance for explanation hadn't extended to *our* conversations.

"Why do you use green boards?" Toby asked once.

"They'll give with the beating they're going to take. Dry lumber would crack at the first falls."

"Falls! Is there going to be falls?"

"Sure there's falls. Couldn't call this a river unless it had falls. None real high, though."

"How are you going to keep the water off your things?" I called from the boulder.

"You've got a look at Cap Gulecke's boat, haven't you? Then you should of seen that the floorboards were raised above the hull to keep bilge water out of the supplies, and the gunwales were double-walled to store groceries and the like."

"Won't water come in the cracks between the boards?" Toby asked.

"That's where you'll come in handy, lad. We'll make a pitch mortar, and you can go around with a putty knife and smooth the goo into all the cracks."

As Afton's rest periods became more frequent, the boat-building extended on and on. I'd given up asking about his health for fear I'd get my head snapped off, but the worry he might have a heart seizure while floating the river haunted my days. I couldn't bear the thought of more drownings in my life. If Afton had an attack while on shore, how would Toby find help in that wild canyon? I continued to hope something would prevent the trip from ever coming to pass, even toyed with the idea I should go along, though I said nothing of it to Afton.

Then came the wind. It struck with fury in the night, made the house shudder, blew dust through cracks in the chinking onto my bed. It gusted and died, gusted and died. During the worst blasts, it seemed the world had come to an end, that I'd be torn from my bed and tossed onto the highest mountaintop.

The most frightening assault hit at dawn. I thought it might tear the house from its foundation. During the peak of the blast, I heard a loud screeching at the back of the flat, the sound of nails parting from wood, of wood torn asunder. I hurried downstairs to the kitchen and peered through the window, saw timbers that had been part of the barn roof standing at odd angles from the walls. The rest of the roof was gone, nothing but a black hole. The goat pens were holding, but leaned at a slant. All that remained of the chicken coop was splintered wood scattered over the ground. At that distance I could see no hens, had no way of knowing if they survived.

Next came a startling stillness, broken now and then by mere breaths of wind, faint reminders of that terrible blow. I went outside to tour the barnyard. Tree branches lay scattered everywhere. Pine needles and shredded leaves carpeted the ground. A strip of timber along the mountainside lay flattened, as if a giant had cut it with a scythe. My flower beds and vegetable garden were a shambles, the cornstalks blown to the ground.

The animals seemed to have survived, but were putting up a caterwauling that jarred my strung nerves. Sadie and Highpockets tore around the pasture, neighed, and kicked up their heels. I found the hens huddled beneath a low-branched pine, so disheveled they looked like they were molting.

The damage to the buildings was about what I'd seen from the house, the roof torn from the barn, the henhouse flattened. I felt beaten with a club. After the misfortunes of the last year, I couldn't believe I'd been dealt another blow.

I could hire John and Oakie to put on a new

roof and build a henhouse. I'm sure they'd be willing, if they could accomplish it at their leisure. But
why should I bother? Why not sell the homestead
and let someone else assume the headache? With
men traveling to the gold fields, someone was
bound to pass through who'd think the homestead an ideal wilderness home. The thought made
me feel a traitor. Chester had invested so much of
himself in developing the flat. How could I sell?

On the other hand, why shouldn't I? I'd
promised Jennie I'd attend the wedding. If
pressed, I could restrain my dislike for Carl. And
winter lay ahead, with all its tribulations. John and
Oakie would leave. Afton and Toby would be on
the lower Salmon. Men like the Harpers might
come around. As much as I hated the thought of
being involved with Carl Foreman, I'd be much
safer in Lewiston. Not that I'd live with Jennie or
Marybelle. Part of me had become a hermit, used
to doing things my own way, when I wanted, without interference, without demands. I needed independence, a place of my own.

It had occurred to me often in the past year
that I'd spent so much of my life caring for others—for husband and children, hearth and home,
nursing Chester's patients—the pattern had
woven itself through my being as surely as eating
and breathing, the need for earth and sky. But I
hoped to give those leanings new expression. I'd
often thought I'd like to open a small gallery with
artists' supplies, give lessons in painting and wood
carving, perhaps teach art at the school. Before
Chester and I moved to Weasel Creek, the super-

intendent had been looking for a lay person to
teach music. He might like to have an artist come
into the classrooms once in a while.

But what should I do about Toby—and Afton?
I couldn't bear the thought of them disappearing
from my life. So many possibilities! So many problems to consider! I felt like demons had taken hold
of my person and were pulling in all directions.

I was no closer to a decision when Afton and
Toby completed the scow in late August, six
weeks after the first board was sawed. The wind
had destroyed Afton's shack, but I'd loaned him
the tent Chester and I lived in while building the
cabin. Without giving the windstorm another
thought, he and Toby had finished work on the
scow. They'd double-lined the floor, built a raised
floor above the first to keep seepage from equipment, built double walls on each side to store
equipment and supplies. They'd set the exten-
sions on the gunwales, and completed the four-
foot raised platform across the center of the scow
where Afton would man the sweeps.

One sizzling hot day they began work on the
sweeps. Toby held one end of a fir pole to keep it
from turning, while Afton stripped away the bark
with a double-handled blade.

"Isn't this an awfully long oar?" Toby asked.

Afton explained, pausing in his explanation
each time he made a stroke with the blade. "Aye,
'tis sixteen feet . . . the blade eight . . . but 'tis not

an oar . . . 'tis a sweep . . . sweeps have no sculling action at all . . . just used for steering."

"Like the ones on the ferry."

"Now you have it . . . but they're harder to handle on a free-floating boat . . . you must hold the blade above the water . . . except when you want to steer clear of a rock . . . or keep the scow on course . . . a blade can get caught in a back eddy . . . can whip the sweep around and knock you into the—" Afton stopped the knife abruptly, put his hand on the bow of the boat to steady himself, then sat. "Whyn't you go play for a while, lad. I won't be needing you."

Toby gave his uncle a look of uncertainty, then took off at a walk, then a skip, dogs and coon at his heels, expecting some kind of game.

I'd stirred from my rock and was filling a gunnysack with the glut of wood scraps that covered the building site. I noted Afton's fatigue, but knew better than to comment. Instead, I smiled, saying, "The boy's full of questions, isn't he?"

Afton returned my smile with a sad warmth. "No worse than you, Hattie. But sometimes I get tired of answering." The weak voice, the sag in his features, made it clear what I must do. I shook inwardly at the thought.

I went on picking up chips while I mustered the courage for what could be an unpleasant encounter. It took a while. "It seems to me there's more than questions that tires you," I said at last. "Since I can't persuade you not to take this insane trip, I'm going along. If something happens, I'll be there to watch over Toby."

Afton jerked his head around to face me, unbelieving. "You along! A woman! You'd faint at the first rapid. Then what good would you be?"

I gave him back stare for stare. "I'm just as capable of courage as a man."

"Och! You don't know what you'd be facing. You know nothing about floating. You'd just get in the way."

"I could learn."

"Not on my scow, you won't!"

I dropped the gunnysack and stood directly in front of him, hands on hips. "You're being a stubborn old fool! You don't have a thought for Toby, just for yourself."

"That shows how blind you are!" His jaw was stiff as a board, his eyes dagger points. "You're just like all the rest of womankind. Want to coddle the boys. Make sissies out of them. You think men don't know what's good for a lad. Well, that's where you're wrong. I was a boy once, believe it or not. I know what it takes to grow up in this hard world. It means taking risks, facing danger." He wagged a finger at me. "You say I have no thought for the boy. You're wrong! That's all I'm thinking of. Him! I've got to make this trip once more. For him! I have deep feelings for the lad, and don't you forget it." He tried to rise, seemed to dizzy, dropped back onto the bow.

His speech had numbed me. My arms fell to my sides and hung limp. My conscience hurt. It took a while to find my tongue. "I—I didn't mean to upset you so. I just felt I could be of help. I still do. I could set up camp and cook, while you rest."

Afton motioned me toward home. "Go away. Leave me be," he said, wheezing. "I'm tired of your badgering."

"All right, Afton, I'll leave," I said calmly. "But I'll not let you make the trip alone. You need me. I'm just as capable of floating the river as Toby and a lot stronger. I can face danger, too. And I'll prove it." I sounded brave, but as I climbed the bank and looked downcanyon at the Salmon, splatting itself into huge geysers of froth, my insides turned to jelly. I'd spoken my piece. Now I'd have to face that mad river.

13

On the way home, I found Toby playing near the bridge that crossed McCabe's Creek. I told him I wanted to know the minute Afton set a date for departure, that I wanted to bake cookies for the trip. With Toby's craving for sweets, I had no doubt he'd do as I asked. That is, if Afton would let him come to the ranch. I said nothing to Toby about my plan to float the Salmon. I didn't want to cause an argument between the boy and his uncle.

To Afton's credit, two days later, Toby showed up at the ranch to say goodbye and to tell me they'd be leaving the next day. What a whirlwind of preparations when Toby left! First to Len Johnson's to ask him to care for the ranch and to leave the Winchester and Colt .45 for safekeeping—a hurried picking of stringbeans and summer squash, as well as a few of the more mature carrots (I'd leave the raspberries for Len)—the baking of cookies and bread—the packing of a few clothes and Chester's satchel of medicines and herbs.

I spent the night trying to convince myself I had nothing to fear. I argued the trip might not be as dangerous as I thought. That it was the only way I could watch over Toby and Afton. And it would allow me to visit my girls in Lewiston, to decide what I should do with my life.

In the light of morning, the night's persuasions seemed the reasoning of a fool. But at seven o'clock, half-dazed, saddlebags loaded, I rode Sadie across McCabe's bridge. Len Johnson followed on Highpockets, and would return the mare and mule to the ranch. I knew Sam and Bones would have followed, so I'd bid them a tearful farewell and shut them in the barn until Len could turn them loose. I had confidence in Len's care of the animals; still, I feared the dogs might roam and get themselves into trouble when they had no need to watch over me.

My insides swam with worry, mainly at the thought I'd have to face McCabe's wrath if I were to argue my way on board the scow. I'd told Len of the situation, especially about Afton's health, and asked that he support my decision, but I doubted the timid man would take sides in the event of a spat.

Afton wasn't in sight when we rode onto the sandy beach where he and Toby had spent so many hours building the scow. Now the boat lay a few yards off shore, bobbing up and down amid a dazzle of sundollars reflecting off the surface of the river.

I slid from the saddle, took the saddlebags from Sadie's rump and set them beside a collection of oil-

skin sacks waiting to be loaded aboard the scow. I
was helping Len untie straps that fastened my clothes
bag to the back of Highpockets' saddle, when Afton
strode down the bank in blue denim pants and shirt,
feet clunking in short-topped rubber boots. He was
carrying a lantern and a burlap sack that appeared to
hold the parts of his sheepherder's stove. Toby followed with hatchet, hammer, and saw. The boy was
hound-faced and sulky, and dragged his feet. A new
straw hat rode his thatch of chestnut hair.

Afton stopped with a jerk when he saw us, and
stared in outrage. "What do you think you're
doing, Missus Clark? Toby said you were bringing
cookies."

"And I have. What I didn't tell him—but told
you—was that I'm going along."

"The devil you are! We've been through all
that."

Toby climbed down the bank to his uncle's
side, surprise and excitement written on his round
face. "Can Hattie go? Please! I want her to."

"Och! She'll crowd the boat. See all she's
brought. A woman has no business on the river.
Long days without stopping. A woman can't take
the sun and discomfort like a man."

"And what have I been doing the past six years
while I worked like a ranchhand?"

"Please, Uncle." Toby begged. "Please let her
come."

"She'll be afraid of the rapids. Probably faint
and fall overboard. That'll put us in a pickle!"

"She had the grit to stand up to the Harpers,"
Len said as he set my clothes bag on the sand.

"The Harpers weren't in the middle of the river!" Afton marched down onto the beach, muttering to himself, and laid the lantern and sack with the rest of the cargo.

Len and I stood by, keeping our silence. I was surprised he'd had the nerve to speak in my behalf. His shy, bristly moon-face hinted he was pleased with himself.

Len's boldness seemed to hearten Toby. He dropped the tools at his uncle's feet. "If you won't let Hattie go, then I won't go," he said in quiet defiance.

"See what you've done, woman! You've driven a wedge between me and the boy. Wouldn't surprise me if that weren't your purpose in the first place."

"How can you say that? After all I've done to keep Toby on the river with you." Despite my protest, I felt a pang of guilt, recalling how I longed to have Toby as my own.

Too furious to reply, Afton yanked on the scow's mooring rope until the bow touched the riverbank. Then with an agility born of anger, he climbed on board and set out the gangplank. From the furrows of extreme irritation that lined his face, I thought I had no chance of going. I was certain of it, when he walked the plank to shore and stood glaring at me with a look that could stop a rattlesnake in its tracks.

"All right! You can go," he said at last. "But by heaven, if you cause trouble, I'll drop you on the riverbank and let you climb out of the canyon."

I nearly sank to my knees. My heart raced. I

felt like shouting Hosanna. I wanted desperately to hug Afton, but he'd already spun on his heel and was carrying tools and lantern onto the scow.

To make myself useful, I hauled things on board—slowly, until I became accustomed to walking the narrow plank, as I'd never liked heights. Afton accepted my help grudgingly, jerking things from my hand when I held them out for him to stow where he wished.

Worried he'd be left behind, Reb followed his master so closely he kept getting in the way. The coon, who'd formed an attachment to Reb, was underfoot as well. Toby kept his distance. The apprehension had returned to his face. When I walked down the plank to where he stood, he looked at me with beseeching eyes, as if he wished I could change his uncle's mind about the trip.

The supplies on board, I sat on shore, watching Afton bustle about, tying down the cargo. Despite a late August sun that drove heat onto the bar, despite the fact I was going on the trip against his will, he worked with the enthusiasm of a young man about to sail the Pacific for the first time.

I felt no enthusiasm, just relief and gratitude that I'd be able to watch over Toby. My mind still reeled from the sudden preparations. Len had left for the ranch, and I wondered if I'd remembered to tell him where I kept canvas for repairing dams used to divert creek water to the field and garden. I'd forgotten to remind him to stay at the house for a while to keep the dogs on the property. Some other crucial instruction had probably slipped my mind as well.

Because space limited what I could take along, I'd packed one extra set of clothes to wear after a wet day on the river, a jacket and sweater for cold mornings, a set of town clothes to wear when I reached Lewiston, and the snake stick I'd embellished with carvings of ivy. I wore a light blue cotton blouse and skirt—a dark color would absorb the heat of the sun—a sunbonnet with long brim, and my heavy ladies' boots for climbing around on the rocks. I brought my house shoes to wear in camp.

Chester's gold pocket watch was the only thing of value I'd brought along. It hung from a cord around my neck. I expected to have time to carve in the evenings, and had wrapped the relief of Toby and Afton in a sheet and several layers of oilskin. I'd tied Chester's old yellow slicker around my suitcase in the hope it would keep bilge water from seeping inside. On the move to the ranch, I'd worried about dust seeping into everything. On this trip the problem would be water stains and mildew.

Now and then Afton looked my way, pinched his eyebrows together and raised them at the same time, as much as to say, "This is a stupid thing you're planning to do, Hattie Clark." I noted a certain air about him, as well, as if he had more concern for my welfare than he liked and fought the feeling.

I knew there was reason for concern. I listened to the lap of water on shore and barge, thinking, *You can't back out now, Harriet. You've packed all the possibilities for your future and all your hopes for*

Toby in with the rest of the scow's clutter. If the boat
capsizes, so be it.

Afton's scowl burned into me as he walked the
gangplank to shore. "Woman, quit looking like
you'd been called for and couldn't come. If you
must go along, then let's be off. We'll see how you
like being a swamper." He started me up the plank
with a hand that felt like stone. I wondered if
annoyance caused the stiffness, or if he secretly
feared the trip as much as I.

It was obvious Reb had no fear. He stood in the
bow with his front paws on the gunwale and looked
out over the river like a Viking dog. Since Reb preferred the bow, I took a seat in the stern beside
Toby, the rear sweep angling up between us. Afton
had tied one end of a rope around Toby, the other
end through a metal eye in the gunwale. He gave
me a section of rope to tie myself in like manner.
Toby had leashed Chitter in his corner away from
the sweep, and the coon crawled along the sideboard, peering into the eddy with beady eyes.

Afton untied the mooring rope, pulled the
gangplank in behind him, and released the sweeps
from their ties. Standing sideways on the raised
deck, a hand on each sweep, he swung the stern
sweep on its pivot until the water licked at the
blade and parted with an oily heaviness. The scow
quivered and creaked as it drifted free of the shallows, then rocked when it met the outward swirl of
the eddy. At first, the scow seemed stationary, the
river possessed of motion, but as the current
tugged at the hull, the scow rushed past the shore,
fluttering my sunbonnet.

For half a mile or so the river was broad, the current strong and steady, only a few ripples of whitewater here and there. I could feel the river, a fluid, living thing beneath the scow's flat hull, a force used to having its way. On each side, an awesome mix of crag and pine went streaming by, above it a brilliant ribbon of blue. The shore was so distant I felt cast adrift, no soil to give me foundation, no tree to offer support, my life dependent on one man's skill with two clumsy poles.

That man stood with feet spread wide, shoulders thrown back, an imposed look of daring on his face, as if he were summoning the strength and spirit of his youth. From time to time he'd glance across his shoulder at Toby in an expectant way, seeming to will his zest for the journey into the boy. Toby gave no sign of accepting it.

Ahead of us, a creek tumbled down a talus slope and cut through a rumpled fan of silt and rock to join the Salmon. Upriver from the fan, the water had ponded, and a flock of mallards sunned themselves in the quiet. The surface reflected the birds and the canyon walls with the clarity of a mirror. Each knifed draw and knobby ridge, each crooked branch and speared tip of pine shone up at us as we cut the reflection.

Beyond the ponded water the river disappeared, rumbling around a turn in the canyon. There was something ominous in the way we glided from the quiet water into the swift channel entering the turn.

Afton swung the bow sweep on its pivot and sent the scow around the right-hand side of the bend. "Hear the rapids?" he called over his shoulder. There was a giddy pitch to his voice, the same excitement on his face.

We were approaching the rapids with terrifying speed. Nothing I'd seen or heard could compare with that bedlam. Chitter moved her mouth, but the roar drowned her squeals as well as Reb's restless whining. I took a tight grip on the gunwale and braced myself for what lay ahead.

If a channel existed, it escaped my inexperienced eye. Plumes of greenish foam shot from boulders that poked their slick heads above the surface of the river. Water swirled around the base of the boulders threatening to suck us onto the rocks. Waves crashed against the gunwales and soaked me to the skin. Walls of spray broke across the bow, blotting out the sun. The boat lurched and rolled. My stomach heaved along with it.

By throwing his weight into the sweeps, Afton escaped the suction forces that would send us splintering onto the rocks. That danger past, we raced toward a string of waves that looked like the ridged back of a dragon. We shot to the crest of each frothy swell and hurtled down the other side, like a dinghy on a storm-swept sea. Afton's eyes glittered. He whooped like a cowboy on a bucking bronco. Not I. Only fifteen minutes on the river, and I'd confirmed my fears. The river was a grave danger. My mind wheeled with dire imaginings. I saw myself tossed into that seething river world, tumbled end over end into an underwater cavern lined with eerie nooks and crannies, slammed against rock after rock.

A quick surge in the current spit us forward as though we were distasteful, then settled us onto a steady, but slightly choppy, flow of water. My heart was still in my throat. My knees trembled. My knuckles had turned white from their hold on the scow. I was amazed to be alive. I looked back at the wild confusion of spray and boulders and felt a new respect for Afton McCabe. Not many men could have kept us afloat.

As for the man himself, he crumpled, panting, onto a low wooden box he'd nailed to the sweep deck for a seat, and ran his shirtsleeve across his face. Toby looked like he was being held prisoner, which, in a way, he was. He'd locked one hand on Chitter. The other gripped the sideboard. Chitter licked the water from her coat in a frantic way. Reb sat on the sweep deck doing the same.

"Get the buckets!" Afton's tone allowed for no dawdling. Toby and I exchanged wan glances and put our backs into emptying the scow of water.

The quieter stretch of river offered a chance to think of the rapids I'd survived and of the possibility they could have cheated me of life. It also allowed time to realize, with a shock, that I'd left behind everything for which Chester and I had slaved, everything I owned in the world except the clothes in my suitcase and those on my back. For the first time since Chester died I felt the depth of my ties to the ranch. To remain at the ranch was to relive that cherished season of my life. To remain at the ranch was to touch Chester. Why on earth had I left? I was old enough to know better. I

wanted to ask Afton to drop me off on the riverbank so I could somehow make my way back, but
that would seem cowardly. I didn't want to give
him the satisfaction of saying, "I told you so." And
Toby's wistful eyes were upon me.

With calm water ahead, Afton relaxed his grip
on the sweeps and slanted a look over his shoulder.
"Some ride, wouldn't you say, Missus Clark?" he
said, gloating.

I straightened from my bailing and made a wry
face. "Are they all going to be like that?"

"Some are worse. The Big Mallard's coming
up. She's like messing around a bear cub with the
sow near."

"If it's that bad, why don't you rope the boat
through? I've seen bargemen do that on the
Snake."

"I use a rope sometimes when I catch the bad
spots at the wrong time of the year, but I want
Toby to ride the river all the way. A country lad
needs something to earn the respect of the boys in
town."

"It isn't worth the risk!"

He snorted. "Worth it to a boy!"

I went back to my bailing, while Afton
stretched his neck to look ahead. "I'll be needing
to stop and scout the Mallard," he said. "'Tis dif
ferent from season to season and year to year. A
channel that works one time might swamp you the
next."

"I thought you said you'd never had a wreck."

"I've never lost a boat. But I've swamped. A
man can't get so cocky as to think he'll not swamp.

On the other hand, he can't lose his nerve. That's when he loses his head. That's when the river can run him out the sluice."

In spite of what he said, running the rapids had put the cock back in Afton. He showed more vitality, had more healthy sheen in his face than I'd seen for months. The ride had the opposite effect on me. I felt like a wet noodle, and I was certain the sun was poaching my brains. Added to that discomfort, my wet stockings had balled up inside my shoes. I could do nothing about the sun, but I took off my shoes and pulled the stockings into shape.

With the drumming of the rapids behind us, my ears focused on the loud creaking sound the sweeps made when they moved in their notches in the gunwale, much like the hair of a fiddle bow scratching across the strings of a double bass. We were passing a bluff thick with yellow pines and dusky green rabbitbrush, behind it a rising sweep of dense forest. A mix of resinous and herbal scents drifted out over the river. At the edge of the bluff, a black bear was tearing apart a decayed log, tossing bits of orange punk into the air. A cub meddling in his mother's affairs had covered his nose with orange rot. The nearsighted bears must have thought us a log floating downstream. They went about their business and paid us little attention until Reb barked. At his warning, they spun around, half rearing, and watched us out of sight.

Beyond the bluff, sheer cliffs closed in on both sides, and the walls echoed the whisperings of the river. The air turned cool and damp. A water ouzel lit on a boulder in midstream, dipped up and down like a mechanical toy, then dove into the water and disappeared among the ripples and rock shadows. I imagined myself an ouzel, weaving among rocks and sandbars, dropping into deep holes to rub noses with speckled trout, and wished I, too, had no fear of the water.

Before we reached the Big Mallard, Afton swung the scow into an eddy, put the coiled end of the tow rope into Reb's mouth, and said, "Shore!"

Reb must have recalled some previous training. He shot from the scow like a flying black rug, splashed up to the bank with the rope in his mouth and towed us ashore, not an impossible task for the big dog, since the scow drew only twelve inches of water. Afton had built the boat with that much draft so it wouldn't tip sideways going over rapids.

"How long's Reb been doing that?" Toby asked from his seat in the stern.

"About three years," Afton said as he tied down the bow sweep. "He belonged to a drifter before that."

"How come you got him?"

"The man was leaving for the Klondike and needed a home for the dog." He straightened from tying the rear sweep.

"Why didn't you go to the Klondike with him?"

"That's for young men. I was through with that kind of wandering long ago. No more questions now. Come help me with the mooring." He set the end of the gangplank on the rocky shore and motioned Toby across to take the rope from

Reb. He turned to me before he, himself, crossed over. "You don't have to come along, Hattie, unless you want. The Mallard's just down the shore a piece, around that curve. I won't be long." His tone was placating, as if he'd accepted my presence on the trip, might even be concerned at the prospect of taking risks with my life. I also marked the fact he'd called me Hattie for the first time that day and was glad I hadn't mentioned parting company.

"I'd like to go along, if you don't mind. I want to see that she-bear of yours. But first I must tend to a private matter. I'll catch up to you and Toby."

By some quirk of geology and wind current, the rapid's blaring song escaped me until I rounded the curve in the river. A chaos of spray and rock spread out before me. It was easy to see why Afton respected the Big Mallard. With the speed of a locomotive, the Salmon flowed straight and smooth until it reached a sharp ledge of rock. There it turned, made a tight swirl around the right-hand side of the ledge, and smashed into two great rocks. Below the rocks, the river dropped into what seemed a bottomless hole. From there it rose and struck a boulder that pounded it into froth.

Afton sat on his haunches at the bottom of the rapid, looking upstream. He was taking out his anxiety on a toothpick. Toby stood back in awe. Even Reb and Chitter had the sense to keep their distance from waves that could drag them under in a second. Afton acknowledged my presence by shaking his head. "'Tis a whole lot worse this time of year. Not enough water. I can't make it on the other side of that rock. I've got to come through here." As he spoke, he pointed out the chosen route, his voice so tense, so quiet, I had to strain to hear his words over the roar of the rapids.

All I could see as a possible channel was a passage not much wider than the boat, something like a green tongue laced with foam. On one side of the tongue, a jumble of rock broke the surface. The hole yawned on the other. If Afton made the quick turn around the ledge, he'd have little time to steer the scow onto that tongue. It looked hopeless.

14

On the way back to the scow, a gnarl formed in my stomach no amount of will could relieve. When we reached the place where the boat was moored, my feet refused to climb the gangplank. "If you won't rope the scow down, I think Toby and I should walk along the shore and let you take it down yourself."

Afton's scowl said if I was dumb enough to tag along on a man's trip, I could take my chances with the captain of the scow. His tone was more sympathetic. "I want the boy to have the ride. You can walk, if you must, but I'll be going too fast to stop for you until quite a ways downstream. You'll have to climb over lots of boulders, wade some places. Otherwise, you'll just have to grit your teeth and bear it."

I decided to grit my teeth and bear it, but when I saw the urgent way in which Afton checked the fastenings on the cargo and the ropes that tied us to the gunwales, it didn't make the prospect of sliding down that suicide chute any easier. As we pushed off from shore, I gripped the sideboard until my nails bit into the wood. The other hand reached across the sweep handle and clutched a strap on Toby's coveralls.

Afton had tied down the rear sweep to give his full attention to the bow, and he hunched over the lone sweep, not compressed, but strung out and lean, like a panther stalking prey. When we neared the curve and the perilous ledge of rock, he darted a look at the landmarks he'd noted while on the shore and calculated the amount of stroke to give the sweep. His eye and brain would have to be quicker than the river, his hand steady and strong. A slight mistake to one side or the other would throw us onto the rocks or suck us into that foaming green pit. Either way, we'd drown.

Afton lowered his crouch, back and legs flexed, his shirt soaked with sweat between his shoulder blades. I wanted to close my eyes to the danger, but when we whipped around the point and into that bullying chute I was so fear-struck I couldn't force my eyelids shut. I could see no passage, nothing but the huge, frothing teeth of waves that clamored over the rocks and showered me with sheets of cold spray. They stole my breath away.

I was about to say farewell to life when the tongue appeared. Another second, and we were riding it to safety. We shot past the rocks on the left and cut the hole on the right so closely I stared down directly into the swirling death pit. In that instant, I felt an inexplicable urge to dive to the bottom, the same strange impulse I'd experi-

enced when on a bluff overlooking the Snake
River, and while standing at the hay doors in the
barn loft.

I hadn't time to puzzle the feeling. The scow
had met the whitewater beyond the hole, leaping
and creaking. It smashed through one wave to the
next, streamed water like a whale breaching
the ocean's surface. Each time the bow slapped the
water, I was certain the impact would rip us apart.

"Get the buckets!" The order came none too
soon. The scow looked as if the river had used it
for a channel.

While Toby and I bailed, Afton sat on the box,
his nerve and energy spent, and wiped spray from
his face. I still shook and could find no voice for
conversation, though I tried once or twice. Toby's
lips had formed such a tight, white line, I doubted
they could part. The coon looked like a cat after a
bath. Reb paced back and forth in the bow, shaking water from his coat. In a way, I was glad for my
wet blouse and long skirts, as well as my soaked
bonnet. They gave relief from a sun that scorched
down from the sky and reflected off the water,
burning my face.

As I bailed, I tried to assure myself we'd survived the Big Mallard. In my mind's eye I saw the
waves slapping us senseless, felt the violent
motion, recalled the fear that gripped me to the
point of paralysis. But we lived. The fact filled me
with gratitude and awe.

The next five miles presented long stretches of whitewater that plucked at the nerves, though they couldn't compare with the Big Mallard. The first rapid hardly fluttered my heart. At the next two, I noticed only a tobogganing between rocks, waves striking the gunwales and rattling the pans, and the din that all rapids loosed on the world.

It struck me that Lewis and Clark had been foolhardy when they considered canoeing the river to its mouth. It was well known around Lewiston that the Shoshone chief, Cameahwait, had told the explorers that to attempt navigating the river would end in tragedy, that the whole surface of the river was beaten into foam as far as the eye could reach, that in many places jutting rocks hemmed in the river, preventing passage along the shore. Clark was slow to give up the idea, but eventually turned back, admitting the river was even more violent than Cameahwait's description. I could attest to that.

As was his habit, Afton commented on the last rapid when we slipped into calmer water. "Well, now, Hattie Clark, did that nice little ride tickle your fancy?" His relief at having the Big Mallard behind us reflected in his relaxed jaw, in the gentle way my name rolled from his lips. It made me wonder if the hostility he'd shown before we launched had derived in part from his apprehension about the rapid.

"You're a tease, Afton McCabe. You know I'm not enjoying a minute of this." I lied a little. I did enjoy floating the polished water. "But I'm not about to complain."

With the scow fairly empty of water and a calm river ahead, I could have sat like a lump in a bowl of pudding as long as the river allowed. Toby's young body apparently made no such demands for recovery. He leaned over the sideboard trailing a rope, snapping it up and down on the surface of the water like a whip. When he tired of the play, he squirmed on the seat with a restless look in his eyes.

"Would you want to try the sweep, lad?" Afton asked. Toby hung in the corner with an expression that said he wanted to try but was half-afraid. "Come, I'll help you hold it."

After a couple of false starts, Toby climbed over the clutter on the floor and approached the sweep as if it might bite. "That's the lad. Now take hold of the handle." Afton put the boy's hands on the sweep and covered them with his own broad palms. "Just give it a little flutter." When the scow obeyed the sweep, Toby met his uncle's approving eyes with a smile.

And so they stood, Afton with his arms around Toby, murmuring instructions as softly as the lap of the river against the scow. "Port a little. Not too far. A bit to starboard. That's a lad. Hold her steady."

I was thankful for Afton's change of heart. It reminded me of winter days when the three of us sat at the kitchen table, warm in our friendship. To keep the coon from disturbing the contentment, I coaxed her onto my lap and scratched her ears. Jealous, Reb left his station in the bow, leaned against my legs, and looked up at me with soulful eyes. The animals' coats had a swampy smell, but I didn't mind. Nothing could spoil the pleasure of that moment.

I savored the peaceful stretch of water—the quiet drift of the boat, the rugged sweep of the canyon, birds wheeling and calling. The swallows and Lewis' woodpeckers had begun to think of the flight south and gathered in chatty conventions. High overhead, a golden eagle uttered a piercing cry, folded its wings in a dive, and brought itself up sharp at a mass of boulders. Clutching a marmot in its talons, the bird launched itself from the rock and disappeared around a bend in the canyon, bound for a roost on some wild crag or sentinel pine.

I wished we could drift along in serenity forever, pretending time and events made no demands. It didn't seem too much to ask that the river remain tranquil, our lives the same. But ten miles of hard travel lay behind us, and Afton had decided it was time to camp. When we arrived at the bluff where he'd stopped in the past, we found someone had built a cabin and ferry and was floating a packstring across the river. Having no desire to intrude, nor to be intruded upon, Afton steered the scow around the ferry and chose a flat down-river to make camp. As before, Reb towed us to shore.

The flat was grassy and level, not a collection of humps and draws like some of the smaller bars. Here, the mountains sloped more gradually, about the pitch of a cow's face. Pines dotted the south-facing slopes like pegs on a board, even growing where ribs of granite poked through the thin soil. They loomed more densely in a draw that entered the flat at a diagonal. On the upper reaches, cliffs sheered toward the crest, breaking the mountain into a multi-leveled slope. Five russet deer trooped down one rocky terrace on their way to a spring.

Water had seeped into the oilskin bags that held the tent and bedding. Hoping the tent would dry before bedtime, we raised it on a mat of blond grass surrounded by clumps of chokecherry and elderberry bushes, then hung our bedding on ropes between sparse pines where the sun could suck it dry. Afton took his fishing rod and a collection of hoppers, caddis, and May flies of his own design and headed upstream with Reb to catch trout. Toby fetched what I needed from the scow to make supper and breakfast, then went to the wooded draw at the back of the flat to gather deadwood. Chitter wanted to stay in camp to beg food, but Toby coaxed her along with a piece of the venison jerky Len Johnson had sent with us.

I hummed while I puttered about my business, enjoying the languor of the place, the smell of sun-warmed brush and pines. I paused a moment to puzzle the unexpected happiness. I'd thought running the rapids would have drained my spirits. Instead, it had brought a lightheartedness and a rare sense of freedom. I had no idea how much being with Toby and Afton added to my contentment, but I was certain their companionship played a large part, especially with Afton's mood of acceptance.

I hadn't slept the previous night, and by the

time I'd built a fire within a circle of rocks, set a pot of coffee and pan of stringbeans on a grate to simmer, I needed to nap. I was lifting the tent flap in delicious anticipation of sleep when I recalled I hadn't seen or heard Toby for a while. I thought he was probably watching Afton fish, but with my tendency for worry, I had to find the boy.

Using my stick to probe for snakes, I walked upriver, wending my way through a mix of bunch-grass, sand vines, and rocks to the heap of boulders where Afton stood with pole bent, playing a fish. Toby was nowhere in sight. I stayed only long enough to watch Afton land a fifteen-inch trout, then headed for the rear of the flat, calling Reb to follow. Toby might still be gathering wood, though there was no snap of branches to indicate that. I sent Reb ahead with orders to find the boy.

When I reached the mouth of the wooded draw, Reb padded back with his tongue hanging out. "Did you find Toby?" I asked.

The dog pricked up his ears.

"Where is he?"

Reb turned to stare at the rugged hillside. I motioned with my arm. "Go find him."

The dog gave me a quizzical look, then left, climbing across a slide of gravel and rock until he disappeared behind some brush.

Too tired to climb, I skirted the base of the hill, angling up the wooded draw until I came to a massive outcrop of rock covered with emerald green moss and lichen. Water trickled down the granite into a pool carpeted with cress. A beam of sunlight shone through the trees at my back and turned a thin spray of water into a rainbow. A lovely place! Obviously others had thought the same. Around the edge of the pool lay obsidian chips an Indian toolmaker had left long ago.

Out of sight on the hillside, Reb barked.

"Where are you?" Higher on the outcrop, a tangle of brush clung to the rock. Reb's black head and shoulders parted the thicket. "Good heavens! Is Toby way up there?"

Reb watched me a second, barked again.

"Toby! Are you there?"

No answer.

I retraced my steps until I found a Bighorn sheep trail that angled up the talus slope in the direction of the outcrop. Inching along to keep from sliding from the narrow trail, I reached a crumbly ledge of rock screened at the approach by mountain mahogany. Reb had heard my feet send loose rock clattering down the slope and came padding along the ledge to meet me. Chitter appeared with a coon grin. But no boy.

"Where's Toby?" My manner was so urgent Reb backtracked through the mahogany and disappeared around an angle in the ledge. I heard him whine.

I crept along the ledge, digging my fingers into breaks in the wall to keep from falling, kicking aside loose rock that might cause me to slip. Beyond the angle in the rock, the ledge widened. Several yards ahead, Reb waited impatiently, patting his feet up and down. Indian pictographs covered the wall between us.

When I reached Reb, I saw that he stood at the

front of an ancient, fire-blackened cave eroded from the rock. Toby huddled at the back of the cave, quite alive and well. A canvas bag lay open at his feet, revealing clothes, a mound of dried apples, jerky, and leftover biscuits, also the cigar box that held the picture of his mother. He stared at me wide-eyed, primed for a scolding.

A sickness swept over me. *Toby had intended to run away.* But where would he have run? If he hid here for the night, what then? Perhaps strike out over the mountains, or upriver? Maybe to the pack trail serviced by the new ferry? Clearly, he hadn't expected me to find his hideaway. He so feared the return home, he'd left us without saying a word, ready to take his chances in the wilds. What manner of abuse would cause such fright in a child?

Wanting to reassure rather than threaten, I stooped forward a little to reach his level and said gently, "I was worried about you. What are you doing way up here?"

He said nothing, simply bit his lip and stared at me. Shame spoiled the clarity of his brown eyes.

"It looks like you were going to run away. Were you?"

His nod was barely perceptible.

"You don't want to go back to your father?"

He wagged his head.

"Are you afraid he'll send you back to Pardees? Or are you afraid he'll keep you?"

"Both . . . he might . . ." A terrible fear showed behind his eyes.

"What has he done to make you so afraid?"

He looked at me from beneath reddish lashes,

bit the corner of his lip. "I—I told you before. He's done bad things."

"What bad things? I'd like to know." From the set of his face, and the nervous way he wound the strings of the canvas bag around his fingers, I could tell he wasn't going to answer. "All right. I guess it's your business. But tell me this, if you planned to run away, why wait until now? Why not leave before we started on this trip?"

He worked his mouth silently, seeming to judge the degree of my upset. "I—I thought I might find an easier way out."

"There is no easy way out, child. No telling what might have happened to you."

"Are you going to tell my uncle?" His expression said he hoped not.

"He needs to know you're afraid to return home. But it would crush him to think you'd tried to run away. It would have caused us both a terrible fright. Promise you'll not try it again."

Toby gave me a wall-eyed, uncertain look, then bobbed his head.

Trying to hide my own misgivings, I took his hand and helped him to his feet. "Come, your uncle will wonder where we are. But first, let's look at the Indian paintings. You can tell me what you think they're about." I thought it a good way to relieve the tension.

The paintings covered the entire face of the rock like a sheet from a doodler's pad, their red color from some mineral or plant. Many of the line drawings and stick figures depicted a battle, with braves on horseback and braves on foot shooting bows and arrows, some pictures vivid, others dimmed by a natural veneer. Part of the wall had been sheared by lightning or ice, and on the face of this split were drawn mountain sheep in various poses. One pictured a ewe suckling a lamb. Rows of red dots, vertical zigzag lines, handprints, and lines connecting a row of circles, had no meaning for me. I put my palm over one of the handprints, found it larger than the print.

The pictographs made such an impression on Toby he talked about them through supper, and later, while we sat on boulders around the campfire, steeped in wood smoke and steam from drying shoe leather.

"I still don't understand what you were doing up on that ledge," Afton said. Suspicion lurked in his voice.

"I told you. I—I was up there looking for packrat nests." Toby turned owlish eyes on me, but I said nothing to destroy his story. He quickly steered the conversation back to the pictographs. "Are you sure you don't know what Indian war those pictures are about?"

Afton shrugged his stooped shoulders. "Like I told you before, there's no way to guess. Only the Sheepeater Indians would know. And they might of lost track over the centuries."

For a while, Toby watched the firelog snap white-hot coals into the air. When he looked up, he had another question. "Did you ever kill an Indian?"

"Aye, but I have no pride in the fact."

"Why not? Pa used to brag about Grandpa fighting White Bird."

"I see no glory in killing my fellow man."

"But Indians did bad things."

"No more than the whites. White men killed my partner Archie. I've seen others slit a friend's throat for a bag of gold. And heard of men who killed one of their own and ate him when they was snowbound and starving." Toby shuddered. He looked across the flames at Afton in disbelief. "'Tis true. Like I've told you before, white men do terrible things when there's the need, or the greed."

Afton stared into crackling fire, seeming to see things he'd rather not. "What about the range wars down your pa's way. Cattlemen burning corrals and barns, killing sheepherders and sheep. And the sheepmen doing almost as bad. I told your pa last time I saw him, he'd do well to get out of the sheep business before he ended up in a grave." He reflected a moment, shaking his head. "The Indians have no corner on savagery."

Toby took a long while to digest that piece of information, moving his mouth without speaking his thoughts. "Why'd you kill an Indian?"

Afton's eyes turned murky, his silence marked, as though the tale was ready for the spilling, but restrained willfully.

"Did you have to?" Toby prodded.

"Aye . . . it couldn't be helped." Afton seemed distracted by the thought.

"What happened?"

Afton squirmed on his boulder and scratched at the ground with a stick. "I was on the wagon train . . . coming through buffalo country . . . the Cheyenne didn't want us there." He shut his mouth tight on that, continued to make random scribbles in the sand.

Toby wasn't satisfied. "What'd the Cheyennes do?"

"Well, lad . . . they come streaming out of the hills quiet as ghosts, and we had to circle up. I had to kill two of them before we turned the poor devils away." Afton frowned, then went on with his tale, shaking his head, speaking around the eternal toothpick. "I'll never forget their screams nor those of the horses going down. 'Twas terrible. The worst kind of nightmare. Men should never have to shoot one another."

Toby seemed to chew on that bit of wisdom for a while, his lip tucked beneath his teeth. "Did you ever see Indians here on the river?"

"From time to time, riding the ridges. None ever come down to bother me. They camped some along the river, like here, but mainly along the South Fork. They called the river the Big Fish Water."

"Will we see them . . . the camps, I mean?"

"We'll spend the night in the one I was staying in when Rains got murdered."

"I remember reading about that," I said. "But it's been a long while. I don't recall the circumstances."

"Rains had a ranch a short ways up the South Fork . . . raised hay for the mining camp at Warren. Indians killed him and drove off his partners. I happened along after the murderers set the cabin afire . . . I was too late to help Rains."

Toby turned glum, sucking in his cheeks.

Light from the fire flashed across his sunken cheeks and turned his eyes into fiery caverns, making him look older than his years. "When Pa was a little kid, Indians burned the ranch house. I guess you saw the old chimney." Afton nodded. "Pa said Grandma and Grandpa and him and Uncle Will hid in a cave while White Bird's gang went around shooting the cattle and stealing the horses."

"That White Bird was a bad one. 'Tis a shame Chief Joseph couldn't keep him in bounds. I've often rued the day I talked your grandma and grandpa into coming to Idaho to face such danger."

"You shouldn't blame yourself," I said. "There was no way you could foretell the future."

"I should of known the Indians would cause trouble. Especially in those early days when we took their lands."

"Did your sister come over from Scotland when you did?"

"Och, no! She came in '74. I came in '61. I paid my passage to Canada as a cabin boy . . . just nineteen, I was . . . but I'd been on my own in Scotland for six years."

"Why did you come?"

"Times were hard in the Isles . . . I couldn't find work . . . there was lots of work over here. My dad was a tanner and taught me leather work, so I drifted down from Canada to upper New York and made harness and bridles for a while."

"I understand that section of New York is lovely. Why didn't you stay?"

"Had the wandering bug. I worked my way

west, making and repairing harness. When we come through southern Idaho, everybody and his brother were crawling over the hills looking for gold. I hitched up with a packer taking beef on the hoof to the miners and made such good money I stayed with the man. We wintered the packstring just north of Salmon City with another bunch of packers, and I got all the harness ready for the next season." A sudden melancholy shrouded his face. "That was when I met Archie." He stared into the flames a moment longer in silence, then left to gaze at stars that crackled brilliant against the black vault of the sky.

I stole to his side, and for a while we stared at the night sky, breathing in the pungent air. Every now and then, we turned our gaze on each other and let it rest there for a moment before we returned it to the sky. It was clear Afton had forgiven me for coming along. And I had forgiven the hostility he'd shown. That day we'd run the rapids together and survived. Tonight we felt the ties born of a common danger. I savored the feeling.

Afton went back to the fire before I did. Wishing to sleep under the stars, he'd laid his and Toby's bedrolls on the ground near the fire ring. He dropped onto the larger bedroll with a groan and began to unlace his boots. "We got to get ourselves to bed, lad. We need to cover the miles tomorrow."

"Will we come to any bad rapids?" Toby's voice had a shivering quality.

In the firelight I couldn't tell if the sparkle that

came to Afton's eyes was an expression of tease or anticipation. He had a way of looking amused without smiling. "Aye," he said shaking his head with great drama, "the first one will spin us around 'til we're dizzy."

15

I woke to the *thonk* of ax on wood, a cruel transition from the dream I'd been having. In that dream Chester and I were stocking the woodpile for the winter, he using the ax, I doing the stacking, both of us young and spry as colts. What a shock to wake and find myself middle-aged and tired, my back jabbed sore from the pallet of fir boughs.

Part of my weariness resulted from spending the early hours of the morning worrying about Toby. I wanted to protect him from his father and the Pardees. But where would we go? To be safe, I might have to take him farther away than Lewiston. Afton was right about the boy needing to get out into the world. There were grand things to do in a city like San Francisco. But would Toby be happy there? He was a country boy. He'd feel more comfortable in a small town like Lewiston, with open fields to explore and a place to keep animals. Besides, my girls lived there and needed me.

I'd pondered the problem until I realized the

mental exercise was futile. I'd been planning without regard for Afton. He might not want me to have the boy.

I heard his burred voice saying, "Roll out, Toby! I'll be needing more deadwood." Then toward the tent, "Coffee'll be on soon, Hattie."

I found Afton standing before a blazing fire, turning one side toward it then the other. It would be a while before the sun rose above the canyon walls, sending stringers of warmth into the river bottom. The leather boots he wore on shore were wet from a dew that lay heavy on the grass. They steamed in the intense heat. Reb sat beside them, watching Afton expectantly for a movement that meant breakfast.

"Why are you so glum, Hattie?" Afton asked. His eyes said he thought he knew. I didn't want to complain after imposing my company on the man, and simply shrugged. He looked up at the canyon's narrow lid of sky. "Perk up. 'Tis a beautiful morning."

It did offer the promise of a nice day, the sky cloudless, with a lilac hue. Still, I had great reluctance for the day ahead and said little while I broke my fast with Afton's sourdough pancakes sweetened with the chokecherry syrup I'd bottled a week earlier. Besides fearing the rapids, I hated the thought of sitting on a bench in the searing heat for hours. Afton was right when he'd said I'd have little tolerance for that. Even he showed less enthusiasm than he had the previous day. I thought he might have second thoughts about taking Toby down a river that offered no possibility for change of mind. He didn't like occasions when he'd taken the bit in his mouth and couldn't spit it out. I was certain he felt the burden of our welfare.

Toby ate in silence. Dread still marked his face. Only Reb and Chitter greeted the day with relish. What a pair! They'd formed an attachment from the start, Chitter to the dog even more than to Toby. They tore up and down the flat playing tag, Reb running in circles while Chitter turned cartwheels. They had an advantage over the rest of us. They didn't know what was in store for them until they saw us pack things out to the scow.

I thought I might have time to adjust to the feel of the river before I panicked, but we'd hardly pushed off from shore and settled into the main current when we sped around a bend in the canyon and headed for a wall of rock that appeared to block our path. The river swirled around a basin at the foot of the wall, struck the end with the sound of muffled blasts, then curled back upon itself, making a tunnel of foam and spray.

Afton had said the rapid would be puny compared to what it was in high water, but I saw him hitch up his belt and wipe his hand across his mouth, something he did when he needed to concentrate.

He put all his strength into the sweeps to keep us in the outer edge of the whirlpool. Even so, we spun toward the arch of foam and wave like a platter on a river of grease. Holding tight to Toby's straps, I pushed my feet against the floorboards and pressed my back against the gunwale, as if that feeble action could keep us from hitting the wall. I was certain we'd crash.

Spray showered us like a waterfall. The shock of it made me shiver and gasp for breath. Squinting through straggles of hair glued to my face, I saw we'd avoided the foaming cavern and were rounding the rock wall on an aisle of racing water. I had no idea how Afton had prevented certain calamity, but it wasn't without effort. His shirt had pulled free of his belt and flapped in the wind generated by the surge. His hair stood out in all directions like a wild man's.

He turned slightly, his face gaunt, and said something I couldn't hear above the blare of the river. In that moment, his daring fell aside, and I saw the vulnerability he tried to keep hidden. Despite the fact he'd come down the river many times, he was getting older, his ability to meet the challenge growing less each year. The rapid had put a strain on the man.

Empathy swept my feelings, as well as a startling awareness that Afton McCabe, whether he wanted it or not, owned a piece of my heart.

The Salmon River had cut such a deep gash in the landscape, from the bottom of the canyon we couldn't see the storm approach until a billowing cloud reared its white dome above the southern ridge. The air turned damp and cloying.

Afton had promised we'd stop at the South Fork of the Salmon to eat our lunch, but long before we reached the Fork, the cloud had swallowed the strip of sky. Its base hung deep and purple, in places trailing sheets of rain that blotted out the slopes. Thunder rumbled on the mountaintops. A thousand whistling voices blew a gale, the blasts so strong I had to gulp for air. Gusts of wind trenched the river and whirled spray into the darkening sky. Along the shore, pine trees swayed with a savage rustling. Young alders and willows bowed before the storm until their tips touched the ground.

When I pulled my slicker from beneath the seat, I nearly lost it to the wind. I had no hope of keeping the rain hat on my head. Toby's straw hat flew from his head and lit in the water far from the boat. He took the launch pole, and with a great stretching of arms and a beating of the stick on water, snagged the hat and pulled it back to the scow. Afton had folded his cap and stuck it in his back pocket.

At first, heavy, single drops of rain hit the scow with a sound as loud as stones. Within minutes, the clouds opened up and dropped a deluge. The river boiled with pelting drops. Rain hit my face with the force of coins falling from the sky. My scalp ran with water. Hair straggled down my face and stuck to my eyelids.

The rumble of thunder sped toward us until an explosion directly overhead tore at my heart and lungs. Reb crawled beneath the sweep deck, trembling. Chitter went into a panic and nearly dragged Toby overboard. I reached across the sweep handle to take a grip on boy and coon.

"We can't make it to the South Fork," Afton yelled above the storm. Rainwater plastered his hair into bangs and streamed from his nose and beard. "We'll have to put in at that . . ." The last bit of information was lost in a clap of thunder.

Cutting diagonally across the wind and waves took time. The eddy Afton had chosen for a mooring place had nearly pinched into nothing before he closed on the shore. Reb jumped from the pitching boat and began the mooring process. Afton made several attempts before he was able to set out the gangplank.

Clouds in the shape of heavy gray udders hung over us and dumped their load. Lightning struck the slopes with tines that vibrated like tuning forks. One bolt pierced a tree on the hillside above us with a loud snap and a flash of brilliant light. A topmost branch split from the tree. I felt struck through myself. I imagined the scar of flesh, the stifling of breath and pulse, and wished I were back at Weasel Creek within the shelter of my sturdy logs.

When Afton had tied the scow, we slogged through torrents of rainwash to the back of the flat, where he knew of a sod cabin. Taking refuge in a sod hut was not the best course in a lightning storm, but safer than staying on the river.

Toby was about to step inside the hut when Reb went into a slink. The dog stuck his nose across the doorless threshold and sniffed.

Afton pulled dog and boy aside. "Wait! Let me check for snakes." He found a dead pine bough at the side of the hut and stirred it around inside the crumbling walls.

A strident rattle pierced the unceasing roll of thunder.

"There 'tis! In the corner. Stay back! It might try to get out."

I'd already taken several steps backward, dragging Toby with me. I didn't know which frightened me most, the lightning or the snake. At the moment the snake had the edge.

Afton hurled a large rock at the snake.

Again that horrid rattling.

He threw a second rock. This time the rattlesnake's warning came from just inside the door. He threw another rock, another, and another, until the rattling trailed off to nothing. Using the bough, he lifted the flaccid body through the doorway—not one body, but two.

I turned aside, groaning. My skin crawled. First the rapids, now this! I should have stayed home.

If Afton hadn't insisted we take shelter from the punishing wind and rain, I would never have entered that snakes' den. While I stood amid bits of crumbled roof prickly with cactus and burr weeds, I imagined snakes crawling at my feet. By the time the storm passed, the nerves at the corners of my eyes and mouth twitched, the rest were strung tight as springs.

Glad to leave the hut's moldering remains, we stooped through the doorway into air redolent with the smell of spent lightning and rain-washed brush. One minute the late afternoon sun slanted its rays into the canyon, the next minute it slid behind a tattered cloud. Birds darted about the cleansed slopes, shrilling and hunting, some missing a few feathers.

Afton studied the sky. "There's another storm gathering. We'd best set up camp and be ready for the next beating."

Debris on the floor of the hut made it impossible to sleep there. It was just as well. I couldn't have lain where the snakes had denned. Instead, we pitched the tent, making sure it wasn't near tall trees that might attract lightning. Alongside the tent, Afton strung the wagon sheet he'd brought as shelter for himself. After the episode with the snakes, I'd have felt more secure if he'd slept in the tent, but my small hold on propriety kept me from suggesting it. He did use the tent to change, then hung his wet clothes on lines we tied between trees.

It was almost impossible to find wood dry enough to burn, but we cleared a space near the clothesline and built a small fire. Smoke from the damp wood drove us away, so I put my shoes by the fire, then walking around in the gum boots Afton had brought to wade the river, looked under trees for sticks that might burn.

We spent little time on supper and settled for the night early, before the new storm hit. Images of the snakes remained behind my eyelids, and at first I couldn't loosen my knotted nerves enough to sleep. My muscles burned. Pain circled my head and pressed against my eyes.

When exhaustion finally drove me to rest, sleep was short. I awoke sensing someone had called my name, but the cry didn't extend beyond sleep. Though I listened, all I heard was the renewed storm. Rain drummed its fingers on the canvas roof, sending a mist onto my bed. Thunder grumbled and snorted. Wind tore at the tent flap and sucked the walls in and out. I was certain only my weight kept the tent from flying off into the storm.

The glow of lightning lit the tent briefly. In that instant, I noticed Toby was missing from his bed. I recalled Chitter had curled under his blankets. I felt for the coon. Nothing.

"Afton! Are you awake?" I called through the canvas.

"You think I could sleep through this!" His voice came from the front of the tent, rather than from the side where he'd pegged the wagon sheet. "What are you doing out in the storm?"

"Trying to keep the tent from flying away. The tarp's already taken off into the trees."

"Is Toby with you?"

"No. Why would he be out here?"

"He's gone. Chitter, too."

Afton waited for a clap of thunder to roll into the distance. "Reb's not here, either. The lad's probably answering the call of nature. Wait a while. He'll be back."

"I know boys well enough to know he'd hold it rather than go out in a storm. At the most, he'd stand in the doorway and do what was needed. I tell you, something's wrong."

The incident at the Indian paintings flashed through my mind, and I experienced the same sick feeling I'd had then. *Surely Toby hadn't run off in this storm*. I crawled over his bedroll and found the canvas bag, still packed, nothing missing.

"Something's happened to the boy! I'm going to look for him." I felt beside my bedroll for socks, shoes, slicker. Afton cursed, grappling with the tent.

"I think you're worrying for naught. But I'll light the lantern and go with you. To hell with the tent!"

Heads bent against the storm, we started upstream, wading through puddles between rocks. The thunder was more ominous outside the tent, the lightning more livid, flashing in blue-white sheets and yellow spikes that lit the shore with a flickering light. Trees tossed in erratic circles, squealed and groaned in the wind. Branches snapped from their trunks. The rain drilled down from the sky. We called Toby's name, though I doubted our voices carried above the storm.

Two hundred yards upstream a rock slide blocked our way. We backtracked, passed camp, and continued downstream, calling Toby all the while. Thinking Reb more likely to hear us than the boy, we'd sometimes yell for the dog, but heard no answering bark. My alarm grew with each step.

16

$\mathscr{W}$e walked downstream for several minutes before Reb crashed through the brush and into the circle of lantern light. Chitter waddled in, too, wretchedly wet. It had begun to hail, and the animals' coats were salted with stones. When I scooped Chitter into my arms, she poked her nose between the buttons of my slicker and wedged herself under the rubber. Her teeth chattered. "Where's Toby?" I asked the coon. Fright gave my voice a ragged edge.

"He must be near," Afton said. "Reb, take us to Toby!"

The mention of Toby's name struck a spark in the dog. He spun around, ran a few yards downstream, and barked. When we followed, he repeated the process, scrambling over rocks and through brush. Again, it reminded me of the day at the Indian paintings. Terrible doubts filled my heart and mind.

At a dense thicket, we lost sight of Reb. Afton swung the lantern around to spread the light.

"He's up on some kind of mound. Could be a prospector's diggings. Wait here. You don't want to break your neck." Clinging to brush, he climbed out of sight, leaving me in the flickering light of the storm. "Toby!" I heard him call.

A small voice wavered out of the night. "I'm down here."

My heart raced at the sound. Ignoring Afton's words of caution, I climbed the rain-slicked dump of rocks and earth and found him holding the lantern over a hole that looked like the burrow of a giant badger.

"How far down are you?" he asked Toby.

"Just a ways . . . the hole slants in . . . I can't get hold of anything."

"Don't worry, lad, I'll get a rope from camp and be right back." Afton gave me a look that bordered on panic. "Will you be all right in the dark? I'll be needing the light."

"Of course." I touched his arm, felt it rigid as a pine slab beneath the cold wet of his slicker. "Take care," I murmured. Next instant, he'd disappeared, taking a part of me into the night. It seemed each crisis, each shared danger, drew us closer, and for that I was grateful.

I could see well enough in the storm's wan light to keep my balance and make out the crumbly walls of the diggings. "Are you hurt, Toby?" I yelled into the darker black that was the tunnel.

"Scratched is all."

"Then we should be thankful."

"Hattie . . . is my uncle mad?"

"I wouldn't say he's happy about what you've done, but he's glad you're alive. Whatever possessed you to come out on this terrible night? You weren't running away, were you?"

A moment passed before his wary voice drifted up from the void. "I—I went after Chitter. She crawled out of my bed."

The voice, so hesitant, caused the doubts to build, until I recalled that in the storm I'd forgotten to feed the coon. She must have gone in search of food.

"How did you find her in the rain and dark?"

"Reb did. I just followed him. She climbed down in this hole to get out of the storm, and I couldn't get her to come out."

"So you fell in trying. Well, next time she does that, you let her find her way back. It's better than doing yourself harm." I doubted Toby would heed my words. His dread of the return home, the fear he'd have the coon taken from him, had strengthened his attachment to the little rascal.

Morning dawned in a sky washed clean by the storms. Trees and brush sparkled like cut emeralds. Even the bleached grass seemed to have found new life. The wind had died, and blood-hungry insects filled the air with their whining. We kept busy brushing black flies from face and hands. Tired from the previous night's adventure, we were slow to gather the belongings scattered by the storm, slow to breakfast. We'd wait for our clothes to dry before setting off down the river, though I didn't know why. They'd be soaked after the first rapids. Still, it seemed nice to start out dry. Afton sneezed several times, and I worried he might have caught cold. I felt a little stuffy in the nose myself, and my head still ached, though I'd taken a small dose of laudanum.

On the river, we encountered signs of the storm's violence. The South Fork rolled into the main Salmon, a rich chocolate scummed with insects and froth. All manner of debris floated past, caught in the wash of heavy rains and flooding creeks. Toby kept the launch pole handy, I my snake stick, to push aside clutter that attached itself to the gunwales. Like part of the storm's scourings, a family of otters swept by on a log, their black eyes bold with curiosity.

A mile or so beyond the South Fork, we met the first storm-caused obstacle, a giant pine the winds had felled two-thirds of the way across a narrows in the river. Only by veering the scow far to the right, where filaments of current swirled around the tip of the tree, was Afton able to prevent our being pinioned on the limbs.

We encountered a second obstacle in the late afternoon when we approached a side stream flowing in from the north. The storms had washed gravel down the stream and across the Salmon toward the south bank, almost damming the river. In one place, water flowed over the gravel bar a few inches deep, and the otters' log had lodged there, but there was no sign of the animals. Along the south bank, the gravel bar had left a narrow passage where the river burst through in humping waves. The current sucked us toward the funnel as if we were a chip of wood.

Afton raised his voice above the tantrum of foam and waves to curse his luck, the storm, and the damnable fate that was about to do us in.

The terrible force concentrated in the narrow channel propelled us over a drop and against a curling wave that threw the bow in the air. The stern hit a boulder on the right. Submerged rocks grated against the hull. Water boiled over the side-boards. It was all Toby and I could do to keep the waves from dragging us overboard. It seemed we'd turned a backward somersault before the scow thrust its nose down. When it did, it was with a seesaw motion that rocked us along an eternity of waves. My stomach rolled until I thought I'd vomit. My clothes were soaked through. They clung to me like the skin of an over-ripe peach. A foot of water covered my shoes.

How much more of this brawling river could I take?

Shaken by the day's near-calamities, Afton headed for a campsite before he'd intended, on a flat he said had been placered by companies of Chinese in the mid eighties. Their doghouse size cabins clustered on a bench above the flat.

"I spent a few days with them one summer," he explained as we pulled into shore. "Two dozen men, there were. Never saw any fools work so hard. They used handmade wheelbarrows and shoulder yokes with buckets to carry the gravel to their rockers and sluices. They had only a half-dozen beds . . . had to sleep and work in shifts."

"Did they find much gold?" Toby asked, always eager to know about riches.

"They earned two or three dollars apiece many days. Most of it they sent to their families in China. The company paid their wages and the big license fees Uncle Sam charged. They seemed happy enough . . . guess it was a lot better than living in China."

"Is that all they did—work?" I asked.

Afton chuckled. "Not those Chinamen. At night they'd sit around the campfire and gamble . . . smoke opium 'til the wee hours of the morn."

Afton had definitely caught cold from being out in the storms, and rested often while we set up camp. Exposure to the elements could lead to pneumonia. His age made that possibility even more threatening. What would I do if he became ill in this wilderness? What would I do if it affected his heart?

Next morning, his congestion seemed worse. I insisted he take some Ayers' Cherry Pectoral I kept in Chester's satchel. The label listed the ingredients as tincture of blood root, antimonial wine and wine of ipecac, syrup of wild cherry, and acetate of morphia. I'd always found it worked quickly to ease a cough.

I tried to convince Afton he needed to spend the day in camp, but he wouldn't hear of it. "We need to get out of the canyon before one of those early snowstorms catches us. I want to cover the miles today . . . maybe make camp this side of Carey Falls."

"We're not going over the falls!" Toby and I squealed in unison.

Afton made a sound between a sigh and a moan. "Aye, we are, and some falls it is." A twinkle in his eyes belied the attempt at gravity.

I pictured the falls as an abrupt drop from a ledge of rock, such as those I'd seen on the Columbia and on the Snake. As it turned out, the danger in Carey Falls lay not in the drop of several feet, but in the monstrous granite boulders that hulked haphazardly across the river between a cliff-like slope on the right and a rocky point on the left. The boulders offered two precarious routes through the drop.

Unlike the first two days of travel, Toby seemed to face the cataract with calm and courage, his arms folded around the coon. I wondered if he'd decided that falling in the river would be no worse than the return to his father. I felt no such resignation. I'd found new purpose in life and wasn't going to give up easily.

From what I could see of the falls, we'd have to make a straight run between one of the Gibraltar-like rocks and the rocky point on the left, or be lost.

I sat rigid as a post while Afton steered the scow through the stretch of tumbling whitewater that preceded the thundering drop. I hoped to heaven he'd show the skill he had at the Big Mallard. He didn't. The scow approached the falls too close to the dump of rock on the left. Halfway down the drop, the scow rammed a boulder. With a loud scraping sound, we swung around onto a shelf of rock and stuck fast. The jolt threw me to the floor. My shoulder hit the edge of the sweep deck, my shins a can of kerosene. Toby and Chitter fell across me. Afton tumbled onto the clutter in the bow.

When I pulled myself to my knees, I saw that the scow pointed upstream, the bow angling toward the sky. The stern hung dangerously over a great basin of green water with a curling reverse wave at the lower end. On all sides the falls bellowed.

Afton crawled onto the sweep deck, his face ashen. "We nearly did ourselves in that time."

And what made him think we were out of danger!

"I'll tie the mooring rope to something down the shore," he said. "Then I'll see if I can push the boat free. The river can take it down without us."

He tied the sweep handles to the sweep deck, then set the gangplank across two scum-covered boulders that reached within four feet of the riverbank, with two feet of air between the plank and shallows. Reb and Chitter immediately raced to the end of the plank and jumped the four feet to shore.

"You and Toby get busy with the buckets while I snug the line," Afton said. "It won't do to lighten the load too much, though. She'll slide off and swamp you in that hole for sure."

Toby and I had just finished bailing when

Afton returned from tying the bowline to a drift-log. He waded the channel of water between the riverbank and the ledge that held the scow prisoner. "You'll have to go onto shore so I can shove her off."

Toby crossed to the riverbank like one of his nimble goat friends. Not I. When I saw the slick boulders I'd have to use as stepping stones, the waves slapping between, I couldn't will myself to step from the plank.

Afton saw me falter. Dripping water, sneezing, coughing, he climbed onto a boulder. I felt a faint tremor run through his hand as he helped me from the gangplank onto the boulder, an apparent reaction to fatigue.

"You shouldn't push yourself so hard," I said, clinging to him to keep from slipping. "Nor wade with that cold of yours."

He looked at me with an impatience fueled by anxiety. "How else do you propose we get out of this fix?"

I had no answer, so remained on the riverbank, while Afton stood in two feet of roily water and put his muscle into the push. I watched him struggle to find a strength long gone, his back and shoulders quivering, ready to cave. I heard him groan, saw his chest heave, working for air. His effort tore at my feelings.

Without another moment's thought, I plunged into the channel and put my shoulder to the scow, desperately aware of the man beside me, alert to his condition. The river filled my boots and sucked at my long skirts. I fought the pull, fought to keep my balance on the slick rocks shifting beneath my feet. Fought to keep the river from dragging me under. I was so cold I would have screamed if I hadn't been concentrated on Afton.

He was so intent on trying to move the scow, his feet went out from under him. Swearing, he grabbed the gunwale and leaned his head against it. His lungs pulled at the air. I grabbed his arm to keep him upright, feeling his misery, his frustration.

When he was able to pull himself to his feet, his mind was still fixed on the task at hand. "I'll have to cut some poles to pry her off." He felt between the double walls of the gunwale, pulled out the ax, then dragged himself onto shore, I at his heels.

We worked our way downstream, wading pools and crawling over boulders, Toby and the animals in the lead. We cut two slender pines to a suitable length and limbed them, then dragged them back to the scow, working them over and around the boulders.

Wheezing and blowing, Afton dropped to a rock at river's edge, his head bent over his knees, his face blue-gray beneath its tan. I ran my hand along his shoulders. The muscles tensed, then relaxed.

"You shouldn't be doing this," I said. "Your heart won't stand it."

"My heart's fine. 'Tis just the heat that gets me."

"Then rest. We're in no hurry to move the boat."

"We can't leave it sit there all day. We'll be wanting to make camp."

"Maybe Toby and I can pry it loose."

He looked up with a jerk of his head. "I'll not let a woman and boy do what's rightfully mine to do."

"You'll need a hand," I said warily.

He looked out at the helpless scow and gave a sullen nod. "Aye, guess you can help."

Standing in the channel between the ledge and shore, he wedged the poles at separate points under the hull, one near the bow, the other near the stern. Using the pole as a lever, he'd push on the pole near the stern, the one closest to the drop. Toby and I would push on the pole at the bow.

"All right," he yelled above the roar of the falls, "push down on the poles at the count of three. One—two—three!" He gave a fierce grunt.

Mimicking his uncle, Toby grimaced and groaned. I felt like doing the same. I thought my muscles would give way, thought my back would break with the effort. The green poles bent beneath the force. The noise of the falls pounded at my ears. Spray that smelled of fish spattered my face, making it difficult to see. As before, the current tried to drag me under.

The scow didn't budge.

Our second attempt failed as well.

With the third, the hull moved a few inches. With the fourth, the scow slid free of the shelf, but still hung on a submerged rock.

"Take heart," Afton said, "we just about have her." He reset the poles. "A couple of deep breaths now . . . and push!"

I bore down on the pole with all my strength. My head seemed about to explode, my arms to leave their sockets. I thought I'd faint.

The scow hung on the boulder for an excruciating moment, then with a great shudder and grating of wood on rock, it slid into the falls. With the tremendous force of the chute at its bow, it plunged into the green basin at the base of the drop, knocked back and forth between boulders, and came up streaming water. An inward swirl of the current spun it completely around, then rocked it across the waves until it pulled into shore below the driftlog that held the bowline fast.

My attention riveted on the scow, I didn't know Afton had fallen until I heard him cry out. He slumped across a boulder—wheezing—coughing—strangling—his arms wrapped around his chest. Within seconds, he crumpled into the shallows, hitting his head on a rock. With a cry, I scrambled over the rocks that separated us.

He was unconscious, his clothes waterlogged, heavy. My fingers were so cold they refused to grip, and I had to hook my elbow beneath his armpit to lift his head from the water. While I dragged one arm, Toby pulled on the other, his face grave with the responsibility. Reb pulled, too, on Afton's clothes. Unable to help, Chitter leaped from boulder to boulder, squealing.

Toby and I would heave and rest, heave and rest, until we dragged Afton through a gap in the rocks barely wide enough for him to pass. We could find no place on the rocky shore to lay him flat, so we propped his back against a low-lying boulder and draped his legs across a spit of sand. He breathed, but barely, wheezy, bubbly breaths that strung thin through his lips. His pulse was feeble and irregular in beat, his skin like ice. A cold already congested his lungs. With the immersion in water and what I was certain had been heart failure, the possibility of pneumonia loomed stark. To make matters worse, blood spurted from a gash on his forehead. I feared the blow on the head might have caused concussion. Whatever the problems, I had to work fast.

17

I couldn't bear the thought Afton might not live—the personal loss, as well as the danger it would put us in. My mind wheeled, listing the steps I must take to keep him alive. I first thought of the smelling salts in the medicine satchel, but recalled Chester had said it dangerous to give salts in the event of concussion, as they increased the chance for inflammation in the brain. I next thought of heat, necessary in both heart failure and concussion. Though the sun scorched down, Afton was cold. I needed blankets, matches for a fire, and Chester's satchel. I didn't dare leave Afton alone, but I had no choice. Reb would have to watch over him while Toby and I went to the scow.

When we returned, we undressed Afton and wrapped him in the driest of the blankets—most were dripping wet from the plunge into the falls— then I rubbed witch hazel on his chest. When I pinched his skin accidentally, he stirred, opened vague eyes, made a few wordless sounds, and immediately settled back into his stupor.

"Afton? Can you hear me?" Again, he stirred out of his stillness. His eyes remained closed, but he moaned and wobbled his head.

"Are you getting warm?"

His eyes opened to slits, their expression still opaque and meandering. He mumbled something I couldn't understand.

"Afton, are you warm?" I said more loudly.

"Feet . . . cold," he murmured, and followed with a stream of incoherent babblings. I rubbed his feet until he drew them away. He breathed with great effort.

I kneeled beside him, feeling soaked, disheveled, and bruised. Reb, smelling like the wet dog he was, stood astride Afton's legs and licked his master's face. Chitter sniffed at his ears. When I waved the dog and coon aside, Afton roused and wiped his cheek with a trembling hand. He touched the wound on his forehead and puzzled at the crimson smear left on his finger.

"You fell on a rock. Does your head hurt?"

He nodded, touched his head again, let the hand drop to his side.

"How do you feel otherwise?"

"Like . . . like one of them boulders is sitting on my chest." His speech was now coherent, though somewhat slurred. His eyes were dull, without depth. He looked around at the river and rocks in a bewildered way. "Wha-wha-happened?"

"You fainted when we pushed the boat off the rocks." I didn't want to give my diagnosis until later.

The puzzlement that marked his face dissolved

into an expression of pain. He asked nothing more.

I pulled one of his arms from beneath the blanket, intending to rub it with witch hazel. He drew it away. "I'm freezing. Why'd you take off my clothes?"

"They were soaking wet."

"Fine thing to do to a man when he's—he's addled."

"We'll have a fire soon." I pointed to a strip of sand where Toby was using his knife to sliver a few sticks of wood into kindling. "When you feel up to it, we'll move you over to the warmth."

Now that Afton had revived, I cleaned the wound. He gasped at the sting of witch hazel, but the shock helped him focus more clearly on our predicament. "Where's the scow?"

"Where you tied it."

"Is it hitting any rocks?"

"Now and then . . . a few small ones. As far as I can tell, not enough to hurt anything."

"Better get the boy down there to do some bailing." He raised his head to look in Toby's direction, then leaned back, sighing. "I've put us in a real fix, haven't I?"

"Nothing we can't handle." The words seemed strange coming from my mouth. Afton was usually the one to speak thus. "The scow is doing just fine. Now hold still, and let me dress that wound."

He winced as I spread a styptic of collodion, carbolic, and benzoic acid on the wound. "You almost smeared my eye! Och, I hate the smell of the stuff."

"This bandage will keep the smell down." I wrapped a strip of flour sacking around his head and tied it at the back. He looked like a pirate. "There now, that should feel better after a bit. As soon as Toby has a fire started, I'll have him look for a place to camp."

"He'll not find one near. We'll have to go farther downriver."

"You're not up to it. Besides that, your clothes are still soaking wet."

"I'll put them on anyway." Snugging the blanket around himself, he rose, intending to stand. Instead, he dropped to his knees and remained there, weaving, wheezing, coughing.

Gently, but firmly, I lowered him onto the rock. "You're not going anywhere until you're dry and warm. Then we'll see what needs to be done."

"What needs to be done is get us to a camping spot."

"You can't man the sweeps."

"No, but you can."

"I've had no practice!"

"Don't need any. About a half-mile downriver there's a flat where you can land easy." Then he added with a faint grin, "Even if you are a woman."

Despite my clumsiness with the sweeps, the river beyond the falls carried us quietly to the flat Afton had described. Thinking it wise to have a more comfortable shelter than the tent, I steered the scow through the polished water toward a moss-streaked cabin on the upstream end of the flat. Afton noted the change of direction and raised up from his slouch in the stern.

"Don't head in there," he said in a voice so weak and hoarse I could barely hear him. "'Tis Ab Pocock's cabin. He won't let you trespass."

"The place looks abandoned. If he's there, surely he won't mind if we camp nearby. We may need his help."

"He's not one to help others. Tetched as a cow with a bee in her rump, he is. I'm surprised he's not shooting at us right now."

"Maybe he doesn't live there anymore."

"Well . . . that could be. Two years it is since I been by." He made a limp gesture toward a side canyon that came in at an angle and ended behind the cabin. "Or he might be up that creek. He has a placer up there a ways and . . . and . . ." With a moan, he leaned dizzily against Reb. The dog had been pressed against him since we'd left the falls.

Please, Afton. Don't faint now. I had no confidence I could steer us into shore without his help, but I tried not to sound frantic. "Where should I pull in?"

"'Tis a grove of trees at the lower end of the flat," he said, eyes still shut. "A bend in the river will keep us out of Pocock's sight."

"Won't he see the smoke from our fire?" I'd begun to think like a fugitive.

"Keep the fire down and hope he's away."

"Maybe we should camp farther on."

"There's some whitewater you'll not want to handle."

Good enough reason. Still, when we pulled up to the stand of pines, I had a strong feeling we'd stopped where we were not wanted.

Toby and Reb took over the mooring process, Toby's chest puffed out with a man's responsibility, Reb bewildered at the switch in masters.

We pitched the tent, sour-smelling from bilge and rainwater, helped Afton inside, and put him on the floor beneath his scrubby blanket. Because he'd insisted on leaving the falls before his clothes were completely dry, I had him take off his damp shirt and trousers. Lying half-naked beneath a blanket galled him, and when I brought out the witch hazel to give him a rub he pulled the blanket up to his chin and held it tight.

"I've let no decent woman see me in my shorts since my mother, and I don't intend to let you again."

Now that he was fully conscious, I felt shy myself, but wasn't about to let him notice. "Don't be absurd! I've seen lots of men in nothing but their underwear. I used to fill in for Chester's nurse when she was ill." I reached for the blanket. He shoved my hand aside, and in his irritation, broke into a fit of coughing that made me fear he'd tear his lungs apart. "If you want to live, you'll let me do what's necessary!"

The frightful cough seemed to humble Afton. Grumbling, he let me pull back the blanket, inch by inch as needed, to apply the rub. When I reached his belly button, he ordered me out of the tent. I left, but not until I put a piece of flannel soaked in kerosene on his chest to act as a poultice.

He tore the rag from his chest and reared up, roaring. "What kind of revenge is this to heap on a sick man?"

"Better to suffer revenge than the grim reaper."

With something between a hiss and a moan, he sank back to the floor and let me put the poultice in place to do its work. I gloated a bit, knowing I'd won the first of many skirmishes we'd have before he recovered.

With several hours of daylight ahead of us, Toby and I changed into half-dry clothes, then worked leisurely to set up camp amid the locust trees abundant in the lower reaches of the canyon. Avoiding nettles, and thickets of blackberry and thimbleberry that rustled with the stirrings of grouse, we emptied the boat of its cargo, took all the wet clothes and bedding, and put them to dry in the scorching sun. An abandoned sluice turned upside down became a kitchen table, green pine boughs an arbor. Near the table we made a fire ring for cooking. We pegged the wagon sheet at the front of the tent to serve as entryway and sleeping room for Toby, hung the lantern from a hook at the peak of the tent.

When the blankets had dried, I took them into the tent and spread them over armloads of withered grass for our pallets. Throwing propriety aside, I laid my bed opposite Afton's. In the aisle between beds, I stored items I'd need for nursing, and other goods I wanted under cover. The night hinted of fall, so I heated rocks by the fire and tucked them inside a pair of heavy socks to put at Afton's feet.

Despite the poultice, the next morning his congestion was worse. His skin burned red with fever. I could wait no longer for his heart to recover before I treated him with quinine and the dregs from the bottle of Ayers' Cherry Pectoral. I kept the breakfast coals alive to prepare the same decoction of Jade Girl I'd given Toby last May and to cook a broth from jerky and onion. All day long, on the hour, I gave Afton a spoonful of the thick tea. Chester's watch ticked at the end of the cord that circled my neck, reminding me of the hour for medication, sounding off the drag of time.

Toby gathered a store of wood and stacked it beneath a wide-branched pine near the kitchen table for protection from rain and the heavy dews. When not gathering wood or carrying bucketsful of drinking water from the creek at the back of the flat, he fished for our supper and wandered up and down the shore with Chitter and Reb. In his wanderings, he discovered lodge rings from an old Indian camp and chips from arrowhead workings, and most precious of all, two obsidian arrowheads the storm had washed free of dirt. He fastened the points to sticks with pitch and ran around playing Indian, scaring off the doves that frequented the flat. He appeared more relaxed than he had for days. Still, he watched my comings and goings with a vigilance that made me suspect he was waiting for the right moment to run away.

Once, as I hunched beside the fire ring heating

the decoction, he handed me a bouquet of purple asters and white daisies he'd gathered from the banks of the creek. The smell of the tough stems pricked at my nose. I detected something peculiar in his manner the moment he gave me the flowers. His eyes had a strange cast, an intensely searching look mixed with a bit of wildness. His cheeks held the flush boys have when considering things bold or foolhardy. While I admired the flowers, he worked his mouth and sucked in his cheeks, a mannerism I'd come to recognize as prelude to serious talk.

I moved the pot that held the decoction to the edge of the fire grate and prodded the coals back to life. "Is something bothering you, Toby?"

He made no reply, simply fixed me with those probing eyes.

I searched the clutter on the table for the coffee can I'd emptied that morning. "I wish you'd tell me what's on your mind." He hesitated, skimming the reddish-brown forelock back from his round, secretive face. "Umm . . . you know the trail that goes up the creek?" I said I did. "Maybe I could find somebody up there with a horse. They could take Uncle out to the doctor."

"Heavens no! You might run into that crazy hermit. If you don't, you might have to hike twenty miles or more before you'd find anyone. It would be of no help, anyway. Your uncle isn't up to the trip." I poured water from a bucket into the empty can and put the flowers into the makeshift vase.

"Couldn't I just take a look?" A measure of guilt lurked behind his eyes.

"You're not thinking of running off, are you?"

His flush deepened. "No—I mean—not really."

I was certain he planned to do just that, or at least to explore the trail for future reference, yet he seemed to want my permission, even if he gained it under false pretext.

"Toby, traveling the wagon roads between Pardees and Elk City was risky enough. Finding your way out of this canyon would be frightful, maybe impossible. If you were to leave, your uncle and I would worry ourselves to death."

He hung his head, curling his lower lip slightly. "I'd be all right."

I ran my hand over his crown of thick hair, feeling the contours of his skull. "I wish there was some way you could avoid going back to your father. Maybe . . . now that Afton is sick . . . there's a chance you won't have to. Maybe I can . . ." I paused, realizing I had no right to promise the boy anything without first speaking to Afton. I altered my tack. "Maybe your father's had a change of heart. Maybe he'll—"

"He won't never change!"

"I wish you'd tell me why you despise him so."

He stared at me a long while with those hate-filled eyes. "'Cause . . . 'cause he . . . 'cause he's done bad things."

"What bad things?"

His eyes rolled upward, sideways, downward, until they filled with tears. "He's just mean . . . and bad."

I cupped my hand under the boy's chin, tilting

his head. "I know your father's been cruel. Some men are. They don't understand children. They don't really take the time. But they have problems of their own. Ranching in this country can be brutal. A man will take his feelings out on his family." I paused, wondering whether to open wounds. "It must have been painful for your father when your mother died."

Toby jerked his chin free. His eyes sparked with outrage. "Pa wanted her dead!"

"How can you say such a thing!"

He gave no answer, just looked at me with extreme resentment.

My fingers slid down his bare arm to his wrist. "You shouldn't let bitterness eat at you, child. It'll make you sick."

"I don't care! I won't never stop hating Pa!" He jerked his hand free, then ran as fast as his legs could fly to the back of the flat and up the bare hillside toward an outcropping of rock that soared from the slope like the watchtower of a castle. My heart went out to the child. Giving vent to his feelings, he'd not stop until he reached the top of the battlement and could scowl down on the world. I doubted he'd run off that day, but when? How could I live with myself if I allowed him to slip away? I must speak to Afton as soon as he was well and insist he make different plans for the boy.

Worry over Afton and Toby continued into the night as I lay awake with the fumes of the

kerosene poultice assaulting the linings of my
nose. By then, my fretting rose more from the
mind than from the heart. I was dead to emotion, numb with fatigue, with little sense of
touch. It seemed we'd come a thousand miles
since we'd left McCabe's Bar. I worried that I,
too, might fall ill. Then what would become of
Afton? Of Toby? Of me? Often, since Chester
died, I'd wondered what would happen if I
became seriously ill with no one around. It was
one of the concerns that turned my thoughts
toward civilization.

Now others depended on my staying well. I
felt as if I were trying to pull us all from the bottom of an abyss. I'd been left to trouble over matters while Afton's inner processes dwelled on
fighting the pneumonia. He hardly recognized
me, hardly knew I tended him. He moaned and
groaned, his breathing so labored I wished I could
breathe for him. Now and then he cried out in his
sleep or smiled a twitchy smile and muttered a
string of babblings.

Once in his sleep, he called a woman's name,
"Libby. Libby!" then burst into a convulsion of
tears. His fevered brain seemed determined to
burn through its file of memories while it still possessed spark.

Earlier, he'd told me he wasn't afraid of death,
but from other remarks he'd made, I gathered he
was afraid of life, afraid he didn't have enough
time left to spend it as he wanted. He especially
wished to complete the trip, and from the way he
expressed it, I knew it would be his last.

Tormenting worries, the man and the boy. They'd become the center of my life, and now I might lose them both.

It was the eighth of September, our fifth morning in camp, our tenth on the river. I stood at the makeshift table scrubbing my way through fire-blackened pots that filled a dishpan. I was stewing over the fact that we were about to run out of beans and salt pork. I already skimped on flour and on kerosene for the lantern. The fresh vegetables were long gone.

Fingers of sunlight touched my back with a soothing warmth and eased my cares somewhat. The long beams had just cleared the ridges to the east, and lanced through the trees, drawing patterns of light and shadow. The light had softened the early-morning frenzy of bird song, the trilling infrequent, sweet as the breeze that ruffled the loose folds of my blouse and skirt.

The past three days had followed a pattern. The bright blue skies of morning preceded billowing white clouds that gathered each afternoon and disappeared by the next morning without leaving a drop of rain. This day, the clouds had piled up early into towering mounds the texture of whipped cream. Their shadows darkened the south shore and threatened to steal across the river to where I stood.

Toby had gone into the grove of trees at the mouth of the draw to gather wood, or so I'd thought. He'd been gone a long while, Reb and Chitter with him. Again, I feared his intentions. I reminded myself Toby wasn't one to hurry, that his mind routinely drifted far from where his feet were planted.

"Toby!" I called, as much to relieve my anxiety as in the hope he'd get the wood under cover before it rained.

As if answering my summons, Reb and Chitter pattered from the grove of pines east of camp. A man followed them, prodding Toby into the clearing with a double-barreled shotgun, not the usual length, but sawed short. Whenever Toby slowed his walk, the little man jabbed the boy in the back with the tip of the gunbarrel.

18

he man prodding Toby with the shotgun
seemed an apparition from some other
time and place, aboriginal. At the least, he
looked a fool or a madman. Nut-brown from the
sun, he wore nothing but a pair of cut-off black
twill pants slung low on his hips for lack of a belt.
His exposed hip bones stood out like those of a
dead steer. Hanks of white hair streamed over
shoulders as bony as the hips.

I hurried across the clearing and pulled Toby
to my side.

"Who are you?" I asked the man. "What are
you doing to this boy?" I held Toby so close I felt
his heart race.

The man grimaced through a bramble of
white beard. His nose was just a knob of bone—
probably damaged by severe frostbite. "I caught
the boy poking around my diggings up the creek.
If he knows what's good for him, he'll stay clear of
my property."

Then Toby *had* tried to run away, or was

exploring the possibility. I'd speak to him later about that, but I gave him a look that told him I knew what he'd done. He hung his head, squirming under my scrutiny.

I turned to face the apparition. "I'm sorry you had to bring Toby back. I'll see that he stays near camp from now on."

"If he's like my boy used to be, you might have to hog-tie him. I couldn't keep the little devil to home. Whippings didn't do no good. I finally booted him out when his ma died." He scanned our camp from scow to makeshift kitchen and tent. "This here's my property, too. You'll have to get off it."

"We can't leave. This boy's uncle is terribly ill."

"What's wrong with him?" The man's eyes glared, bulgy and brown. Their cast said they'd either seen too much of life or too little.

"He's had a heart attack, complicated by pneumonia. We can't move until he's well."

"What's his name?"

"Afton McCabe."

Curiosity lit the man's eyes with a subdued glow. "Didn't think that old chawbacon'd ever marry."

I felt my cheeks flush. "I'm not his wife."

"Then what are you doing floating the river with him?"

"It's none of your business!"

The man fingered the trigger on the shotgun.

"Th-that is, it's too long a story to tell. Let it suffice that my name is Harriet Clark and I live on a homestead upriver from Afton's placer claim. This boy is his grandnephew. Afton is taking him to his father's ranch."

"That still don't explain you being here."

"I came along to help care for the boy and to visit my daughter in Lewiston. Now, would you mind telling me who you are?" I was certain I knew the answer.

The man worked a quid between cheek and gum, then spit a string of tobacco juice into the curling grass near my feet. "Name's Ab Pocock." He jerked his head toward the tent. "I wanna see McCabe."

I stepped directly in front of Pocock to block his path. "He's too sick."

Pocock pushed me aside with a stringy, but powerful arm. "I ain't going to bother him. Just wanna make sure you ain't lying."

Pocock's noisy entrance roused Afton. He turned his head from the wall and looked up at Pocock with glazed eyes.

"So it *is* you, McCabe." Pocock's gaze left the gaunt figure on the pallet and roved our quarters, noting with an expression of disapproval my bed on the opposite wall. He studied the open satchel with its assortment of medicines and herbs, the tin plate that served as a tray for the pot of Jade Girl, the canteen and cup for water, the suitcase at the foot of my bed, and Afton's canvas bag pulled open to receive the underwear I'd taken from the line.

While Pocock took inventory, I could see Afton's delirious mind fumble for a time—a place—a name—and finally arrive at distasteful recognition. "What're you doing here, you old shitepoke?"

"Making sure this female was telling the truth. I thought she was your ball and chain at first. Why'd you want to take on all the extra baggage?"

I knew Pocock referred to me, not my belongings. His sarcastic laugh sent a wave of heat up the back of my neck. "It's time you left, Mister Pocock. Afton needs his rest."

"No cause to ruffle your feathers, *Missus* Clark," he said sarcastically. "I'm going. But I want you out of here soon's this old goat can walk."

"My, he's a strange sort," I said to Afton after Pocock had left the tent.

"That he is." Afton wheezed, spoke with effort. "Many's the time I've found him living in caves . . . probably has one up the creek . . . he'll just dig out a bank . . . make a hole big enough to crawl in . . . cover it with an elk hide." He paused to rest, eyes hazing over. "Once . . . once I found him in a cave that had a nice soft floor . . . donkeys had left dried manure . . . a strange sort, all right."

And so are you, Afton McCabe. So are you. But I like you in spite of it, perhaps because of it.

When Pocock showed up in camp next morning I thought he'd come to hurry us on our way. Instead, he waddled up to me on his bandy legs and shoved a bottle into my hand.

"Give McCabe a swig of this twice a day. It'll cure what ails him. Shake it up good."

I wanted to return the greasy bottle, but thought better of it. It wouldn't do to insult Pocock. I held the bottle up to the sky and watched the sunlight turn the muddy liquid to a sickening greenish-brown.

"What's in it?"

"Wake-robin . . . Jack-in-the-pulpit . . . bark . . . wild honey and such . . . an old Indian tonic."

I knew of Indian remedies that cured when other medicines failed, but Afton wasn't likely to swallow this horrid-looking stuff without a fight.

Pocock handed me a round, flat tin with lid. "Rub some of this on his chest."

I stuck the bottle in my apron pocket and opened the tin, wrinkling my nose at the smell of bear grease and some other overpowering scent. "Another Indian remedy?"

"Yup. It's helped me kick death in the ass more'n once."

"I—I suppose we could try it. I am grateful. I don't suppose you'd have any—" I'd wanted to ask for beans, but Pocock had spun on his heel and was retracing his steps across the clearing. I thought about running after him, but his step was so determined I didn't want to risk annoying him. No telling how long we'd have to remain on his land.

"I'm not going to take that snake oil," Afton said when I showed him the bottle. His voice was weak, but he seemed more alert than before, more aware of my movements. "It'd kill me for sure."

"I doubt it has any snake oil in it. And I doubt it will kill you." I wanted to suggest he was too stubborn to die, but didn't. "Mister Pocock claims he uses it."

"That's why he's tetched."

"He's *tetched* because he's spent too much time alone. Like others I could mention."

Afton's eyes sparked like dying coals set in beds of puffy gray ash. "Are you calling me loco?"

"Take it any way you want. Isolation makes people act in strange ways. At times I feel myself growing odd."

"So, you admit it! Now, if I was to—" He broke off in a spell of coughing that ended in a hollow bark that came from deep in his chest. He turned his head to the wall and wheezed a sigh.

I felt his pain. "It won't hurt you to try a sip of this. It might ease the cough."

"You taste it first."

I made a face, unobserved. "Will you take it, if I do?"

Understanding a grunt to mean he would, I poured a tiny bit of the remedy in a spoon and swallowed it. A flaming sensation shot up my nose and down my throat. I gasped. My eyes watered. I swallowed again and again to clear my throat.

Afton heard me rasp for air and rolled his head in my direction. I slid the look of pain from my face. "It isn't bad at all," I lied. "I'm sure it will help." I filled a teaspoon with the liquid fire and attempted to raise his head. He put out an arm to prevent it, but was too weak and groggy to do out-right battle.

"You said you'd take it if I tasted it first, and by heaven you will!"

Afton's mouth slackened in surprise at my nerve. I shoved in the spoon. While he clutched his throat, I took the flannel from his chest, rubbed on Pocock's bear grease, and stood back, panting.

"Jesus Christ! First you strangle me with that poison. Then you rub me with this stinking bear grease. How do you expect me to live with myself?"

"At least you might live!" Blowing a gust of air, I turned to leave. "I'll let you rest now."

"That's real kind of you," he said with sarcasm. "Don't be surprised if I'm dead when you come back."

Despite Pocock's strange ways, I was thankful he lived nearby. His threats kept Toby in camp, and more important, his potions worked. For three days and nights Afton blew and coughed the poison from his system while he made a battle of just about everything I did toward his care. A sure sign he was improving.

The fourth night I was so weary from listening to his racket, I crawled into bed right after supper and slept through the night without waking, not even to the rolls of thunder Afton told me about later. When I did wake, he was sitting up, pulling on socks and shoes. A minute passed before the import of the act slogged its way through my drowsy brain.

"What do you think you're doing?" The words echoed in my head.

"What does it look like, woman?"

"Surely you're not getting up!"

"Aye, I'm getting up. I'm so sore from my bed I feel like I been stomped on by an elephant."

I sat up abruptly and shrugged on my wrapper. "You're not well enough to get up."

"I'll be the judge of that, not you. I never thought I'd see the day I'd let a woman tend me— learning every mole on my body—sharing her tent without half knowing it."

I gave an exclamation of disgust. "It was a matter of necessity. I found no pleasure in your wheezing and coughing."

For a long, shrill moment the air quivered between us. It occurred to me that Afton looked aged, the yellow-gray skin in loose folds on his cheeks. A living skeleton. Like a mop dressed in pants. Then I thought of the reflection I'd seen in the river the previous day—my face haggard, hair braided haphazardly, my eyes surrounded by waxy white puffs. Events had taken their toll on us both.

A look of apology slid over Afton's face. "Och, pay me no mind, Hattie. I guess a man can't come so near to dying without showing his upset. 'Tis grateful I am for your care. Grateful you came along in spite of me." A pause. "Am I forgiven?"

I could think of two good reasons why I shouldn't forgive Afton McCabe. Foremost, I'd suffered his sharp, sick man's tongue for several days and had been repaid for my efforts with more of the same. Secondly, he'd been relentless in his decision to return Toby to his father's ranch. It was he who'd determined to float the boy down the river rather than return him in the comparative safety of a packstring. Because of him, we were in this fix. I considered a host of other reasons, but the humility in his eyes made me weaken. "Oh . . . of course I forgive you. And I'm glad you're feeling better."

With a smile more eloquent than words, he reached across the space between our beds, took my hand, and gave me a slow, thoughtful look that made me flush. I wondered if he knew how that look affected me, or even knew it was there on his face for me to see.

"I'm sorry I took ill on you, Hattie. I know I'm a bear when I'm under the weather. The trip's been hard on you without that. I'll try to do better. I think too much of you to cause you hardship, or to want you angry with me. I've never known a woman who made me feel so . . ." His heartfelt look slipped into one of embarrassment. He released my hand. "I—I'll go start a fire."

Something feathery swept over me as I watched Afton stoop through the doorway, a feeling revived from girlhood and Chester's wooing. I was amazed the sensation arose so easily after such a long time. Affection for Afton seemed to have grown slowly within me, despite the differences which might have prevented it. For a long, shivery moment I let myself dwell on the feeling. I wondered about the depth of Afton's sentiment—to what extent it might grow—wondered if I really wanted that to happen. When a woman felt affection for a man, it stole from her independence. Now that Afton was recovering, needing me less, it dawned on me that I liked my freedom. On the other hand, before he came into my life, I'd known a terrible loneliness.

As I dreamed on, sorting out my emotions, my confused needs, Chester appeared in my mind's eye. He would have thought me the silliest of fools, would have thought I was growing senile. Perhaps I was. It was mindless of me to think I could fill the emptiness left by his death. We'd lived as one for too long. I told myself Afton was simply grateful, that I'd be making a mistake to consider it anything more.

I tried to persuade Afton to remain on Pocock's flat to regain his strength, but his stubborn nature kept him from further rest and care. He acted as if time were snapping at his heels like a herdsman's dog. I vowed not to cause him upset, but did prevent him from setting off down the river that day. I thought about telling him of Toby's attempts to run away, but decided to wait a day or two until he was stronger.

He spent the afternoon replacing the short logs he'd attached to the sweep handles for balance—the green wood had dried and was lighter than he liked. The following day, we shoved off, the morning dry, the sky overcast but lofty, the veiled sun a disc of copper that gave ample light to brighten river and shore.

I lay back against the sideboards, Chitter asleep in my lap, and watched bleached hillsides splashed with rust and green drift by. I felt at peace with nature and myself.

The float was uneventful, with little whitewater, and Afton allowed Toby to man the sweeps while he sat in the bow with the remnant of his cough keeping him from complete rest. I smiled to myself as I watched Toby at the end of those giant sweep handles, pretending with great seriousness to be the man. It reminded me of my own boys during their in-between years, wanting with every atom of their being to act like men, their childish needs and impulses preventing the transformation. The memory brought a lump to my throat, made me more determined than ever to keep Toby under my wing.

I noticed Afton's gaze on me much of the time, his look pensive, as though he were giving me a thorough summing-up. At times the stare became diffused, and despite an effort to suppress romantic thoughts, I believed he might be imagining us in a setting remote from river and scow. I thought I might have given him cause to consider things he hadn't contemplated for years. After all, I'd taken charge of his life for a bit, and he'd come out none the worse for it.

We passed several placer camps. At one camp, the smell of scorched wool told of the miners' habit of burning a sluice blanket to retrieve the gold it had trapped. At another, a lone sourdough hunched beside a crude water wheel with old coffee and lard cans attached for lifting water into a sluice box. The miners at most of these camps were busy grubbing away at their diggings, but they looked up with curiosity when we passed and waved. One miner had strung a cable from one side of the river to the other and was pulling himself across in a bucket big enough to hold a man. He stopped at midstream and waved as we passed underneath.

At French Creek, a wagon road wound down the southern hillsides from the Warren mining district. The road crossed the river on a bridge, then slithered up the north slopes in the direction of the Florence diggings. A wagon rumbled across the bridge as we skimmed underneath. It seemed strange to hear horses' hooves and wheels biting into the wooden planks.

The sound brought back recollections of Lewiston, where winds carried the clop and thud of wagon traffic to our house on the bluff. Images of that other time and place paraded before my inner eye, snippets of memory I'd stuffed in a pocket of my mind to carry forever—the faces of family and friends, the voices and mannerisms that made them unique.

I thought of my sons, each so different from the other. Alan, the younger of the two, was still at Stanford. He'd received a master's degree and was working on a doctorate in philosophy. If he could, he'd remain a university student the rest of his life. He was born craving knowledge, craving understanding beyond most of us, craving all the vibrance and music of the earth. He'd always go on searching, believing there was more to life than he could possibly experience in his lifetime.

On the other hand, Walter was content with small things. Since a boy, he'd wanted to try his hand at farming, had spent summers as a hired hand on wheat farms in the Palouse, saving his money to buy a little spread. He needed more land, barely broke even each year, but he demonstrated a natural bent for farming and a good head for the economics involved. He'd keep his family secure, happy.

The sentimental thoughts about my boys led far, far into the past to my own childhood in San Francisco, to Chester's courtship, to the thrill of those first years of marriage. If I could relive those days, I'd take such a hold on them they'd stretch on forever. But no amount of wishing could bring that to pass.

Life was like the river. The current sped us along in unexpected directions, one minute drifting peacefully, the next caught up in a tumult of experience and emotion that allowed little time for reflection or to cherish things dear. Without a prophet's talent, how could I predict which moments or which sensations on this eventful trip would later hold the most meaning. Thus far I'd been overwhelmed by the rapids, by the calamities that had taken their toll, by the very fact that I, Hattie Clark, was sitting in a scow floating the mighty Salmon, the River of No Return.

19

The river was kind to us that day, yet Afton tired easily, and we stopped to make camp after only eight miles of travel. He threw himself down on his bedroll the minute we laid it beneath the wagon sheet. I'd slept well the night before and had been resting all day, so I sat outside the tent on a rock, studying the partially completed relief of Afton and Toby.

The carving of Toby pleased me, but I couldn't decide on the expression to give Afton's eyes and had left them blank spheres until some spark of creativity answered my dilemma. I'd come to see many facets of Afton's character during the trip, with the attending facial expressions that at one time had seemed foreign to his nature—a reckless daring, an alertness to beauty, humor, also kindness and affection. Having come to understand him better, I'd already softened the creases I'd carved around the mouth.

I took up a piece of driftwood to experiment with the expression in the eyes before I set to work on the carving. Dissatisfied with the first two attempts, I put knife on wood to begin again.

Toby came from a pile of rocks where horned lizards had been sunning themselves and stood beside me, petting one of the spiny things. "Why are you carving that stick?" he asked after a bit.

"I'm trying to find the best expression for your uncle's eyes." I continued to pare with the knife. "The eyes are hardest for me, and I don't want to make a mistake on the relief. Too deep a gouge in the wrong place can spoil the features."

Toby studied the pine relief at my side, then pointed to the blank space that spanned the bottom. "Aren't you going to put anything there?"

I glanced over at the relief, than back to my carving. "Yes, but I haven't decided what . . . something both you and your uncle would like . . . something important in your life together. I've thought about carving a strip of mountains with a river running through it . . . perhaps a gold cradle on the riverbank . . . I don't know . . . you and your uncle can help me decide."

"You're important to us."

I glanced up. "You mean, put myself in the carving?"

"Uh-huh."

"It's nice of you to say that, Toby . . . very nice. But the space is too long and thin. A face wouldn't look right. And I'm not sure your uncle would agree I'm that important."

"Yes he would! He told me you were the . . . umm . . ." He pressed a finger against his chin searching for the word his uncle had used. "The finest woman he'd ever known."

The blood rushed to my cheeks. Afton *had* intended more than gratitude when he held my hand. I knew I'd have trouble keeping the knowledge from showing next time I faced him. It did something to a woman to know a man thought highly of her. It brought out her femininity and interest almost against her will.

I didn't have to face Afton that night. He was so tired he slept through supper, and roused only momentarily when Toby and I went to bed for the night and woke Reb, who lay beneath the canvas shelter with his master.

Afton was somewhat stronger the next day, and when we began our float, he seemed to appreciate the balming warmth reflected from the water and the canyon walls. The day seemed timeless, tempting me to think September would last forever. The hillsides were muted with a soft haze, the air filled with the smell of ripened grass and sun-warmed pines, the buzz of dragonflies' wings and the drone of wasps. The day induced the strange mix of inner warmth and melancholy I always felt at the dying off of summer.

In my languid state, I heard the rapids long before they made an impression, an irregular drumming and roaring that mounted and waned, mounted and waned on a fickle breeze.

Afton rose from his lethargy, setting the muscles in his jaw. His fists explored the sweep handles for the best hold. "Tie yourselves good and tight. 'Tis a bad one coming up."

I checked Toby's fastenings and, in doing so, noticed Chitter had gnawed her leash nearly in two. "Don't let go of her," I warned the boy. "It won't take much to break that rope."

A bend in the river opened onto a sight that shattered what remained of my peaceful state. A hundred yards downriver, the current battled a huge dump of boulders in a tremendous eruption of spray and foam. The boulders, some jutting their brown heads above water, some skulking just beneath the surface, seemed to bar the way completely.

Afton riveted his attention on the heaped-up waves along the north side of the river. Gripping the sweep handles in fierce recognition of what lay ahead, he steered the scow to the right.

The boat hit the waves, reared, started to turn broadside. Afton fought the sideways motion, sending the scow into the foam. A wall of water flung itself across the bow. One huge wave, rolling cross current, caught our port side and tipped us dangerously.

The force of the wave hurled me from my seat and on top of Toby—he'd fallen onto the oilskin tent bag tied to the floorboards. The sweep handle passed within a few inches of my head. I grabbed the pole where it entered its channel in the stern. "Hold on to me," I yelled to Toby. I thought it the only chance he'd have against the river. The angle of the scow's tilt was so great I was sure we'd be gobbled up in the waves and the roar.

Waves breaking over the tipped sideboard tried to suck us into the river. I held onto the sweep handle with such effort, I feared the muscles in my arms would tear. Toby clutched my skirts. I thought I heard him cry out.

With a lurch, the scow righted itself, throwing me against the pole. I hit my head.

Dazed, drenched, and deafened, I climbed onto the bench and sat, trying to slow my galloping heart.

Afton had been thrown from the sweep deck, but had managed to keep his grip on the bow sweep. He pulled himself onto the deck and caught the handle of the careening rear sweep before it could slam him in the back.

Reb slithered out from under the deck and shook a gallon of water from his coat.

We'd shaved through a gap in the rocks and were crashing through the unyielding green waves beyond. Above the whack of hull on wave, I heard Toby's cries grow to a scream. He was bent over the gunwale, pointing into the river.

"Chitter's going to drown! She's going to drown!" he cried over and over.

I stood up, working to keep my balance in the bucking scow. Chitter was on the left, slightly ahead of the bow. Haystack waves alternately pulled her into the bottom of a swell and lifted her to the crest. She splatted the water frantically in a struggle to stay afloat. Reb saw her from his perch in the bow and leaped into the river, intent on saving the coon.

Afton was in a panic, trying to control the scow while he followed the plight of dog and coon. I had my own problems, trying to keep Toby from falling overboard.

"Don't worry!" Afton yelled across his shoulder. "Coons can swim like fish."

We'd cleared the string of waves, ahead of us a stretch of smaller whitewater. Chitter crossed in front of us in a frenzied attempt to reach shore, her head barely visible on the choppy waves. Reb gained on the coon, paddling with such strength the water curled out from his chest in great scrolls. He was about to set his mouth on the loose hair of her neck when a crosswave flung her into a souse hole at the base of a rock. She vanished in the whirling pool.

Reb swam in circles at the edge of the whirlpool, fighting the tremendous suction. He turned his head from side to side, looking for the coon.

"Forget the coon and save yourself!" Afton yelled at the dog. "Shore!"

Reb continued to swim in circles a few seconds, as if undecided, then let the current sweep him downstream. Gagging, sinking low in the water from exhaustion, he reached the riverbank and dragged himself through the rocks. He took a minute or two to retch the water from his lungs, then lumbered over the boulders at water's edge, keeping us in sight.

The boat had stopped its leaping, the grumbling of the rapids grown fainter.

Afton stood on the raised deck, shouting, "Goddamned river! Take an innocent, will you!"

I thought Toby would curl up and die. I folded him in my arms, but he just rocked and rocked. Tears streamed down his face. In between sobs he murmured, "It's all my fault. I should of put a new rope on her." He looked into his uncle's face as if he expected blame, but there was none there, only sympathy.

Afton found an eddy where we could beach the scow and threw the rope to Reb, who'd caught up to us despite his fatigue. Dismally, we searched the riverbank between our landing spot and the rapids, expecting to find a sodden body washed up on shore. I hurt terribly for Toby, and it wrenched my heart to think of the little coon, a victim of the river on a trip she needn't have made. Reb, too, was hurting. Every once in a while, he'd stare in the direction of the whirlpool and bark.

When we found no sign of Chitter upstream, we searched downstream from the scow. We looked around every water-washed rock, every mound of flotsam. Reb waded along, a few feet out in the river. He whined constantly, stopped now and then to look upstream.

We'd gone a half mile when Toby yelled and pointed out over the river. Fifty feet from shore, a log had wedged between two large boulders. At first, I thought a soggy rag had caught on the splintered log. Then the rag moved, took on the shape of a coon preening her coat.

"Chitter! Chitter! It's me," Toby yelled, waving his arms.

Afton and I called and waved, too, our voices shrill with relief and happiness.

The coon looked up from her preening, pricked her ears this way and that, finally spotted us on the riverbank. With a squeal, she launched herself from the log and paddled for shore.

Reb bounded through the water to meet her.

Toby rushed into the river unheeding, Afton right behind.

Tucking my skirt between my legs, I let joy propel me through the shallows. The survival of one small animal could never make amends for Chester's drowning. Still, I felt victorious, avenged. A strange sense of power swept over me. I wanted to climb the highest mountaintop and shout, "Chitter lives!" I wanted to take up spear and headdress, stomp my feet in dance, utter a primitive cry.

20

We camped that night on the rocky shore where we'd stopped to look for Chitter, an almost impossible place, with little room for the tent, and scant wood. Smoke from our sluggish fire twined upward, disappearing in a bank of clouds that trailed along the hillside.

When we woke next morning, the cold, gray clouds smothered the canyon, dipping fingers of mist into the deep ravines. They compressed our world to river and shore. Along the Salmon we could expect a week of false winter before Indian summer arrived, promising days forever balmy and sweet. Since our original plans had called for us to arrive in Lewiston by the seventh of September, and we were well beyond that date, this storm had caught us unprepared. Shivering in my cotton blouse and skirt, I unpacked the sweater to wear under my jacket and wound a woolen scarf around my head and throat. Still, the cold seeped through to my bones.

I was dropping spoonfuls of flour-lean batter

onto the fry pan when Toby dragged himself from the tent, head hung. His hair stuck out in all directions. His mouth curved downward like a sullen Cheshire cat's. His dread had returned since we'd left Pocock's flat. Even his joy over Chitter's miraculous survival had dwindled during the night. He stood by the fire and shivered beneath his thin coat. Before he'd left McCabe's Bar, I'd tried to persuade him to take Chester's fleece-lined jacket, but the coat was so large he was afraid he'd be laughed at if anyone saw him in it.

He stared at the ground, moping, while I kept up a one-sided conversation, talking of Sadie, Highpockets, and the goats back at the ranch. I reminded myself aloud that if I stayed in Lewiston for the winter, I'd have to write Len Johnson about further arrangements for the animals.

I'd toyed with the idea of visiting San Francisco after the wedding. I could visit my son, Alan, and my sister, Beatrice. There were advantages and disadvantages to such a plan. On the one hand, I could revisit my childhood home, the opera, Golden Gate Park, the Academy, places fixed indelibly in my mind as giving profound pleasure. On the other hand, Beatrice would expect me to follow like a puppy on her shopping sprees, dress up to meet society, keep up mindless chatter at parties. I'd have to patronize untalented artists and musicians along with those more worthy. I'd have to pretend tolerance with my son's collegiate attitudes, with professors whose minds were in some other universe—at least, that's how Alan described them. I wondered if I could waken my dormant social and mental skills to that extent.

In the wilds, our strivings were simple and to the point—to stay fed—warm—alive. Here, every creature knew its place. Every tree had its spot of earth. Man was true to his nature, or failed to survive.

Afton crawled from under the wagon sheet and put an end to my ponderings. He wore a sweater beneath his mackinaw, a woolen cap, and gloves. Even so, I worried the cold might slow his recovery. He sat on a boulder, propped his elbows on his knees, and cradled his head. I hadn't expected cheer, but this gathering had the optimism of an undertaker's meeting. We sat on our cold rocks and ate without speaking. I'm certain our thoughts followed similar shadowy paths, but none of us wished to give voice and substance to our feelings.

Afton was the first to interrupt the gloom. He put his fist at his mouth and cleared his throat in the ritual I'd come to know as a prologue to talk. "It bothers me to see you so glum, lad," he said to Toby. "I'm sorry I brought all this misery upon us."

"You mustn't blame yourself," I put in. "You can't expect—"

"Don't go making excuses for me. I need to confess my guilt before it keeps me from another night's sleep." He took a sip of coffee and wrapped his hands around the warmth of the cup. "'Tis I that insisted on bringing the lad downriver. I see now I was just trying to stay young . . . relive my youth in the boy. I wanted to stir in him the same excitement and love of the river I feel. Instead, I've showed him fear and brought him close to grieving the loss of his pet." He raised his head and looked at me with an expression of regret so deep I had to lower my eyes. "You, too, Hattie . . . I've made you endure things you needn't have."

"You didn't ask me to come along. I chose to do so of my own free will. If I've been foolhardy, it's my own f—"

"I forced you to it! I should of listened to you when you tried to talk me out of the trip."

"What's done is done. You've been an example of courage Toby will never forget."

"Sure I have!" he said cynically. "Showed him what it's like to be old, and stubborn as a mule."

I reached across the space between us and put my hand on his knee. "Don't talk like that. You've faced more danger in seventeen days than most men would face in two lifetimes. And you've done it with little concern for yourself. I admire you for it, Afton McCabe. Toby does, too. Don't you, Toby?"

Toby took his glazed stare from the campfire and nodded. "He's braver'n I'll ever be."

I detected a flush of pink beneath the pallor of Afton's illness. He fingered his cup self-consciously. "You don't need to say that just to make me feel good . . . but I thank you. And lad, you're twice as brave as I was at your age. Did you not cross the highlands by yourself to find me? I may be an old fool, but I'll try my best to get you home in one piece."

At the mention of home, Toby's scowl deepened. He hauled himself to his feet and walked down the riverbank, threading his way through the slender aisles between rocks.

Afton watched the boy with eyes inscrutable beneath their heavy lids. "Do you still think I'm wrong to make him patch things up with his father?"

"It would be fine if Frank were a changed person. But from what Toby tells me, I doubt that's possible."

"I have to admit, the closer we get, the more I'm inclined to agree."

I couldn't believe my ears. I hesitated, almost afraid to ask the question that had burned in my mind for so many weeks. "Are you . . . that is, what will you do, if you don't leave him at Frank's?"

"I've not decided. I may hole up with him in Whitebird for the winter."

"He's welcome to stay with me in Lewiston. I could find a flat with enough room. He could visit my daughters. They both love children, and Marybelle has little ones to play with."

"You don't need to do that. The lad is mine to care for."

"I know you love him, Afton, but you need to consider what's best for the boy. I could give him the same care as a mother. I could sew for him, see he got off to a good start at school, things that are hard for a man to do." I tried not to sound too anxious.

I realized I'd failed when hurt showed in Afton's eyes. He spent a while alternately sipping coffee and gazing in Toby's direction. The boy had stopped a hundred yards downriver and was skipping rocks across the surface of the water.

"I'm still hoping Frank will do what's needed for the lad,"

"I'm terribly afraid he won't. I've put off telling you this because of your health. But it's time you knew." I hugged my jacket tight around me, as much from apprehension as from the cold. "Twice on this trip, Toby has tried to run away."

Afton spun his head around. "The devil he has! When?"

"Our first night out . . . again at Pocock's flat."

"Did he give a reason?"

"He's afraid of his father. Afraid he'll send him back to the Pardees. Mainly afraid of what his father will do to him."

"I don't intend to let Frank send him back to the Pardees. I've seen what they did to him. But I didn't know the boy was that scared of his father. I thought he'd just gotten the usual whippings a lad can expect when he's growing up." Again, he looked in Toby's direction. The boy was throwing sticks in the river for Reb and the coon to retrieve. Every time Reb brought in a stick, the coon would pull it from his mouth.

"Maybe the lad's more fearful of whippings than most."

"It's something much worse. But he won't tell me what."

Afton's face clouded. He kicked the pebbles at his feet, taking his time to reply. "Guess that changes the color of the sands. I'll have to give some hard thought as to what I should do with the lad."

He sat a long while with head bent, rubbing his tall forehead. I'd given up on talk and was gathering the tin plates and forks in the dishpan. "I've been thinking, Hattie," he said to my back, "no matter what happens, you can catch the stage at Whitebird. It's about ten miles past Frank's. No sense traveling any farther by river than you want."

The idea took me by surprise. It disturbed and saddened. Amazingly, I didn't want to leave the river, and I hated to think of leaving Afton. I turned slowly to face him. His eyes said he felt the same.

"Is Whitebird as far as you'll go?"

"I may float the scow to Lewiston. I've . . . I've friends there." His expression turned more vulnerable, as if he wished for something beyond reach.

I was suffering my own illusions. My heart pumped faster at the possibility Afton might stay in Lewiston. "Why don't you take the stage with me? It would be safer—and a pleasure to have your company." I felt myself blush. "That is—I—I'd like you to be at the stage stop to meet my daughters."

"You wouldn't want to be seen with an old river rat like me."

"You're not a river rat! I admire you, Afton McCabe, and I'd be proud to travel with you."

Afton's face took on the color of brick. He stared at me skeptically, squirming on the rock.

"I want my grandchildren to know someone with your courage. Think of the tales you can tell."

He stared at me a moment longer, as if unconvinced, then relaxed into a smile. "Well . . . in that case, I'll give some thought to taking the stage and meeting your girls."

In the miles ahead, the canyon showed more sign of settlement. Cabins stood on bluffs above the river and near the mouths of streams. Livestock dotted the slopes. In young orchards, apples shone red through the gloom. Except for locust and pine that filed up and down spring draws and along creek beds, the lower elevations on the south-facing slopes were bare of timber and strewn with volcanic rock. A gray-brown gumbo lined some of the draws, with an occasional patch of wiregrass to mark a spring. The float was tranquil, though frigid, the river like a sheet of polished metal beneath the leaden sky. Every now and then we skirted an island where willows turned their leaves against the chill.

On a bluff at the great northward bend in the river—the general direction the river would follow until it made one last turn into the Snake—a few farmsteads clustered around a one-room school. We stopped to warm ourselves at the McVeighs, sheep ranchers whom Afton had known for many years. They were slight, straight-backed, their arms ropy with sinew. Afton's fellow Scotsmen seemed to have won his approval, for it was he who suggested we stop to visit.

The McVeighs' cabin sat at the back of the barren flat amid lodge rings and other signs of Nez

Perce encampment. The exterior of the house was
made of shakes, the chimney of volcanic rock. The
interior was spartan, but comfortably warmed by a
fire sputtering on the hearth.

A wall divided the house into a large living
room-kitchen-bedroom and a smaller room where
the four McVeigh boys slept. Mary McVeigh called
them "boys," but they were really young men
in their late teens and twenties, away at the time
herding sheep. A red and yellow quilt splashed
color on an iron bedstead that filled one corner of
the sitting room. A range stood in the opposite
corner flanked by resinous stacks of pine. A table
of slab-wood fronted the range.

We sat around the table to share pot-luck, end-
ing the meal with Mary's shortbread. As in many
ranch homes, and in most Scots', dinner was
devoted to food, not talk. Children, especially,
were to be seen and not heard. That didn't seem to
bother Toby. Worry had strung his nerves tight.
He picked at his dinner and asked to be excused as
soon as good manners permitted. When he closed
the door behind himself, I wondered if I'd see the
boy again. A trail, connecting river settlements in
the north with these farms, left the Salmon at this
point and headed south over the mountains. It
would be no trick for Toby to hitch rides until he
reached Boise, where he could lose himself in the
crowds.

Worry over Toby made it difficult for me to
concentrate on the after-dinner talk, but Afton
appeared content. He seemed to have accepted the
fact he was worn out and was in no rush to leave

the McVeighs. While Mary and I cleared away the dishes, he and John sat on sheepskin chairs by the hearth, spun yarns, and shared news John had gleaned from the ranchers' grapevine.

While I worked, I noted the deep lines that had stamped Mary's face with a look of bleak resolve, noted her swollen, twisted fingers, the raised veins that ran like rivers of blue ink through the wrinkled skin of her hands. I saw the way she put her hand at her back and closed her eyes in obvious pain. Age and ranch life had taken its toll. I knew the feeling, though I'd been ranching only five years, Mary for a lifetime. If I were to stay at Weasel Creek, I questioned how much longer I could do the heavy chores, grow a large garden, and raise enough stock to see me through the year. Unlike me, the McVeighs lived where they could get supplies to their cabin by wagon road.

"I wouldn't be in a hurry to get to Frank and Will's place," I heard John say in his clipped speech. "The cattlemen have been pulling dirty tricks to run them out of the country. Frank'll likely be more unsociable than ever. Poor Will's about to give up. Keeps talking about going to the Klondike." Will was Frank's brother, a man Toby spoke of in kind terms.

"I was hoping the vigilantes had done with that sort of thing," Afton replied.

"They haven't. 'Tis why we moved our sheep operation from Lucile. Got tired of tangling with them."

"What sort of things have the vigilantes done to Frank?" I asked. I hoped to learn something that would persuade Afton not to leave Toby at Frank's.

John gave me a sideways glance that said I had no business intruding in a conversation between men. "Oh . . . they tore down his fences. Put a rattlesnake in his oven." Then to Afton, "They did worse to one of his neighbors. Happened just a few days ago." His mottled face turned grave. "'Tisn't nice to tell. If they'd done it to me, I'd have killed the lot of them."

Mary whanged a dishpan onto the table. "I'd horsewhipped them first."

"Och! What would you know about such things, Mary?" John said with acid in his voice. "'Tisn't a woman's place to say, anyhow."

Mary's thin, fox-like face took on a hard, closed look. She went to the stove for a tea kettle and poured scalding water into the dishpan with a vengeance. Chester would never have spoken to me in the way John did to Mary. But Chester wasn't the usual husband. He'd never kept me under his thumb or kept me from speaking my mind. And Afton? He'd tried to put me in my place a few times, but eventually apologized. I doubted the word "sorry" was in John's vocabulary.

Afton had leaned forward in his chair, intent on questioning McVeigh. "I'd like to know what other danger there might be. I might want to change my plans for Toby."

"Hard to tell about them cattlemen." John looked my way briefly, pulling at the loose folds of his neck, as if wondering how much he should say in my presence. "Rumor has it a bunch of cowboys from Lucile raided a sheep camp in the high country. They killed the herder when he tried to run them off. Killed two hundred sheep, they did, and left man and sheep for the buzzards to pick on."

My stomach shriveled at the thought. I took a plate from the cloth where Mary had set it to drain and dried it absently while I thought of the horrible deed—of Toby—Frank—the vigilantes. In the background, John and Afton's voices droned on.

"What kind of men are these cattlemen that they'd do such a thing?" Afton asked.

"Ordinary men," John said. "Take each man on his own and he's not such a bad sort. Put them together, goading each other with hate and drink, and they turn into a pack of wolves."

"I've often wondered why Frank and Will switched from cattle back to sheeping like their parents," Afton said. "They must of known they'd pucker them cattle boys good."

"'Tis my recollection they made the switch when the price of beef was down."

"Also, the rains ruined the hay crop and they couldn't feed," Mary said to me on the side. "They must of thought sheep easier to keep."

John heard and clucked his tongue in disagreement. "I'd say it's six of one, half-dozen of t'other. Depends on which animals rile you the least. 'Til we can bring peace to the range, it's no good to be in either business. Leastways, not on the Salmon."

Afton had begun to fidget, and I sensed the conversation made him nervous. It was time we left, anyway. He planned to float a series of rapids before we stopped to camp, but from the weariness in his face, I wondered if we'd get that far.

As soon as I'd dried the dishes, I told Mary I needed something from the scow and went outside. Actually, I hoped to check on Toby before Afton left his chair.

Nothing moved on the threadbare slopes behind the sheep corrals, and except for clumps of locust and hawthorn that could hide someone, the bluff offered no sign of the boy. The steep bank kept me from seeing the river. Clouds hung overhead like a shroud, and a soft, sleety mist touched my cheeks. My throat tightened at the thought of Toby running off, caught in the storm when it broke.

Concern became reality when I descended the bank that hid the scow from view of the house. Toby was climbing from the rear of the scow onto the raised deck, bag of clothes in hand. Reb and Chitter romped on the shore. Since the near-drowning, the coon seemed to rank over Afton in the dog's loyalties.

"What are you doing?" I asked Toby as I closed the distance between us.

Toby spun around. A shock seemed to go through the boy. A wary play of thought troubled his face. He dropped the bag into the clutter on the floor and picked up Afton's fishing rod. "I—I thought I'd go fishing," he said in a struggle to master his voice.

"Are you going to use socks for bait?"

He shot a guilty look at the bag. "Uhh—no—I—"

"You needn't lie to me. I'm not going to scold you." I crossed the plank and stood on the raised deck with my hands on the boy's shoulders. He hung his head, his gaze on the timbers at his feet. "Did you give any thought to where you'd go?"

It took him a while to arrange an answer. "Umm . . . maybe to Boise and get me a job."

"You'd have a hard time of it. A nine-year-old can earn only pennies. Maybe enough for a few scraps of food, but not enough to fill your stomach. Where would you live? Who'd take care of you?" I ran my fingers along his cheek and through hair that strung from beneath his farmboy's hat. "Who would you find to love you as much as your uncle and I do?"

His lips curled into a soft pout. "How can you say you love me when you're going to take me back to my pa?"

I bent low to look into his eyes. "I've told you before. Your uncle thinks facing your father will help you become a man. It's because he loves you that he's gone to the trouble of bringing you out of the wilds. If he didn't care, he'd never have kept you in the first place, nor would he be risking his life on the river."

"You say that because you don't know—" His voice choked. His head continued to droop. "You had a family that wanted you. Your father didn't . . ."

"Didn't what?"

"Oh . . . beat up on you . . . yell at you all the time . . . worse things."

"I'm sorry you've had to endure that. If your uncle and I have anything to do with it, you won't have to again. But we need to talk things over with your father."

Toby looked up then, eyes full of fright.

"I know how afraid you are of your father. But in this life, we all have to confront things we'd rather not. There've been times when I've wanted to catch a stage . . . jump on a train . . . board a ship and go to the ends of the earth . . . anywhere so I wouldn't have to face frustration and sorrow. But we can't run away from life. Wherever we go, trouble skulks around the corner. You just have to thumb your nose at it and go on your way, making life as worthwhile as possible."

"I can't do that at Pa's! Or Pardees! And if we tell Pa I'm not going to stay, he'd just kill me like he—" His eyes startled, as if the words had slipped from his mouth against his will. Snapping his mouth closed on further talk, he picked up the bag of clothes and hurried down the plank.

21

I had no time to dwell on the boy's troubling words. Desperate to stop him, I cried, "Very well, then, run away! But I warn you, the upset might cause your uncle to have another seizure."

On shore, Toby brought himself up short. He'd noted the change in my tone and altered his rebellious expression to a defensive frown. "I can't help it if . . . he wouldn't . . ."

"You do love your uncle, don't you?"

A wary nod.

"Then think about what I've said. You have to have faith things will turn out for the best. Now come put your bag away." I hoped Toby would discover the wisdom of his child's mind and choose to face his problems. If he ran, I'd have no chance of catching him.

I watched him intently for a moment or two, then as casually as I could, I turned back to search for the saddlebag that held my clothes. From it, I took a potholder, one I'd crocheted for Jennie but had decided to give Mary McVeigh. I could make one for Jennie later.

Toby hadn't moved. I waved the potholder in the air. "Now that I have what I came after, let's get back to the house."

He glanced over his shoulder in the direction of the Boise trail a couple of times, then dragged himself up the gangplank, sucking in his cheeks. He set his bag of clothes on the floorboards, then joined me on the riverbank, his eyes dismal, his gaze on the ground.

I put my hand on his shoulder and stroked it gently. "You did the right thing, Toby. You won't be sorry." I hoped that was true. "One thing before we go. I—I'd like you to tell me what you meant about your father killing you. That was a startling thing to say."

His chin began to tremble. He turned his head aside. "Nothing. Just never mind."

Nothing? How could it be nothing! All manner of images flashed through my mind, images of a father with gun in hand—knife—a rope for strangling.

When would I learn the truth?

John and Mary tried to convince Afton we should stay overnight because of the weather. Always afraid to impose on others, he declined. We visited a while longer, then the McVeighs heaped provisions on us and put on their wraps to see us off. After promising to visit again, we left them standing together on the shore, waving, and watched them until they became tiny stick figures against the dun-colored hills.

I hunched on the seat, hugging myself against the cold, pinching my nostrils at the smell of bilge water and mildew. I hadn't minded the smell when the sun shone, but wrapped in the iron-gray of river and sky, all things seemed disagreeable. At least no wind funneled up the canyon. The storm seemed suspended, waiting for a signal to dump its white load.

The low clouds held sound in the river bottom, making it possible to hear the first rapids long before we reached them. I prepared myself for a rough ride, but found we'd been through worse. Afton did have to avoid a monumental rock on the right and a deep hole on the left. The tricky maneuver wrung more energy from him than he had to give, but the second rapid was upon us before he could rest. By the time he'd negotiated a series of haystack waves at the tail of the second rapid, he looked white and pressed his hand against his chest. He called me to the sweep deck.

"You and Toby will have to man the sweeps."

In the distance, spray marked a third rapid. "We can't take it through that whitewater!"

"Yes, you can! Just aim to the right, so she's about ten yards from shore." Those scant directions given, Afton shoved the sweep handles into my fists and crumpled amid the rummage in the bow. Reb scrambled to his side and put a wet nose in his face.

The river had narrowed, condensing the back-

bone of current into a formidable ridge of humping water. On each side, ominous trenches and ripples betrayed hidden dangers in the bed. Our
speed increased to that of a runaway locomotive.
My skirts twined around my legs. My scarf cracked
like a whip in the breeze. Toby had tied the coon
to the floorboards, and stood beside me, clutching
the rear sweep as if his life depended on it.

I felt like a worthless stump. In Afton's hands,
the sweeps had seemed easily managed, obeying
every movement of arm and wrist. He bent into
them with all his might at times, but for the most
part stayed the master. In my hands, they behaved
like the unwieldy poles they were. Push down too
hard, and the blade leaped from the water. Too little pressure, and the blade dove beneath the
surface. The trick was to keep the blade riding the
surface, the pole never submerged.

Toby had practiced with the sweeps more than
I, but not in whitewater, and there was no time for
practice. The first choppy waves were upon us. Just
ahead, the river splashed upon rocks and
rebounded, hitting with what seemed tons of hiss-
ing spray.

"There'll be lots of rocks all the way across the
river, and lots of splashing," Afton said from where
he lay. "You'll not be able to see the channel. Just
keep the distance I told you. We'll go right
between that big rock on shore and that mess of
rocks on the left." He paused, his lungs pulling at
the air. "Hold the sweeps out of the water when
you're not using them . . . they'll snag on a rock."

Afton was daft if he thought I could control

the sweep. The pole swerved on its pivot, tore at my hands, threatened to toss me into the river. Hoping I was correct in my judgment, I told Toby to pull on his sweep handle so the blade would go to the right. "Harder!" I grit my teeth, and pulled on my own sweep. I had no hope I could take us through without swamping, but, by God, I'd try.

I lost all sense of self as I fixed my attention on the headlong rush. I became part of the cataract— the thundering, the splashing, the violent pitch and toss, the rolling, murky water. It was as though the river had already claimed me, and I had given myself willingly.

A loud *crack!* brought my senses back to the scow. I looked around in time to see Toby's sweep handle cut the air, barely missing his head. A rock had snapped the blade from the pole, leaving it useless.

Afton sat up abruptly, his clothes drenched. He crawled onto the raised deck and tied the broken sweep handle to a metal eye on the deck. He tied my sweep as well, to keep it from accident until we'd passed through water churning itself white. We'd shot between the worst of the rocks and hit diagonal waves that tossed the boat about without direction. To keep our balance, we dropped to our knees. I held onto Toby and Afton with a desperate grip.

In that instant, I recalled a painting I'd seen somewhere in my youth of an immigrant family clutching one another on the sinking deck of a sailing ship, their eyes fixed in terror on the storm-tossed seas. We were experiencing a similar fright.

Somehow the scow muddled through the worst of the waves and we rocked into quieter water. Still huddled together on the deck, Afton took my hand. His eyes were soft, filled with esteem. "I'm proud of you, Hattie. You set our course just right. You have real grit." He took Toby's hand and squeezed it. "You, too, lad."

A mix of pride and embarrassment brought warmth to my face. I gave a little "huh" of a laugh. "I don't know if it was grit or desperation."

Despite Afton's words, I knew luck deserved the praise. We'd come so close to disaster, I thought it a dream we'd made it through.

"I won't let you take the scow past Whitebird," I told Afton as we sat around the fire that evening. We'd set up camp beside a wagon road that followed the east bank of the river. No one had come along the road as yet, possibly because the sky spit tiny pellets of snow and promised a full-fledged storm. Afton sat on a stump, about to fold from exhaustion. Toby had gone to the river's edge to put the fry pan to soak and had stayed to throw stones at a boulder a few yards from shore.

"You've done too much after your illness," I went on. "You're going to ride the stage with me. In fact, if we could catch a wagon going toward Whitebird, I'd say we should give up the river here and now."

"No need to fret," Afton muttered. "I've already decided to take the stage."

"And will you take a wagon from here?"

"'Tis no bad water between here and Frank's place."

"But the sweep . . ."

"We can get by with one. Besides, there's no telling how long we'd have to wait for a wagon to pass by."

I didn't argue the point further. A greater concern weighed on my mind. I leaned toward Afton, voice low. "There's something I need to tell you before Toby comes back. When we were at the McVeighs, I found him trying to run away. I convinced him to stay, but in the process, he told me something terrible." I repeated the boy's words.

Afton's eyes narrowed. The trenches at the corners of his mouth deepened. "That's all he said?"

"Just, 'Pa'd kill me, like he—' He broke off without finishing and wouldn't say more. Who do you suppose Frank killed?"

"Maybe it wasn't a 'who' but a 'thing.' Maybe some animal the boy was attached to. Or maybe it's something his mind's cooked up."

"We can't be sure, can we? I'm afraid something terrible will happen to the boy. We simply *must* take him on to Lewiston. It might be a mistake to even stop at Frank's."

As was his habit when worried, Afton rubbed his forehead and sucked a tooth. "I'm not against taking the lad to Lewiston, mind you, but Frank has a right to know. It may be he's had so much trouble he'd be glad to be rid of the boy. Then we can take him on the stage with us." He eased the worry from his face and smiled knowingly. "'Tis what you've wanted all along, isn't it?"

Next morning, the canvas roof sagged beneath four inches of wet snow. The blizzard had stopped, except for an occasional flake drifting down through fog that rose from the river and enveloped camp.

Toby and I stood just outside the tent, passing judgment on the day. Afton's watery eyes peered out from his nest of blankets beneath the wagon sheet. "'Tis too cold to be on the river. We'll hole up for a day and rest." Snuffling, he pulled the rough-spun blankets up over his nose.

I could see the relief spread across Toby's face. A twenty-four-hour reprieve.

I, too, was glad. Not only for Toby, but because I hadn't brought clothes suitable for cold weather. In the tent I could wrap a blanket around myself.

The following dawn broke to clear skies, the smell of frozen greenery strong in the windless morning. We waited for the sun to rise above the eastern hills before we left our beds to venture down the sparkling canyon. Even then, the scow shattered a thin sheet of ice that fanned out from shore. Continuing its northerly course, the Salmon sliced through pasture lands and hay fields, the stubble bristling gold above the fallen snow. Livestock turned their frosty flanks to the sun. Wilted sunflowers could no longer seek the light. I thought how peaceful it was to drift along the Salmon's glossy surface, and actually regretted the trip was near an end.

Every few miles, ferries connected the rutted wagon path with ranches on the west bank of the river. Here and there, farm buildings nestled beneath a sheltering hill or within a grove of cottonwoods. Scarves of smoke spiraled thick and slow from chimneys, a silent protest against the cold.

I had mixed feelings about returning to the settlements for good. On the one hand, the thought of living among women and talking my fool head off, of opening my little gallery, excited me. On the other hand, I already missed the solitude and beauty of the upper Salmon. I missed my vegetable garden, the animals. I wondered if being among old friends, in settings I'd shared with Chester, would affect my relationship with Afton. Returning to one's roots could often destroy something new. I had the feeling it had already begun to distance us. Afton's remark about my not wanting to be seen with a river rat testified to that.

The war between the cattlemen and sheepmen was even more unsettling. I'd heard the problem had already split Lewiston into two camps. I'd seen the harsh side of wilderness, and thought its savagery no worse than men killing each other over grazing land. San Francisco was no better, with its union wars and its brutality toward the Chinese. But I could easily distance myself from the problems in the city. Not in Lewiston. As had happened so often that summer, I felt torn in a hundred different directions.

Toby had worries of his own. He'd pressed himself into a corner of the scow and sat sunken-chested, watching the river ahead with mere slits for eyes. He showed an unhappy familiarity with the landscape, a growing anxiety. He'd looked like a curled hedgehog ever since we'd passed Lucile, where the Pardees lived. I found myself hoping fervently Frank was away. If I could will it, he'd never see Toby again.

Frank and Will McCabe's ranch lay along a horseshoe bend in the river that over the centuries had captured a thick layer of silt. Our first glimpse of the ranch was of bottomlands rich with native grass still yellow-green from springs and river, but frosted with snow.

A pair of plow horses and a buckskin saddle horse fed in one pasture. Behind them, hillsides grazed bare by sheep had blown nearly free of snow during the storm. Now and then, a little swirl from a rising wind scooped up what remained of a mound of white and hurled it into bordering thickets of bitterbrush and wild rose.

Huge willows clogged a stream that formed the northern boundary of the meadowlands. Not until we passed the mouth of the stream did we see the farmhouse and outbuildings huddled in the lee of the trees. Smoke trailed from a skinny stovepipe that rose from the roof of the cabin. Frank was home!

Protected on the north by a ridge that sloped down to the river, a drive left the wagon road, passed beneath a loosely strung wire gate, and proceeded to house and sheds. We pulled into shore where cottonwoods hid us from the drive. The water had receded several feet from its June fullness, leaving a fringe of bleached grass and water plants, now humps of melting white. Reb did his bit with the mooring rope. Afton lowered the gangplank and tied the mooring rope to a tree.

He hesitated a moment, watching Toby, then held out his hand. "Come, lad. We'll see if we can find your pa." A look of deep regret lined his face. Toby rolled his eyes and sucked in his cheeks, but didn't stir.

"I'll be right beside you. I won't let Frank bite."

Toby tightened his hold on the coon. "What about Chitter? Pa don't like coons."

"You can leave her tied here so she won't cause a fuss."

Toby still didn't budge.

With more patience than I thought him capable, Afton climbed into the scow, took the boy's arms ever so gently from around the coon, then led him over the raised deck and down the gangplank. I kept my place, thinking I might make matters worse if I went along.

"Are you coming, Hattie?"

"I don't know if I should. Toby's father might be more at ease if I weren't there."

"Do as you see fit, but I'll help you down so you can stretch your legs."

As I stepped on shore, Toby grabbed my hand. "Come with me, please!"

"Ohhh . . . I don't know if that's wise."

"Hattie, come along." Afton's voice had a nervous edge. "'Tisn't going to make any difference. Let's be getting the job done."

The yard around the one-story log house had gone without care for some time. An old lilac hedge, grown wild, sent up shoots through a litter of chicken droppings, scraps of animal hide, bones. Weeds crowded the foundation of loose rock, except at the front where a stoop offered entrance into the house. Afton was heading for the stoop when a large, rough-coated, shepherd-cross tore from the cluster of animal sheds at the rear of the house. The dog charged into the yard and barked with savage authority. Reb met the dog shoulder to shoulder, snarling. They leaned heavily against one another, each daring the other to make a move.

A man strode from the barn with purposeful, long-legged steps. "Bill, come here!" he yelled at the shepherd.

"Reb, heel!" Afton shouted. Reb obeyed, quivering from his effort at restraint. The other dog backed toward his master, growling, lips curled away from his fangs.

ot yourself quite a watchdog, Frank," Afton said to his nephew in greeting.

"Good enough." Brown, lean, and straight, Frank McCabe closed on us in his stiff-legged stride. His clothes were caked with dirt, the pantlegs spattered in places with mud from the afternoon's melting snows. He was Afton's height, and with his leathery, young-old face, black mustache and spade beard, the resemblance was amazing. He stopped a few feet away. Bill stood at his side and snarled softly at Reb. Toby waited slightly behind me and peered around my jacket, his eyes fixed on his father with the concentration of a rabbit on an approaching coyote.

The men exchanged a cool handshake, then Afton waved a hand in my direction. "Frank, this is Hattie Clark. She has a homestead near my diggings. I'm taking her to Lewiston to visit her children. 'Course, you recognize Toby."

Frank grunted, gave a slight nod. I sensed his indifference was feigned, that he was furious at the boy's presence, and certainly he felt no pleasure at seeing his uncle or me. There was no smile of welcome, no invitation to sit on the bench at the back of the stoop. Not that I needed to sit—it simply would have been good manners to offer.

Afton stood with feet firm, gaze steady. "How are you doing these days, Frank?"

"Not too good."

"I hear you been having trouble with the cattle boys."

"Yeh, the bastards are trying to run us sheepmen out of the country. Killed my neighbor's herder and two hundred of his sheep." Frank aimed his words at Afton, but his stare drilled holes in Toby.

"Is the law going to do anything about it?" It occurred to me Afton was avoiding talk about Toby until he'd shown sympathy for Frank's condition.

Frank spread his legs and folded his arms across his chest, his face sullen. "Ha! The law do something when the cattlemen boss the county? The sheriff'll claim he can't get anybody to bear witness and let it go at that."

"Have any idea who it was?"

"That bunch of vigilantes from Freedom. They were here a few days back, threatening to salt my fields. Will was up at the high camp checking on the sheep, and I had to stand the bastards off by myself."

"That must of give you a fright."

"Made me madder'n hell! I shot into the ground to scare them off and accidentally sprayed one fool's rump with shot." A cynical smile twitched Frank's lips. "Suppose I'll get arrested for that, and those yahoos'll go scot-free."

"It galls me to think it's come to that. This business of cattle not wanting to feed where the sheep have walked is a bunch of hogwash cooked up by the cattle boys."

"You're damned right! Believe me, us sheepmen didn't start the trouble." Frank closed his mouth in a way that indicated the end of the subject. He continued to stare at Toby as if the boy had leprosy. "What's the kid doing here? Run off to you, did he?"

I felt Toby flinch. He backed off a step.

"He's a fine lad," Afton said. "I've enjoyed his company. But he needs schooling. I was thinking of taking him to Lewiston. He could go to school there."

Frank snorted. "I gave him to Pardees, and that's where he belongs."

I sneaked a look at Toby. He seemed ready to run. The fear in the boy's eyes spurred me to chance Frank's wrath. "You'd think you'd be glad to see your son after all this time—glad Afton has the boy's welfare at heart."

"I don't have a son." Frank's voice had a snarl in it. "I gave him up when his ma died."

"How can you say such a thing! Of all the poor excuses for a father! If you were my kin, I— I'd—" I could think of no insult great enough to express the terrible anger I felt. Up until then, I'd reserved the tiniest bit of charity for Frank McCabe. But with the man standing before me—

unfeeling, selfish, and cruel of eye—I realized Toby had every reason for fright. I turned to leave, taking Toby by the wrist. "Come, Toby, we're not wanted here."

"See here, Missus Clark, you have no right to the kid! The Pardees do." Frank lunged at Toby, but before he could reach the boy, Afton thwacked his chest with a long arm and held him tight.

"Hattie, take Toby and wait for me at the scow." Afton's tone left no room for argument. Not that I intended any. "Frank and me will have us a little talk."

By the time Toby and I reached the riverbank, his shoulders had begun to quiver. I wiped away a tear that rolled down his cheek. "Don't take on about this, Toby. Don't give your father the satisfaction of hurting you again."

"He—he says I—I'm not his son. Well, I wouldn't be his son if he was—if he was—and I won't go back to the Pardees no matter what he says!"

"You don't have to. Your uncle and I will see to that. Maybe you'll get to stay with me in Lewiston."

He looked up, liquid eyes pleading. "Could I?"

"It's entirely possible." I put my hands on his shoulders and stroked the knotted muscles.

"Could you teach me like you did last winter, so I won't have to go to school?"

"I'd love that, but you need to work with other children and have a teacher trained for the job."

Face thoughtful, he looked down, digging at

the slush of snow-mud with the toe of his boot. When he raised his head, his beseeching eyes tore at my heart. "You won't ever let the Pardees take me, will you?"

"Of course not, child. I'll protect you with my life."

"And Pa? What if he tries to steal me? If he came after me, he might . . ." Again, his tone implied something horrible in his and Frank's past.

"Don't worry your poor head about that. Now that I've met your father, I won't ever let him get his hands on you."

It was late afternoon when Afton returned to the scow. He was wearing a long face. "I don't understand what's come over Frank. When I saw him three years ago, he was a different man. Serious-minded he always was, and glum at times. But not like this. He can't say one good thing about life. 'Course, with his luck, I can't say I blame him."

"I didn't improve his mood."

Afton softened his tone. "Aye, your tongue gets in the way at times, Hattie, but you had cause." He turned to Toby. "I told your pa you'd not be going back to the Pardees. That you're going on to Lewiston with me and Hattie. He didn't like it none, but I see him weakening. I'll talk to him again in the morning." He started up the gangplank. "Let's get the tent set up. Frank's invited us in for coffee when we get that done."

I gave a little snort. "You mean he didn't invite us to sleep in the house?"

Afton's look slit my invective like a finely honed knife. "No, nor did I want it! He asked that Toby stay inside . . . I think to get at the lad. But I'll insist he stay with us."

"As will I!"

Toby glanced at me, his face deeply troubled, as if he were seeing through me into the hours ahead and found them frightening. We'd have to be watchful. If he chose to run away, it would be that night.

Toby evidently trusted me to keep my promise and made it to bed without trying to run away. I lay still, listening to him sniffle and grind his teeth. To ease the boy's fears, Afton had laid his bed in the tent. His snoring penetrated the blankets he'd pulled up around his head. Reb had pressed his nose against the foot of Afton's bed, and added to the concert.

I couldn't have ached more physically and emotionally if I'd been beaten with a club. I willed myself to relax, willed my scratchy eyelids to close, only to find my mind bending back to Frank's cruel words. He was every inch the beast Toby had described. And there was still the boy's implication Frank had committed some dastardly crime. I thanked heaven Afton had agreed to take Toby on to Lewiston.

Around one o'clock, the horses in the pasture

whinnied. Beyond the southern border of the ranch, horses whinnied in answer. A distant thud of hooves on the wagon road's frozen mush grew nearer until the clodding stopped on the far side of the trees that hid the tent from the road. Harsh voices admonished the horses to be quiet. Feet hit the ground. Men mumbled orders to each other.

Reb growled. Afraid he'd bark, I reached across Toby's blankets to the foot of Afton's bed and clamped my hand around the dog's muzzle. At the feel of my elbow pressed against his foot, Afton grunted to life.

"Wh-what's going on?"

"Shh! Some men just rode up. You're going to have to do something to keep Reb from barking. I can't hold him much longer."

Afton sat up, groggy. He gripped Reb's collar, warning him to be quiet, but Reb continued to growl, ready to spring at anyone foolish enough to enter the tent. No longer could I hear the men, but the horses stomped lightly in place as if tied. Near the house, a dog barked.

"Do you suppose they're bandits?" My taut voice had little resonance to carry above Reb's growls.

"Hope not."

"Do you think they saw our camp?"

"They'd be down here by now if they had."

Moonlight streaming through a crack in the tent flaps shone on Toby's rumpled hair. If he'd slept, which I doubted, he'd have wakened and heard our whispers. He propped himself on an elbow, and listened for sounds coming from the outside. "Must be robbers," he said. "Nobody else comes along here at night."

"Or those cattlemen laying for Frank."

The words had hardly passed Afton's lips, when Bill's occasional barks of warning turned into the frenzy of a watchdog in panic. Shots rang out. The dog gave several agonized cries and fell silent.

More shots split the air.

An explosion cracked open the night, slammed into the hillsides and echoed up and down the river until the grumblings faded into the distance.

The impact of the blast hit my chest and stole my breath away. I thought my heart would stop beating.

Toby held his hands over his ears, his eyes wide from shock. My own ears throbbed from the concussion. The tethered horses screamed and pawed the ground. At the house, men hollered in triumph.

"God-a-mighty! I'm going to see what's happened." Afton heaved himself from his bed, wearing only longjohns and socks.

I grabbed his arm. "It's too dangerous!"

"I'll keep out of sight."

"I won't let you go!"

He took both my wrists and held them so firmly they hurt. "If Frank's alive, he'll be needing help." His voice was low, level, just above the grating hiss of a whisper. For one suspended moment, his gaze held mine, his eyes so intense they glowed in the wan light. "Hattie, I want you to know I

think the world of you . . . always will." He gave
my wrists a squeeze that spoke of finality and let
them drop to my lap. He pulled a revolver from
under his bedroll. "Use this if you need to. I'll get
a rifle from the scow."

His words of affection had so stunned me, it
took a moment to gather my wits. "What about
Reb?" The dog had pushed himself into a corner
of the tent and sat trembling.

"Blasts scare him. Never has liked it when I
used dynamite at a dig. As long as you're here,
he'll not budge."

Afton pulled on his trousers and boots and
threw on his jacket. With one last glance at Toby
and me, he was out the door, creeping into the
murky shadows, into the danger that waited in the
night. In that instant, I knew nothing mattered
except that he return, alive.

I had no time to dwell on my feelings. At the
homestead, rough laughter and obscenities fouled
the air. One voice boomed above the rest. "We can
kick up a fuss later, boys. Let's torch the barn."

Toby shot from his bed, intent on the doorway.

I put out a hand to stop him. "You're not
going anywhere, young man! Those men will burn
you along with everything else."

He tried to pull free. "I'm going to turn the
animals loose. If they were yours, you wouldn't
want them set afire."

"No, but you're more important than the animals. I'll not let you put yourself in harm's way."

"I have to!"

The boy's pleading eyes and voice tore at my conscience. "Oh, Lord . . . all right . . . but I'm going with you. And you'll do whatever I say." I pulled on my shoes without stockings, shrugged my jacket on over my nightgown, stuck the revolver in a pocket.

Still spooked by the explosion, a dozen snorting horses bobbed up and down at the border fence. Speaking to them softly to keep them from further alarm, we walked through the open gateway, skirted the inside of the fence, then made our way up the line of trees in the creek bottom. South of the creek, Frank's horses screamed and galloped up and down the pasture. Infinitely tall, the sky snapped with stars. The moon was three-quarters full and brilliant, the air crisp enough to hurt the linings of my nose.

We went as far as we dared before we parted the tree branches that hid us from the drive. The cabin should have stood a few yards beyond our hiding place. It seemed to have evaporated. Between that emptiness and the outbuildings, shadowy figures darted here and there. At the sheds, animals cried a bedlam, the smell of their fear as thick as the acrid scent of blasting powder. Several rapid shots turned the squeal of pigs into death cries.

An orange light flared at an opening in the barn loft. I smelled burning hay. Tongues of flame already licked at a smaller building that had come alive with the squalling of chickens.

"I've got to let the hens out before they catch fire!" Toby cried.

I put my hand over his mouth to quiet him. "Those men would kill you like they did the pigs."

What a grisly business. If the vigilantes would kill animals in cold blood, they'd kill Afton. Did he lie dead in the shadows? Or was he hiding? There was no way I could know, no way I could help. The thought paralyzed.

Rifle shots thwanged from a hillside back of the flaming barn. They echoed from slope to slope, growing flatter with each repetition. South of the barn, a volley of shots returned the challenge. For several minutes, the exchange of rifle fire split the roar of the fire.

Someone near the henhouse cried out in pain. From another quarter came a string of blasphemous threats.

The same rough voice that had ordered the arson boomed above the crack of rifles. "Let's get the hell out of here! No sense getting ourselves killed."

Boot heels pounded down the frozen drive and passed within a few feet of where Toby and I hid. Two men moving more slowly brought up the rear. One man dragged his foot. The furnace that had once been barn and sheds belched smoke so thick I was afraid we'd cough and reveal our hiding place.

We watched the injured man and his companion clear the gate and enter the wagon road. Horses whinnied. Riders mounted. They milled around a few seconds waiting for the stragglers to gain their saddles, then thundered up the road.

When we could no longer hear the clack of

hooves, we ventured from the trees and into the eerie light of moon and flame. Whipped by growing night winds, the flames were past quenching, the heat so intense we flinched backwards, unable to approach. We held our hands in front of our faces and gasped for breath. Sheds crumbled to the ground, showering sparks. White-hot cinders exploded like firecrackers and spiraled upward on whirling columns of hot air.

Victim of the blast, the house lay in ruins. Moon and firelight gleamed off a cast-iron stove that hulked amid the rubble. The posts of an iron bedstead poked through a crosshatch of shattered logs. I thought of the man who might lie in the bed. No matter how cruel and unfeeling, Frank deserved no such fate.

And what of Afton? How could I find him in that inferno? What if he were dead? Tears welled in my eyes. My nails bit into the palms of my hands.

23

In the fire's poppy-red glow, I saw someone creep down the slope behind the gutted barn. The figure skirted the blazing sheds and stopped on the far side of the ruined house. With the flames splashing the night orange behind him, I could see no features, nothing but tall shadow. It might be Afton. Or Frank. Maybe a lone vigilante who'd stayed behind to make certain nothing lived. Hardly daring to breathe, I pulled the revolver from my pocket, drew Toby close.

"Is that you, Hattie? Toby?" the shadow asked.

I gasped a "yes."

"Now, now, 'tis just me." The shadow came forward, took on depth, and gathered us in his arms.

"Oh, Afton, I was afraid you'd . . ." I hung in the comfort of his arms for a long while, crying softly, wishing I could stay there forever. He seemed in no hurry to let me go, though he quivered from fatigue.

I pulled back to look into his face. It looked drawn, a pasty orange in the fire glow. "You should never have come out here. Those men are monsters."

"Aye, hate's sickened their heads and rotted their hearts. But they're gone." He ran his hand along my forehead. "And you're safe."

I felt like a candle melting at his touch, secure, serene, mightily relieved that he'd survived. "I was so worried about you. And then, when the shooting started . . ." The words that trailed off were more breath than voice. "Was it you shooting from the hillside?"

"I wanted to scare the devils off before they set fire to something else. As it is, the place is pretty much a loss. It won't—" He broke off, choking on the smoke and ash. My own throat felt raw from the smoke. My eyes burned.

"What about Frank?" I asked when Afton's fit of coughing had stopped.

He looked down at Toby, who was hugging his side, and wheezed a sigh that sounded of regret. "I've not seen any sign of him."

Toby pointed to the rubble that had been the house. His eyes were owlish. "Is Pa in there?"

"I don't know, lad. I'll have to get the lantern and have a look around." Afton's dread of the task showed in his face and in the slump of his shoulders. He seemed terribly weary. I was amazed he'd survived the night.

With the gunfire stopped, Reb had left the tent and was slinking around a still form that lay near the front of the house.

"Reb knows Bill is dead," Toby said in a small, faltering voice.

Afton went down on one knee and ran long fingers through the boy's tousled hair. "I'm sorry you had to see this, lad. I wish to heaven we'd never left the diggings." He soothed Toby a moment longer, then stood, taking the boy's hand. "Come, we'll go back to the tent so I can get the lantern."

"Why don't you wait until daylight," I said. "The air will have cleared some by then."

"I need to see if Frank's alive."

"I doubt he could live through the explosion." I motioned toward the heap of debris. "You shouldn't lift those logs. Maybe someone from a neighboring ranch can help in the morning."

"I don't know who's friend or foe around here."

"Then I'll help."

"I'm going to do it now, by myself. You need to stay at the tent with the lad. He'll be needing your comfort." He spoke with a mix of harshness and softness that signified the end of the discussion.

"Why do people do such awful things?" Toby asked, sniffling. He'd thrown himself down on his bedroll and sat cross-legged, shedding quiet tears. Afton had left to search for Frank. He'd taken the lantern, and I'd fastened the tent flaps back to allow the moonlight to stream inside.

I dropped down beside Toby and put my arms around him, tried to ease his shivering. "If we knew why people act as they do, we could solve a lot of the world's problems."

"But they killed animals for no reason."

"I know. It was ruthless." I tucked his head under my chin and stroked his cheek. "What they did to your father was just as vicious. If ever men should go to h—"

Toby pulled back abruptly. "Pa deserved it!" He caught my look of reproach and let his chin drop to his chest. "I guess it's evil of me to say that."

"Not evil, just vengeful. Vengeance doesn't help matters. I don't know what your father has done to make you think he deserved such a terrible death, but I do know this—later on, you'll miss him as much as you miss your mother. There's something about family . . . we can never dismiss them completely from our hearts, even those we dislike."

"Not Pa! Not after what he did to my ma!"

The words Toby had left hanging at the McVeighs flashed through my mind, "Pa'd kill me, like he—" I hesitated, grappling with my suspicions. "What did he do to her?"

"He killed her, that's what!"

My breath caught in my throat, my muscles froze. I'd thought Frank McCabe capable of murder, but to have it confirmed sent waves of shock rippling up and down my spine. "But—but why?"

"Just because he—because he—" The dike

that had held Toby's tears to a trickle burst, spilling streams down his face.

"You poor child!" I drew the boy closer, kept him wrapped tight against my breast until he went limp, sobbing a wet spot on my coat. I tried to imagine what horrible means Frank had used to kill his wife. I wanted to ask Toby, but could find no words gentle enough. At last, I simply said, "Maybe he didn't mean to do it."

Toby shook his head doggedly. "Yes, he did!"

"Please, tell me what happened."

Trembling, he leaned his head on my shoulder and stared down at fingers he'd clasped together so tightly they'd turned whiter than the moonlight. His eyes seemed opaque, as if he'd drawn a shade over them and turned inward. He began the story haltingly, wrinkling his face and rolling his eyes wide from time to time to keep back the tears.

"Ma was on her bed having a baby . . . screaming 'cause it hurt. She wanted Pa to get the neighbor lady . . . the one that helped out when babies came . . . but Pa wouldn't do it. He said if Ma didn't have the grit to have a baby by herself, she had no business on a ranch."

"He said that! When she was in such pain! And in front of you?"

"Us kids were supposed to stay outside. But when Pa started yelling at Ma—and her doing that awful screaming—I opened the door a crack. The bed was in the sitting room, and I could see her lying there. Pa—he was standing over her—holding her by the shoulders—shaking her—yelling at her to shut up. Then he put his hands around her throat and squeezed. Just kept on squeezing—yelling—squeezing—yelling, 'Die! Damn you! I don't want any more brats in this house. No more mouths to feed.'" Toby stared straight ahead, a wild, frightened look on his face as if he saw the terrible deed happening at that very moment.

I stroked his clammy forehead. "There, there, child. Be at peace. Your father can't hurt anyone ever again." I made a great effort to sound calm, but my insides writhed from a fury that could find no release. If Frank weren't already dead, I might have been tempted to commit murder myself.

I thought Toby would say no more, but he looked up then, his eyes begging for understanding, his voice near hysteria. "I wanted to stop Pa—honest I did—but I was too scared—I thought he'd kill us—I should of stopped him—but I just took the other kids and we hid in the barn."

I pressed his head against my shoulder and rocked him, stroked his arm. "You couldn't have stopped him, child. You were right not to put yourself and the other children in danger. If your father was mad enough to kill once, he'd have done it again. I'm just sorry you had to see such a terrible thing." I paused, fighting the rage that churned within me. "I don't understand why your father wasn't put in jail. Doesn't anyone else know about this?" Toby shook his head. "Where was your Uncle Will at the time?"

"Up at high camp. He thought Ma died from having the baby."

We sat quietly then. Little sobs still caught in Toby's chest, but I was too stunned, too outraged to weep. I crawled within myself, imagining the hideous act, imagining the terror Toby must have felt. No wonder he'd been sick at heart. Having his father's words ring in his ears for three long years must have been as much torture as witnessing his mother's murder. What suffering! How inhumane! Ironically, Frank had found his punishment. Like Toby, I was glad.

"I thank you for telling me," I said eventually. "It must have been very difficult for you. I hope it eased the pain."

Toby looked up into my eyes and slipped his arms around me. "Why are you so nice to me?"

"Because I love you, Toby. As much as if you were my own son."

"I love you, too."

The warmth of Toby's breath penetrated my clothes. The warmth of his words penetrated flesh to my heart. Twice that night I'd been told I was loved, and despite the horror that wanted to tear me apart, I swelled to overflowing with affection. I vowed with all the love and will I possessed that I'd keep Toby from further harm, not allow him to be taken from me until he was grown and ready to tackle the world on his own.

Having faced his own tale of horror, Afton returned to the tent red-eyed, wheezing from the smoke, his face pallid in the glare of the lantern. His features had stilled into a dead stare. "Did you find Pa?" Toby asked.

"He was near the door under the heap of logs. Must of been on his way out to check on the shooting." Afton's voice had the same dead cast as his face.

I shuddered at the thought. A few seconds more, and Frank might have made it to safety, free to harm Toby. "When will you bury him?"

"A blast doesn't leave much of a man to bury. I covered his remains so nothing will bother him tonight. The dog too. I'll dig graves in the morning." He wiped a shaky hand across his face. "I'm going to bed. I can't do anything more right now."

Afton started snoring in a matter of minutes. Relieved of the nightmare that had been preying on his mind, Toby soon drifted into slumber, at least he turned silent. As had happened so often in the past month, sleep was impossible for me. I couldn't erase the images of violence that flashed through my mind, the memory of hate-filled voices, the sound of flames eating the ranch alive, the thought of Frank crushed by logs and deserving it.

I lay in thought, smelling death until dawn broke, clear and still. Without waking Afton and Toby, I left the tent and walked through the clump of cottonwoods at roadside to gather twigs for a fire. I hadn't intended to go past the downed wire gate, but some base curiosity drew me. I set my armload of kindling beside the strands of wire and walked up the drive, leaving footprints in patches of ash-gray snow.

The farmyard looked as if Sherman had

marched through during the night. Stock lay slain amid black, smoldering ruins, charred carcasses stiff-legged in death. Weed skeletons, driven into the yard by the night winds, added to the macabre effect. A singed hen perched on the seat of a plow, cackling. The rest of the chickens hadn't fared as well. The stench of seared feathers and animal hide hovered thick in the windless morning. A jackrabbit darted from a clump of shriveled lilac, sat on his haunches sniffing the air, then tore off across the hillside.

Skirting the heap of wreckage that had been the house, I searched the ground for anything that could be salvaged. Several yards from the ruins, I found a section from a can of giant powder lying amid scraps of household goods the explosion had hurled into the weeds. Bullet holes in the piece of metal showed the vigilantes had sparked the explosion from a distance. Frank hadn't had a chance.

The curve of the mountain had prevented Frank's neighbors—those who'd lost their herder and flock to the vigilantes—from seeing the fires, but they'd heard the explosion, and came early that morning to check on Frank. I don't know what we would have done without their help. Afton was in a state of collapse. They built a coffin and dug Frank's grave, buried Bill—at Toby's insistence—then made a funeral pyre of other animals that had been slain but not burned. The sordid business shook us all, turned Toby and Afton silent. I felt a cloying loneliness, as if I had no place in the family tragedy.

Frank was buried on a grassy bench north of the drive where his wife and parents, Afton's sister and her husband, lay in their graves. I told Afton the story of Toby's mother, and when the boy put up a fuss at having Frank's grave near hers, Afton had the grave dug far to the side. He thought the bench should continue to be the family cemetery, and with that in mind, he fenced the plot while I cleared the area of weeds and planted lilacs from the old garden. The days had warmed and snow had left the canyon, so I carried buckets of water to start the plants, knowing they'd have to depend on sparse rains before true winter arrived.

I had no idea if I'd ever return to tend the cemetery, though I hoped to do just that. There was a good chance no one else would. It seemed a shame the plot that sheltered the remains of two generations of McCabes should, after so much tragedy, become overgrown with weeds, trodden by range cattle, the fences knocked flat.

The similarity between the fate of the McCabe ranch and the possibility for decline of my own, the thought of Chester's grave returning to the wilds, haunted me while I worked. Chester and I had invested so much of ourselves in the ranch, I couldn't bear the thought of it going to naught. I decided I must return to Weasel Creek for at least part of each year to make sure the ranch was cared for, to tend Chester's grave, to live the simple life.

24

*W*ill McCabe arrived home the day after Frank's burial and stared unbelieving at the blackened, shattered remains of his home. Looking a waif in his loose-hanging clothes, he ate lunch at the tent, then he and Afton toured the farmstead, viewing the effects of the raid. They decided we'd leave the scow and travel with Will in his buckboard to the sheriff's office at Mount Idaho to report the murder, arson, and killing of livestock. From there, Afton, Toby, and I would journey to Grangeville, where we'd catch the stage to Lewiston, Afton to stay with a friend, I with Jennie until her marriage—if she still planned to marry. Reb and Chitter would stay with Afton at his friend's livery stable on the edge of town. Toby could go there each day to play with the coon. The ordeal of the past few days had left the boy's future undecided, except that he would stay with me until Afton and I could agree on permanent arrangements.

Distraught by events, Will planned to sell the

burned-out ranch and use the funds to outfit himself for a trip to the Klondike to search for gold. The idea had seized Toby's imagination, and when we started off for Mount Idaho, he sat beside Will on the driver's seat and plied the man with questions. Reb sat in the back of the wagon, gazing at where we'd been, Chitter on the driver's seat, in Toby's arms. Afton had arranged for me to sit with him on the passenger seat they'd put in the buckboard, and I rested there in the solitude of my musings, one thought leading to another.

I'd unpacked my green silk for the occasion and plaited my hair into a French braid. The flowered hat seemed out of place on that somber occasion, but I had no other with me except my old bonnet. After spending a month in calicoes ravaged by wave and sun, I felt quite civilized, though my silk dress was wrinkled from lying in the saddlebag too long, stained in a few places where water had seeped past the oilskin and beneath the leather flaps.

Afton had shaved carefully around his mustache and spade beard and wore his good suit and bowler. The trousers had shrunk slightly from getting wet. Except for his leathered skin, he looked surprisingly cultured, a gentleman of character and distinction. It pained me to think I'd see him only occasionally. From things he'd said, I gathered he felt the same.

We'd made an early start, hoping to reach Mount Idaho before noon. The sun rising behind the tall hills sent long fingers of golden light into the timbered mountains west of the river. On the barren east slopes, the draws lay in shadow, forming aisles of deep lavender. The entire canyon seemed veiled in lavender and gold. I had a sense of time suspended, a meeting of ages past with those to come.

The road gained in elevation as it cut across the hill north of the ranch and offered a view of the river, steaming in the chill morning air. The vapors parted above the swift shallows, revealing a hundred thousand sun-jewels sparkling on the waters. Ducks dabbled for insects amid the sparkles, some with rumps tipped to the sky.

I felt a deep sorrow at leaving the Salmon. Perhaps for the first time, I understood the seductive hold the river had on men like Afton and Chester. It appealed to their sense of beauty, their sense of rhythm, heightened their awareness of the eternal, challenged their sense of adventure. Despite its treacherous moments, the river had become as much a part of me as any living, breathing thing. Its windings, frothings, tumblings, were stamped on my inner eye as indelibly as the blazing river sun. I'd encounter other forks in my stream of life, but none as breathtakingly beautiful, nor as frightening as the river of our return.

Wrapped in his own deep ponderings, Afton absently watched a flock of shiny blackbirds skim the grazed stubble. The flock was constantly dipping, veering, expanding, contracting in a glossary of motion. He turned with a sigh and put his hand over mine. The touch of his warm palm, the way he sighed, told me he had something heartfelt to say.

He cleared his throat, once, twice. "Hattie, my mind's been in such a whirl these past few days, wondering what's to happen to Toby . . . to you . . . to me." He looked straight ahead, avoiding my eyes. "You're right about the boy needing a real home . . . not holed up with a couple of old sourdoughs." He turned then, looked at me in question. "You'd be tied down. You might decide to go to San Francisco. I—I wouldn't want Toby that far away."

"I've decided against that, except to visit during the holidays. My grandchildren are in Lewiston . . . my oldest son's farm is a half-day's ride . . . and I have friends in town. At one time I knew everyone."

"I'll miss having the boy with me, but I guess I can see him once in a while."

"Visit as often as you like. Toby needs to be around a man he loves and trusts." *As do I.*

The muscles in Afton's face slackened. He dropped his gaze to the floorboards. "I don't know how long I can sit in town, staring at the walls."

"You need to sit. Need to rest your heart. That doesn't mean you'll have to stare at the walls. I'll see you have plenty of books to read. There'll be socials in town . . . traveling theaters. Do you like pot lucks?"

"I wouldn't know. Guess I can try. Not sure I'd like being around a bunch of strangers."

"You can come to the house and play pinochle."

Afton looked up, grinning. "How about poker for matchsticks?"

"All right, poker it is. And we'll find other things to do. I wouldn't want you to have to twiddle your thumbs. *I* couldn't. I need to have some project going." I paused, wondering if what I was about to say would sound foolish. "I—I've considered opening an art gallery, where I can teach painting and wood carving."

Afton was silent a moment, sucking a tooth, as was his habit when deep in thought—a toothpick hadn't yet found its way from his pocket. "I suppose keeping busy is as important to a woman as it is to a man. I'm not really without my own plans. I've thought of writing about my adventures in the wilds . . . especially the early days . . . something I could pass on to Toby. But I'm no writer, not like that Jack London fella I read in the magazines. I've had to educate myself. I can't decide if it's worth the effort to write about my life, or worth Toby's to read about it."

I reached across with my free hand and pressed his arm fervently. "It is! It would be a wonderful thing for him to have—for anyone to read, for that matter."

He smiled skeptically. "We'll see . . . writing aside, I plan to spend as much time placering as I can." A hesitation. "You wouldn't be thinking of giving up the ranch?"

After the many times he'd advised me to move, the question surprised me. "I—I've considered renting it out . . . maybe keep the cabin . . . let someone farm the rest. It's possible Len Johnson would be interested."

"I'm glad you won't be selling it off, though

I've worried about you living there alone. The river is a wild and wonderful place to be. My heart aches when I think of the green, soaring mountains and the lambs and deer." He stared into space, reflecting. "The wilds shouldn't belong only to the young and healthy. I'd live there the rest of my days if I could. Not closed in by stone and brick, but by my own canyon walls. I want to be laid to rest where I can listen to the music of the waters and the singing of the wind through the pines."

It took a while for me to find my voice. When I did, it was thick with feeling. "Those are lovely thoughts, Afton. For the same reasons, it would be difficult for me to give up the ranch entirely. Chester is buried there. I can't forget that." Afton's hand quivered. His expression changed to one of near childish vulnerability. I knew what he was thinking—that my heart still belonged to Chester. Part of it did.

I stared at our clasped hands, selecting my words carefully. "I've thought of giving notice to the couple who rents the house I own in town. Chester and I kept the place thinking we might return when we were older. Toby could spend the winters with me, then I'd take him to Weasel Creek to spend the summers with you. I could check on the ranch."

Afton remained quiet, deep in thought. It seemed an age before he said, "The plan has merit, but it sounds like we'd be going our own ways. I'm not sure I'd like that . . . I've gotten used to having you around." His words had the furry quality that came to his voice when he was feeling affection. I sensed where this speech of Afton's was leading. I was fearful, and at the same time strangely hopeful. His eyes had taken on the expression I'd seen in them once before, as if he wished for something beyond reach. "I mean . . . I thought maybe we could . . ." He drew a long breath, blew it out. "Hang it all! I'd miss you. Couldn't you, at least, arrange to spend the whole summer at your ranch?"

My heart pounded against my ribs. "I . . . yes . . . I suppose someone could watch the gallery during the summer months. That way, I could work up a little garden, see the ranch was kept up. I do miss my flowers and vegetables . . . the animals . . . the sheer beauty and solitude of the place."

"Then, I'll be calling on you often this winter to see you don't change your mind."

"I—I'll look forward to that."

I was certain Afton had planned to propose but was too embarrassed. In a way, I was relieved. We needed time to adjust to the town, to get to know each other in that setting, to see if the love we'd found on the river would endure. Before I married again, the townspeople needed to accept the fact Chester was gone. I was in no hurry. I wanted to make a niche for myself before I shared my life with a man. Still, contentment swept through me, filling me with warmth.

I reached under the seat for the pine relief I'd stowed there. I'd planned to give it to Afton after we reached Lewiston, but feeling as I did, I couldn't wait for him to see it. At the time I'd completed the carving, I had no idea what would happen to Toby, but hoping for the best, I'd put a smile on his face, an expression of serenity on Afton's. Mountains framed the top and sides. A scow drifted on the river that wound across the base. Yesterday, I'd looked on the carving with deep satisfaction. Now, I could only hope it pleased Afton. I pulled back the protective wraps and put it in Afton's hands.

He studied the relief a long while without speaking. A mix of sadness and pleasure softened his eyes and pulled at the corners of his mouth.

"When did you finish this?" he said at last.

"The day it snowed. While you and Toby slept."

"'Tis a fine piece of work. A fine remembrance of my last . . . of the trip." His voice had turned thick, gravelly. "I'll put it where I can see it when I wake up each morning."

I patted the weathered hand that covered mine. "In spite of our troubles, things have turned out for the best, haven't they, Afton?"

"That they have, Hattie, dear. That they have."

25

On the first Monday of October, Toby dragged himself from Jennie's whitewashed cottage on Elm Street to face a new challenge, his first day at school. After rebelling in a quiet way, he'd dressed in a new brown suit and hat and had forced his summer-swollen feet into a pair of shiny boots. Jennie had suggested I go along to introduce him to his teacher, so I'd put on town clothes, a pearl-gray brilliantine with purple trim. Afton waited at the gate in his black cheviot to walk us down the street.

Bright, crisp days had turned elms along the sidewalk shades of gold, lilacs a rich mauve. The oblique rays of the sun shone behind the vivid leaves, transforming them into brilliant pendants of light. Crows sat in the top of the trees and mimicked the voices of children who walked in the middle of the street laughing and teasing. Beneath the trees, sprinklers showered rainbows of spray over browning lawns. Young mothers with toddlers clinging to their skirts had already begun to hang out their Monday wash. Mothers of older broods stood in sunny doorways and waved good-bye to children scrubbed clean for school.

Jennie had prepared Toby as well as she could for that first day at school. She'd broken her engagement to Carl and seemed happy in the fact her primary concern was teaching. Needless to say, I was delighted. We'd stay with her until my renters moved into the house they were building.

Despite Jennie's reassurance, Toby looked wan. He'd been in town long enough for the story of his trip down the Salmon to spread. That and the rumors about his father's violent death caused the other children to view him with awe. Still, he felt a stranger. With each step nearer the school, he grew more wide-eyed, turned more silent.

The schoolhouse was a two-story brick with tall, corniced windows, mansard roof, and a play yard that circled the building. A red-haired woman with a plain but friendly face stood in the yard of noisy children and chatted with little girls clinging to her arms. I knew from Jennie's description the woman was Toby's teacher.

I introduced myself and Afton while Toby looked on in his shy, owlish way, and pulled back on my arm. "And this is Mister McCabe's grand-nephew, Toby." I gave him a little nudge forward.

Miss O'Rourke, the teacher, shook his hand gently and smiled. "You must be that courageous boy who floated down the River of No Return." Her voice rose above the nearby play, causing heads to turn.

Toby froze. He glanced up at Afton from the

corners of his eyes, back at the teacher, swallowed. "Yes'm." A smile tugged at his lips. Not a real smile, but the beginning of one, as if he were pleased with himself.

The rest of the children in the schoolyard had gotten wind of Toby's arrival and gathered around him, grinning, or stood back and watched him with looks of reverence, jealousy. I sensed every child would have liked to trade places with Toby at that instant. Embarrassed at all the attention, he backed to my side.

A girl I recognized as the granddaughter of Afton's friend at the livery stable said brightly, "Miss O'Rourke, Toby has the sweetest coon. Could he bring her to school?"

It seemed from the teacher's expression she was about to say no. Then, as if on second thought, she broke into a warm smile. "Of course. That would be great fun." She turned to Afton. "Could you bring her during the noon hour one day?"

"Be a pleasure."

Toby had stood with a forefinger pressed against his lips while he gave the teacher and the children crowded around him a summing up. Now that Miss O'Rourke had accepted Chitter as an important part of his life, his red-brown eyes gleamed. He took the finger from his lips, allowing a smile to flicker there. His cheeks rounded with suppressed pride. The hesitation with which he'd left the house slowly evolved into something that approached a willingness to know these children, this teacher, this school.

Afton gave him an appraising look. "You want us to stay a while longer?" A note of loss, of surrendering something loved, raveled his voice. I knew the feeling.

Toby straightened, his chest swelled slightly, a dismissing look came to his round, child's eyes. "You can go home. I'm going to be all right."

"Then we'll see you after school. Maybe Hattie will bake us some chocolate cookies."

I thought I saw tears in Afton's eyes as he took my arm and led me from the schoolyard. I couldn't resist a look over my shoulder at Toby through my own moist eyes. It did my heart good to see him pleased with himself. I shared his pride. I'd had time to reflect, and considered the trip down the Salmon—especially my deliverance of the scow through the last rapid—one of the highlights of my life.

Leaving the excited chatter behind, Afton and I strolled through town into the open countryside, enjoying the warmth of the sun, the gentle touch of a breeze, the pungence of dried tansy. As our feet parted the withering grass, hoppers buzzed out from underfoot and disappeared in the jungle of stems. The white fluff of milkweed burst from pods and snagged on our clothes.

We stopped to rest on a windy bluff that overlooked the canyon of the Snake River. Naked hills stretched for miles in all directions, their bosoms softly defined by shadows. Beyond them, to the east, long-fingered ridges piled ever upward into the green heights of the wilderness. Far below us, the river wound through a rocky gorge on its way to meet the Columbia. The deep waters glittered in the sunlight. Cottonwoods along the riverbank appeared as torches, a flaunt of color before the drab grays and tans of winter took over the landscape. Just below the canyon rim, a wedge of geese wavered southward, sending their wild calls back on the breeze.

Afton surveyed the scene, reflecting an inner melancholy. "You know, Hattie," he said with a sigh, "when I look down upon that roaring river, I don't just see the Snake . . . I see the waters of the Salmon. They've made the Snake the mighty river it is. When I look out over the countryside I don't see barren hills. I see high forests . . . creeks . . . springs . . . the kind of country that breeds big rivers and keeps them fed . . . alive."

Afton's words struck me as something Chester might have said—he'd held such love for rivers. He would have thought Afton a kindred spirit, would have admired his perceptive mind, his courage, his love for the wilds. Yes, he would have liked this man.

Sensing my gaze, Afton turned and squeezed my hand.

"'Tis a specially nice day, wouldn't you say, Hattie?"

An updraft rustled the grass, fluttered Afton's coattails, and rippled my skirts. I breathed deeply of the warm flow of air, of the solitude, let my smile embrace earth and sky, sound of larks and river.

"Yes, indeed. It is a particularly lovely day."

I wanted to say more of what was in my heart,

but my throat swelled, making speech impossible. I was too full of gratitude to the river I'd left behind, to the man at my side. Because of them, and Toby, I looked forward to life. The journey down the Salmon had been one of destiny for all three of us, a return of hope, a discovery of all we were capable of becoming. Everything we'd learned, every vivid memory, we possessed together.

The thought of spending another summer with Afton and Toby filled me with joy, with an eagerness to see the ranch and animals, to dig my hands in the soil, to stand once again on the banks of the Salmon. I'd find the river as it always had been, flowing along like the passage of time, waiting to take some desperate traveler on a journey of destiny. Having floated its waters, I would never be the same. Nothing in my life would ever be quite the same.